Prai

"The characters are alluring and relatable with absolutely unique personalities. I was hooked from page one, intrigued by Kate's structured family, her eccentric choice of a best friend, and, as the book continued on, the situations she ends up in. All of the plot twists made the book nearly impossible to put down. It was a magnificent read that I would recommend to everyone, and I am thrilled at the promise that this book holds for the next."

~Amanda Nelson, reviewer

"The story grabs you from the beginning and allows you to walk in Kate's shoes and keeps you guessing!"

~Katie Biddle, reviewer

"Kate Unmasked by Cindy M. Hogan is an amazing book. I love how Kate didn't give up hope to finding out who her parents are. I love how even bad situations she never stops fighting. I love this book and have already recommended to my other friends who have read Cindy Hogan's books."

~Jessica Britt, reviewer

"I loved the plot of this one. It's fast moving and there are tons of twists and turns that I didn't see coming. I hope that all of the books in this one are as great as Kate Unmasked!"

~MyBookADay blog, Cathy Jeppsen, reviewer

CODE OF SILENCE BOOK ONE

KATE
UNMASKED

CINDY M. HOGAN

Your past doesn't define you

Cindy Hogan

Also by Cindy M. Hogan

Audio, Print, and eBook

Watched Trilogy:
Watched

Protected

Created

Christy Spy Novels: Spin off of the Watched trilogy
Adrenaline Rush

Hotwire

Fatal Exchange

Gravediggers

Sweet and Sour Kisses:
First Kiss

Stolen Kiss

Rebound Kiss

Rejected Kiss

Dream Kiss

CODE OF SILENCE BOOK ONE

KATE
UNMASKED

CINDY M. HOGAN

O'NEAL PUBLISHING

For reality junkies everywhere

1

Kate Hamilton screamed, ripped up the letter, and threw it, aiming for the trashcan. At least half the tiny pieces missed and fluttered to the ground. She stomped on the pieces, trying to grind them into oblivion. Despite her best efforts, the crumpled paper did not disappear when she removed her foot, but slowly rose a centimeter or so as the plush carpet returned to its former glory. Using her foot, she swept the papers to the side, finding no satisfaction or relief.

She slumped down on her bed, all the energy of her sudden outburst drained, and let her arms drop to her sides. Her hand brushed the brittle pages of her journal, a stained, distended composition book, which she'd left open on her pillow that morning. It contained everything she'd learned during the three years she'd been searching for her birth parents. She picked it up and flipped through it listlessly. Despite the fact that its pages were filled with notes, letters, and taped-in photos, it contained no answers. And now, she'd hit yet another dead end. She momentarily regretted ripping up the letter—she should have taped it into this faithful catalogue of failure. But as her eyes settled on the remaining bits of shredded paper, a surge of bitterness rose like bile in her throat, and she flung the journal across the room.

"I knew hiring that P.I. was a mistake." Her mother's gentle voice drifting in from the doorway startled her, and her cheeks immediately flamed red at the thought that her mother had seen her basically throw a tantrum.

"I'm fine. It's not a big deal," Kate said, though it was an effort to keep the tremor out of her voice.

Her mom crossed her arms and pursed her lips together, looking from Kate to the shredded letter to the journal, now splayed on the floor. She raised one eyebrow, but didn't contradict Kate.

"So, what did it say?"

Kate rolled her eyes and sighed bitterly. She'd only read the letter once before tearing it to shreds, but the words were seared into her memory nonetheless. "Basically—nothing."

Kate was born the year after Texas passed the country's first Safe Haven law—a law that allowed parents to leave their unharmed but unwanted babies in the hands of state-designated officials with no questions asked. The parent was not required to leave a name, and custody of the child transferred to the state. Safe Haven babies could then be placed in adoptive homes. Kate had been one of those babies.

Her adoptive parents knew next to nothing about her—not even her age at the time she was adopted, only that they thought she was around a year old. The state placed her in a temporary foster home for a few months until they found her adoptive parents—Tom and Abrie Hamilton—who were eager to welcome a baby into their home. No one had even bothered to record where her birth parents had dropped her off.

Kate had spent the first years of her search randomly sending out her picture on social media sites, asking people to share her story and help her find her birth parents. That didn't get her any answers, though it did get her a stalker, a man named John Henry who'd followed her everywhere for a week until her parents found out, got a restraining order against him, and forbade Kate from ever trying that tactic again.

After that, Kate knew she had to try something new. She pestered her mom until she agreed to let Kate go through all of her old baby clothes.

"I don't know what you think you're going to learn from this," her mother had huffed as she brought the small box down from the attic. "I don't even remember which outfit you were wearing when they gave you to us, not that that would tell you anything, anyway. This is a bit nuts."

But Kate had examined every piece of clothing doggedly, ignoring her mother's exasperated sighs. Finally, she found it—a faded yellow t-shirt with pink ducks marching across the chest. Kate remembered the triumph of that moment, the excitement of finally being onto something. She'd held the t-shirt proudly up for her mother to see.

"What am I looking at?"

"Right there! Don't you see it?" Kate had actually laughed, she was so delighted. She pointed to the tag of the t-shirt, where something was written in faded marker. "It says right there, Mercy Medical Group." She finally had a clue of where her birth parents had left her.

She spent the better part of the next six months convincing her parents to let her use nearly half her life savings to hire a private investigator to follow the lead. They finally realized she was not going to let it go and, worried she'd start investigating hospitals on her own, they'd finally relented.

She thought bitterly of the two thousand dollars, plus the month she'd spent waiting while the P.I. had investigated every hospital in the chain. She'd been so excited to get his report today, but her hopes had quickly been dashed.

"He tracked the t-shirt back to Junction Hospital, but there was nothing," she told her mom, trying to keep her voice even. "The Safe Haven law doesn't require parents to leave any information about themselves or the children they're abandoning, but I hoped…" her voice hitched and she couldn't continue. Her mom knew what she hoped, anyway—that the hospital might have required whoever had left her to fill out a medical history form. Even that little bit of information would have given her some clue into her identity, maybe even enough to fill in another piece of the puzzle. But no—there'd been no medical history form.

Her mom sighed. "Kate, I'm so sorry."

Kate looked up in surprise. She'd expected an "I told you so" and a lecture about practicality. But her mother's face was filled with compassion, and she looked close to tears herself. She crossed the room somewhat hesitantly and picked up Kate's journal, then sat down next to Kate on the bed. She started bending the creased pages back into place, her calloused fingers working efficiently to put the book back in order.

"Believe it or not, I do want you to get answers. I just... I hate seeing you get hurt like this. I only want you to be happy."

"I know, Mom."

"I think your birth parents—whoever they were—did a courageous thing when they gave you up. Heaven knows how they did it. You were the cutest thing in the world, I swear, so it couldn't have been easy. But they couldn't take care of you, and so they took you somewhere they knew you'd be safe. There must have been a reason they didn't leave any information, and I think... Honey, I think you have to honor that." Kate watched her mom's capable hands smooth the pages of the journal, and her own hands itched to snatch it back.

Her mother continued, "I know it's hard—"

Hard? It was torture.

"—not having all the answers. But I think the time has come for you to let this go." Finally, she smoothed the last page of the journal and closed it, handing it to Kate with an air of finality. "There are no more answers to be found."

Kate took the book from her. She couldn't bring herself to say anything aloud, but she nodded. Her mom smiled sadly at her and gave her a quick, stiff hug.

"I know just the thing to get your mind off it," she said. "A little spring cleaning will do the trick, I know it."

***

Spring cleaning? She can't be serious.

Ellie's text message made Kate laugh, as it echoed her thoughts exactly. After her chat with her mom, she'd told her she just needed a few minutes to gather herself and then she'd be down to help with the cleaning.

You know my mom. She believes in aromatherapy. There's no bad mood that can't be fixed with the lovely scent of Pledge.

Your mother is a freak, Ellie sent.

Hey now. Her mom might be a little emotionally illiterate, but Kate knew she was trying her best. It wasn't easy for her to see Kate so obsessed with finding her birth parents, and Kate hated the pain she knew it caused both her mom and her dad.

Sorry. Meant that in a nice way. Are you really going to give up on this, tho?

Kate's eyes flicked to her journal, now perched on the side of her desk. She'd taped the P.I.'s letter back together as well as she could and added it to the next blank page. She couldn't help noticing there were still quite a few blank pages left to fill—if only she could think of a new avenue of investigation. Her lip curled up in a scowl.

I think I have to. I have nothing left to go off, Kate sent.

Sad face.

Kate rolled her eyes at her best friend's insistence on typing out descriptions rather than using emoticons. Kate thought it was ridiculous; Ellie insisted it was hilarious.

I really hoped this would work out for you.

I know. Me too. Kate's shoulders slumped.

Maybe you should call Braxton. Have a mack sesh. It could cheer you up.

Kate rolled her eyes. Not that she didn't enjoy kissing her boyfriend, but she wasn't about to tell him she was still looking for her birth parents. Ever since the stalker incident, he was more paranoid about her search than her mom and dad were.

Yeah... don't mention this to him, okay? I don't want him getting all weirded out.

I'll keep your dirty little secret. Winky face. Don't worry. Tomorrow's shopping trip will make you forget all about it.

Kate Unmasked

She was wrong, but Kate sent a smiley emoticon back anyway. A life-long obsession couldn't be erased by a shopping trip, but it was nice of Ellie to try.

Thanks, El. Time to be a spring slave. Talk later?

Yep!

She stuffed her phone in her pocket and scurried barefoot downstairs, putting on a fake happy face for her mom.

Her mom was making a list at the table when Kate entered the kitchen, and she barely looked up. "Could you help your brothers and sisters get started on their assignments when they get home? I promised Mrs. Oro I'd help her with her garden, and I don't know how long it's going to take." Her mom stepped over to the counter and peeked at whatever was cooking in the slow cooker.

Leave it to her mom to act like nothing had happened. Moving on was just one of her specialties. Kate held back a sigh and agreed, "Sure." All five kids in Kate's family had been adopted. Her mother wanted more, but the last two attempts at adoption had failed, and she decided they'd have to be happy with a family of seven, that God believed she had enough and others needed a chance to have families, too. At every meal she thanked God for her chance to be a mother to such great kids.

She kissed Kate's temple with a loud smack and then headed out. Kate looked at the master list of spring-cleaning chores. They'd started last week and would finish at the end of this week. Then came outdoor work. Kate's chore today was to clean out the mudroom closet. Easy. She looked at her assignment for tomorrow. The basement bathroom. Argh. That was her least favorite. Her mom's name was scribbled next to the attic for tomorrow. Her mom worked so hard all the time. If she hurried, maybe she'd have time to clean the attic, too. Kate could imagine how happy her mom would be to have an extra hour or so to herself tomorrow if Kate managed to finish it before her mom got back. Yes. She would do that for her mom. She knew that by helping her mom out, she'd also help herself out. Nothing like a little service to lift your spirits, and Kate needed that more than anything after the letter she'd received.

6

She'd hurry with the closet and then get started up in the attic. After dinner, she would do the basement bathroom so nothing would be in the way of her going to the mall the next day. Kate pushed play on the audio book on her phone, wanting something to take her mind off her disappointment and the depressing idea that there wasn't anything to find out about her birth parents. She dug into the closet, organizing the coats, gloves, boots, and other stuff inside it, making a pile of things to go to the cleaners.

As she finished, the front door slammed shut. She paused the book. Fifteen-year-old Jori and thirteen-year-old Amelia rushed into the kitchen and opened the fridge. Kate smiled at their predictability as she walked toward the kitchen. They pulled out the yogurt and carrots their mother had prepared for their snack and jumped onto the stools at the bar, chatting happily.

"I know. He's such a dork, right? I mean, who does that?" Jori said before lifting the foil off her yogurt.

Kate popped into the room and said, "Yep. A dork. Definitely."

They startled and Amelia's yogurt tipped over, spilling onto the counter. Laughing, Kate grabbed a paper towel and hurried over.

"It's not nice to sneak up on people," Amelia said, scowling, her light brown freckles bunching on her nose.

"I wasn't sneaking. I just finished cleaning the mudroom closet." Kate wiped up the yogurt, the sweet smell of strawberry wafting through the air.

They both groaned. "Chores." If they didn't look so different, everyone would assume they were twins like their brothers. They walked with the same lope, they talked with the same music to their voices, and they had the same mannerisms. It would be terrible next year when Amelia joined Kate at high school and left Jori at the junior high. They were inseparable.

"Yep. Chores." Kate grabbed her bag of carrots from the fridge and ate one. It was exceptionally crunchy, and she quickly ate another, leaning on the counter near the crockpot where dinner cooked away.

Kate Unmasked

"Can you pretend not to tell us?" Jori batted her eyelashes and put her hands together as if praying. "We want to enjoy the spring weather. This is Texas, you know, and the heat will be stifling in less than a month."

Kate raised an eyebrow. "Sorry. Jori, you have the front closet, and Amelia, you have the game closet. If you hurry, you'll have plenty of time to enjoy the *cool* weather."

"We can start with the front closet," Amelia said, whipping her head back to look at Jori. A section of her short brown hair flew across her face. It wasn't even a question in their minds if they would work alone or not. Kate loved that about them.

"Sounds good," Jori said, her dark brown eyes sparkling. "Kate, do you think mom and dad will let us go with some friends into Austin for a concert? Brian Kinney's coming in July."

Kate squished up her nose. Her parents never would have let her go when she was thirteen or fifteen, but they didn't seem to be as overprotective of her siblings as they were of her. It might have to do with the fact that she was the first child, but it seemed to Kate that her parents held a different standard and different rules for them and her. "If you present it in the right way, they just might say yes."

They looked at each other and giggled. "Well, I'll be up in the attic," Kate said. "Could you let the boys know they have the closets in the family room downstairs?"

"Yep!" they said in unison, their bright white teeth flashing as they smiled.

Kate flipped through the cleaning binder, turning the pages with more force than necessary. She huffed and glanced back at the girls, still chatting away at the counter. Ten bucks said her parents would let them go. There'd be boys, too, and yet she had to sneak around with her boyfriend. Oh, well. She couldn't explain it or change it. At the back of the binder was a zippered bag with several keys in it. She grabbed them out of the binder. A tingle swept through her. She loved surprising her parents.

"I'm glad it's you, and not me. I'd never go in there by myself. It gives me the creeps." Amelia gave an exaggerated shiver.

"No kidding," Jori said. "I wouldn't be surprised if there was a ghost up there or something. It's bad enough sharing a bedroom wall with it. Scary noises are always coming out of that room."

Kate shook her head. "Oh, brother. It's only an attic. And there's no ghost in there. Or anything scary for that matter." She skipped out of the room and headed upstairs.

The attic was accessible from the second floor by a door that looked like it led to a closet. Except this was a very large closet. Kate pulled out the key Mom had left and jammed it in the stiff lock. She'd only been inside the attic once or twice when her mom had been in there, and it felt a bit strange to go in without her.

Once inside, she flipped on the light switch. Dust swirled around her feet as she walked across the bare floorboards to plug in the vacuum. "Ghosts," she mused, a grin taking over her face. The air was stale and hot. After a quick trip sucking up the dust from the floor and the boxes, she started working on the boxes. Her mind drifted to the depressing letter and her search journal and she sighed, complete hopelessness filling her. She shook her head and with one quick swipe on her phone, the audiobook began again. She would not dwell on the dead-end news anymore. She couldn't if she wanted to keep her sanity.

She opened the first box and matched up the contents with the list on the outside of the box. Several of the items had been used throughout the year and were not candidates for the garbage or good will. She thought nothing had changed in most of the boxes for years. The rule of the house was that if you hadn't used an item in the last year, it was sent to charity, thus the organized and tidy house.

Kate liked to imagine that one day she'd find a new box, full of cool treasures. It never happened, but it didn't stop her from pretending. She kept working, opening one box and then another. She was about to finish the entire left side of boxes when the tornado twins burst into the attic with flashlights.

Kate Unmasked

"It does have lights, I told you," Stetson yelled over his shoulder at Jarem. Most of Kate's friends called the two seven-year-olds T1 and T2 because they couldn't tell the boys apart. Kate could, however. Stetson had a slighter build and a wicked glint in his eye. He was the ringleader and Jarem, the happy follower. Both had jet black hair and a sprinkle of freckles over their very white faces.

She clicked the audio book off. "You two know you're not supposed to be up here. Are your closets clean?" Kate gave them the look that said *get the heck out*, but Stetson said, "We came to help. Honest." His big dark eyes perused the attic. Kate was sure his thoughts were on how he could wreak havoc in there and suddenly, with a bellowing yell, he came at her. Jarem, not wanting to be left behind, joined the charge. "Monster in the attic!" Stetson screamed. "Kill the monster in the attic." Kate knew one thing for certain, she was about to be tackled. The force of the two running into her sent her tumbling back into the rafters and beyond to the wooden walls.

Her shoulders slammed into the large wooden panel. Ignoring the twinge of pain shooting through her back, she started tickling the boys. They squealed and laughed, but did not retreat. She fought for a good attack position and finally rose up on her knees and pinned Jarem. Stetson climbed on her back. Holding on to Jarem, she stood. Stetson hung on for dear life, his hands clasped around her neck. She carried them to the door and walked them out onto the carpeted second floor. She rubbed up against the wall, and Stetson fell to the ground. She let go of Jarem, and they both fell into a giggling mess.

"Oh, no, I'm dying. You got me." Kate stumbled back. "But I'm leaving a poisonous barrier to keep you from entering my deathbed." She pretended to spray something all around the entrance to the attic. "If you cross it, you will die." She stepped back into the attic and heard Stetson say, "Come on. Let's go make a potion that will counteract her poison." The two giggled and planned, their voices fading as their feet pattered down the stairs. She rubbed at her neck and arms. She hoped she didn't end up with bruises. Those boys were out of control. And they better have already done their chores or she'd be in the doghouse with her mom. She looked back at the boxes and realized she only had two left to check. She would finish the last two and then make sure the boys had done their work.

She sat down to work on the last two boxes and noticed the large wall next to her had warped in. "Great. Mom's going to love this," Kate grumbled aloud. She examined the wall; it was made up of sections of bare wood paneling sparsely nailed to the attic studs. The section she'd fallen against had come loose and the bottom corner gaped away from the studs while the middle of the panel bowed inward. Kate winced and started pushing at the bottom corner, trying to get it to lay flat against the stud again, but the wood was unyielding. She moved around trying to get a better angle, and something caught her eye—a baby pink lump on the floor behind the panel. She pulled the thin panel open a bit further. The pink color appeared to be some kind of large bag. She reached for it, but then heard her mom call her name.

"Kate? Are you up there?"

She started, her heart pounding hard into her ribs. She'd hoped to be done before her mom got home. She should have left with the boys. Now the surprise was ruined. She looked at the wall and groaned. She wanted her mom to be happy, not irritated with her. For a split second she thought she'd fess up to her mom about breaking the wall, but she didn't want anything to ruin the surprise she'd worked so hard on. She moved the board, sliding it back into position. She heard her mom open the door and her feet hit the floorboards. Kate inspected the wall. She couldn't tell it'd been disturbed. Quick as a snake's strike, she grabbed hold of one of the last two boxes and opened it.

"Kate? You in here?" Her feet padded on the floor.

"Yeah, Mom. I'm back here." She pulled a few things out and made a show of checking them against the label of contents. Her heart thundered in her chest. Her mom was going to be so thrilled when she noticed what had been done.

Her mom's feet pounded quickly on the floor. Was she rushing?

Could she tell the board had been moved? Why hadn't she mentioned how clean the room was? Kate had expected an exclamation of joy. She held her breath and kept pulling things out of the box, head down, excited for her mom to notice her hard work.

"You were supposed to do the mudroom closet today." Her mother's voice was flat. The shock of it made Kate look up. Was she mad? She resisted the urge to look at the wall, maybe the damage was worse than she thought. She should fess up and quick.

"I already did that. And the boys came up and—"

Her mom interrupted her. "I was supposed to work on this tomorrow." She clenched her teeth, but still somehow smiled. Maybe she hadn't noticed the board after all.

"Yeah," Kate said, her words tumbling quickly out of her mouth. "I wanted to surprise you and have this done before you got home."

Her mom seemed to visibly relax, but her eyes flicked to the board beside Kate. Kate kept her eyes on her mom. Was it out of place somehow?

"I only have this one box and one more to look through before I'm done." Kate smiled, hoping to lighten the mood and get a happy reaction out of her mom.

Her mom's teeth unclenched, but her eyes still held worry. She forced a toothy smile. "You must have worked really hard. Thank you." Her lips pressed together, and she shifted on her feet.

"Sorry, Mom. I thought I was doing a good thing."

Her mom's eyes flicked back to Kate, and she shook her head. "Come here." Her mom put her arms out, inviting Kate into a hug. She stood and took the offer. "It was good. I guess I was just shocked to find you here. And, truth be told, I don't like you being in this space by yourself. It could be dangerous. I understand why you did it, but promise me next time you'll let me know before you come in here."

"Sure, Mom. I can do that." Kate pulled out of her mom's arms and turned to work on those last two boxes. "I'll finish up so you won't have anything extra to do tomorrow."

She grabbed Kate's arm. Kate turned with a quick jerk. Her mom was not the grabby sort.

"No. It's okay. I'll get to that later. It's time to eat."

"I've only got those two boxes."

"The food's all ready." She loosened her hold on Kate and took a step back.

"Funny. I never thought you'd want me to stop working on a job before it was finished." Kate plastered a grin on her face.

Her mom huffed. "And don't think it will happen again. It's roast tonight. Your favorite."

Kate followed her out, unable to keep herself from snagging a last look at the panel. Her mom shut the door behind them and motioned for Kate to lock it. As she did, she could finally smell the promised roast.

2

Kate tossed and turned, unable to get the attic, the panel, and her mom's reaction to her being in there out of her mind. The longer she thought about it, the stranger it was. The fact that something was hidden in some kind of secret attic cubby was odd enough, but the way her mom had rushed her out—Kate wasn't sure if she remembered right, but it seemed her mom had been trying to get her away from the panel. As if there were something there she didn't want Kate to see. Kate moaned in frustration and sat up. If she didn't get some sleep, she could kiss all the studying she'd done after dinner goodbye. Even an hour of losing herself while playing the piano didn't help her anxiety. There was no way to avoid it—she'd just have to get back into the attic. She had to do well on her physics test tomorrow.

She grabbed the headlamp sitting on her emergency bucket—you could never be too prepared, her mom always said—and headed out into the hall. The floor lighting made the headlamp unnecessary. She headed for the kitchen and the key, but as she passed the attic door, she couldn't help but notice it was open a crack. She furrowed her brow and moved with quiet steps toward it. The door moaned as she opened it. She froze, but remained alone in the hallway. She had locked it, hadn't she?

She peeked inside. Totally dark. She walked in and whipped the door shut so that the sound was brief. In the darkness, she held her breath, straining for evidence that someone had heard, but the house was still. She flipped on her headlamp and padded to the far corner. Someone had been up there and moved the boxes around. Her mom?

Ten boxes were clustered in front of the broken panel now. She moved the five closest ones and then pushed on the panel, careful to work as quietly as possible. It didn't budge. She tried again. It was solid. Squinting, she used the headlamp to illuminate the area. Six bright, shiny screw heads had been drilled into the board where the nails had been, holding it fast. She flashed to the other panels. All had screws in them. Perhaps all but this section had had the screws in them already, and she hadn't noticed. She couldn't be sure.

With her slippers, she swished the dust and wood shavings that must have come from drilling the screw holes. She glanced at the other boards and noticed the shavings near them also. Unease settled over her like fine dust, making her shoulders twitch. Her mom knew she'd seen the panel, and now she'd screwed it shut and tried to hide it with boxes. Why? Knowing her mom obviously didn't want her in there almost made her turn around and leave, but a curiosity grew inside her. She needed to know what her mom was hiding. But a habitually obedient nature is hard to overcome; she needed outside support. She dialed Ellie, who answered on the first ring. Kate knew Ellie would be up watching *My Not So Normal Life on the Jersey Shore.* It came on every night at eleven, and Ellie watched it without fail.

"Hold on," Ellie said. "It's almost a commercial."

"Okay." Kate tapped her foot, irritated at Ellie's compulsion.

"Talk fast. Amy's about to tell her husband she wants a divorce, and I'm sure we're about to find out where hottie Jace has been all this time. When my dad hacked the studio's account, the script wasn't there this time."

"Eeelliee. This is real life trauma you're about to hear," Kate said in a hoarse whisper. What would happen to Ellie's parents if the television studio ever found out they were hacking into their accounts? This was the perfect example of money buying them whatever they wanted.

"I'm listening!" Irritation laced her words.

"I found a loose board in my attic, and I think my mom is hiding stuff behind it."

"Well go look behind it."

"I tried. Every board in the attic is now screwed fast."

"What?" Kate could imagine Ellie's determined and incredulous face.

"I think my mom was afraid of me looking behind it, and so she shut it for good."

"They're only screws. Use a screw driver to take them out, and check it out."

Kate should have known Ellie would suggest that. When it came to sleuthing, Ellie and her family were experts. They'd been chasing fame for so long, they'd learned every trick in the book for uncovering people's secrets. No way they'd let some screws keep them from discovering information.

"I don't know. If she was so worried about me finding something, maybe I don't want to know what it is."

"Don't be crazy. Of course you want to know what it is."

Kate's parents had always emphasized self-restraint and obedience, and for the most part she'd fallen in line perfectly. Ellie constantly poked at her discipline, telling her it was unnatural for her not to act a little erratically. But this time, Kate couldn't argue with Ellie. She really did want to know.

"Do you want me to come over?"

"Maybe." Ellie often came over to Kate's house in the night. Kate let her in through the front door, and she hustled up the stairs. No one was the wiser. Ellie helped Kate whenever there was something crazy or scary going on.

"Then you're going to have to wait for a half an hour. I'm not DVR-ing this baby. I can't wait to find out what's going to happen. I need to see my hottie Jace tonight."

Kate rolled her eyes. "Why do you like that guy? He's either chasing skirts or totally depressed. You deserve better."

"Oh, I know, but as eye candy and sweet dream maker, he's the best."

"That is true. He looks amazing. You don't need to come over. It's okay. I can do it myself. But if there's a desiccated corpse back there, I'm going to blame it on you."

Ellie laughed. "It's back on. Call me when you find out what it is. If you don't call, I'll come looking for your dead body."

"Okay." Kate hung up, tiptoed downstairs and out into the shop to get a screwdriver, and was back in the attic in less than two minutes. Drawing a deep breath, she pushed through her reluctance and attacked the first screw at the bottom of the panel.

Her wrist ached as she twisted the fourth screw loose. She left the top two in to hold it in place. The sawdust mingled with dust particles in the air and tickled her nostrils. She held back a sneeze as she pulled up and out on the bottom right corner of the panel. Behind the board, a gaping cavity stretched out before her. The light of her headlamp revealed a stack of boxes hunched up against the back of the space. She swiveled her head around, shining the headlamp around the confines of the space. She couldn't believe how large it was, at least six feet deep and about four feet wide. She could fit her whole body inside. She wouldn't be able to stand, though.

She paused. There were bound to be spiders in there and who knew what else. She took a deep breath, pushing away her worried thoughts. She crawled inside. Her foot got stuck, and the wood scraped her ankle as she tried to pull it through the closing gap. A layer of skin right at her ankle ripped away and blood dripped down it. She pushed her pant leg against it and waited thirty seconds, clenching her teeth against the sting. She never should have done this without Ellie. The blood stopped, so she looked around. A circle of light from her headlamp highlighted the layer of dust that sat on everything and she coughed. She buried her face in the crook of her elbow, trying to stifle the sound.

The baby pink bag she'd spotted earlier that day was nowhere to be seen. Kate frowned. So her mom had not only fixed the panel, but she'd also come back here and moved things around. Intense curiosity impelled her forward.

The top box was taped shut with a shiny strip of packing tape. There was not a speck of dust on it. Kate hesitated only for a moment before ripping the tape free and pulling back the flaps. Inside, smashed and warped to fit the confines of the box, was the pink bag. Kate recognized it now for what it was—a diaper bag.

Kate lifted it gingerly. Unlike the box, it was covered in dust and faded with age. She stood dumfounded as a jumbled mass of questions collided in her brain, one ringing out louder than all the rest. What the heck is going on here?

She opened the bag and ran her hands through the interior and each pocket—it was empty. She turned it over and over in her hands, but there was nothing on the bag—no name, not even a brand. The box, too, was empty.

Stymied, Kate set the bag back into the box and moved it to the wooden floor. The second box was also taped shut, but the tape looked older—the edges curled up and the silver was dulled by layers of dust. Kate wasted no time yanking the box open.

Inside were a child's sweater and a pair of denim pants, neatly folded. Kate held them up—the pants had a little ruffle around the bottom hem, and the sweater was soft white with pearl buttons down the front. A tiny snag on the sleeve made Kate's throat fill with unexpected emotion. She smoothed it out and examined the tags—they were both a size 2T. Not knowing what to make of that, Kate set the clothes on the first box and kept going through the contents: a pair of white mary janes to match the sweater, a sippy cup, and a little pink hair bow. The last thing Kate found, in the bottom of the box, was a locket—a filigreed heart the size of a child's palm on a long gold chain.

It took her a while to get the locket to open. A picture of a woman holding a baby looked up at her.

The woman's bright blue eyes laughed with delight. Pure joy

exuded from her. Kate couldn't help but smile back. Pulling the picture close, she checked the baby out. Chubby and dressed in a frilly white dress, the baby appeared to be going to her baptism. Dust motes swirled around her as she stared at the pair in puzzlement.

Her phone vibrated. After setting the locket back in the box, she checked her phone. Ellie. *Did you get inside yet? Don't leave me hanging. You're dead aren't you?*

Kate started to type, but found she didn't have the patience for explaining everything. She dialed Ellie.

"I'm alive," she whispered.

"Oh, goodie. I wasn't looking forward to having to replace you. All the hassle."

"I hear ya."

"You sound weird," Ellie said, ever observant. "What did you find in there? Was it a dead body after all?"

"I... don't know. I don't understand what I found."

Ellie drew an impatient breath. "Come on, walk me through it."

Kate described the items she found—before she could even get to explaining the locket, Ellie cut her off.

"OMG, Kate! That's your stuff! Your baby stuff!"

"But—it can't be," Kate said, her frustration and confusion made her a little more terse than she meant to be. "I was adopted when I was one. These clothes are for a two year old—there are little shoes and everything."

"Huh, that *is* weird. Maybe you were on the big side?"

Kate shook her head. "I don't think so. This stuff isn't mine."

"Jori's then? Or Amelia's?"

"No—they were both babies when we got them. I can't figure out why my mom would want to hide this stuff."

"Maybe...ooh, I know! You have a secret sibling. One you never knew about, and your parents are keeping her in the attic."

"Uh... right." Kate picked up the locket again and ran her fingers along the chain.

Kate Unmasked

"Well, what about the bag? Are you sure it's empty? Check again."

Kate sighed but complied. She pulled the bag out and looked inside. Nothing. Streaks of something dark, almost black were on the shoulder strap. She avoided it. She swished her hand through each section.

"No, there's nothing here," she sighed. She started putting it back in the box and a glint of silver hit her eye. "Wait, there might be…" There was a zipper in the middle pocket. She opened it. Inside was a gold cross on a chain. She let it dangle from her fingers. It turned side to side, and she noticed an engraving on it. She turned the bag over and shook it. She heard a crinkling sound. She searched one last time. In the deep corner of one section she found a receipt. She flattened the paper out. It was from a pizzeria in New Jersey. She described it all to Ellie.

Kate sighed deeply. "Well, this has been a colossal waste of time, and I'm going to fail my physics test for no reason. Ugh, and now I've got to put all this stuff back."

"No way, Kate! I think we need to look into this further."

"What—why? It's got nothing to do with me. It's probably just some old junk left behind by a former owner."

"Then why was your mom hiding it from you?"

Kate hesitated. She didn't have an answer for that.

"Look, I gotta get out of here. I'm feeling all itchy and claustrophobic."

Ellie huffed. "Fine. But take the cross with you—and the receipt!"

Kate started to argue, but found she didn't want to put the cross back or set the locket back in its box. She liked the weight of it in her hand, and she couldn't deny that the mystery of it tugged at her. "All right, I'll bring them out to show you, but if I get grounded over this you owe me big time."

"Oh! Commercial's over, gotta go—Jace is on!" Ellie didn't even wait for Kate to say goodbye.

Kate pocketed the cross, the locket, and the receipt and packed the rest of the items back in their boxes, smoothing the packing tape back down as best she could. She pushed back out through the panel, careful not to get her foot caught this time, and began the obnoxious cranking of getting all four screws back into place.

Back in her bed twenty minutes later, she gripped the locket in her fist. It didn't have anything to do with her, but the excitement of discovery thrummed through her anyway. If she couldn't solve her own mystery, maybe a new one was just what she needed.

3

With locket and cross necklace tucked nicely into her jean skirt pocket, Kate sailed down the stairs, excited to get breakfast over with and show Ellie her treasures. She sat at the kitchen table with her dad, a strict family rule, and began eating her fruit and nut-filled oatmeal.

"Did you sleep well, Kate?" her dad asked. He'd already eaten and was reading the paper.

"Okay. I could always use more of it, though." She finished her oatmeal.

He chuckled. "Couldn't we all?"

She nodded and dug into her eggs.

"You ready for your physics test?"

"As ready as I'll ever be."

"I'm sure you'll ace it." She took her vitamins with the remainder of her milk. She watched her mom out of the corner of her eye, trying not to stare but at the same time studying her. She stood at the stove, humming to herself, holding a paperback book open in one hand and stirring the oatmeal with the other. The familiar sight jarred Kate. Watching her mother perform her normal morning routine, all the while feeling the weight of the locket and her mother's secret press against her leg—it was like seeing a stranger step into her mother's skin.

She felt a twinge of guilt for hiding what she'd found, but she had a feeling if she confronted her mother with it, she'd get no answers at all. With a shaky hand, she patted her pocket of treasures absentmindedly. It wasn't that she wanted to pry into her mother's secrets—not really. She didn't want to cause problems. After she showed Ellie, she would sneak back into the attic and return the necklaces and receipt. Order would be returned. Her sisters joined them at the table as she stood to leave just like every other day.

"Morning," she said.

"Hey, Kate," the two girls said in unison, as they dragged their chairs out from the table.

Kate passed her mom, who was bringing steaming hot bowls of oatmeal to her sisters. Kate rinsed her dishes and then put them into the dishwasher. Her mom had been chopping vegetables, no doubt for dinner. Kate grabbed her sack lunch and said, "Thanks, Mom." The routine felt familiar and calming.

"You're welcome, Kate. Have a great day at school."

"I will," she said. Once outside, she rushed to Ellie's mini cooper and climbed in. Kate liked it when it was Ellie's turn to drive, one less stressful thing to worry about. She dug the locket and cross from her pocket before climbing in. She held them up for Ellie to see as she backed out of the driveway.

"You did take them. I wondered if you'd let your sense of propriety get in your way and you'd leave them."

"I almost wanted to," Kate admitted. "But I couldn't do it. I have to know what these are, who they belonged to."

"Wait, what's this?" Ellie slammed on the breaks and reached over to get a better look at the locket. Good thing they were in a quiet neighborhood without much traffic because the tail end of the car would have been blocking traffic completely. For once it was good to be in such a slow, secure town.

"Oh yeah, I didn't get to tell you last night—"

Ellie opened the locket while Kate talked and cut her off with an excited, "Holy crap, Kate—"

"—because you did *that*—"

"This is you!" Her eyes were wide and her red-lipsticked mouth gaped open.

"No, I told you—I was adopted when I was one. The kid is at least two in this picture."

Ellie frowned. "This is so weird. I mean, I know it's not a very good picture. It's small, and blurry—"

"*Very* blurry—"

"But I would swear this little girl has the same chin as you."

"My chin? Really? I think that's a bit of a stretch." Kate snatched the locket back. "Would you please just drive? We're already late to pick up Braxton."

Ellie straightened out and drove on. "I really think that's you in the picture, Kate."

"But it can't be me. I told you—"

"I know what you told me. But what if your parents were lying?"

If Kate had been driving it would have been her turn to slam on the breaks. "What are you talking about?"

"You know your mom is hiding something, so don't act like she's some kind of saint, like it's impossible that she could lie to you." Without thinking, Kate gripped the locket; the clasp dug into her palm. She didn't respond to Ellie, and Ellie took that as encouragement to continue. "I'm just saying it's possible that the story your parents have told you is not one hundred percent factual."

"Whatever. I don't want to talk about this now."

"But this is the last chance we'll get until gym! We're almost at Braxton's, and I won't get another word out of you until lunch." When Kate didn't answer, Ellie stuck her tongue out at her. "Fine, we'll discuss this at gym." Ellie grinned mischievously, and Kate made a point of staring out the window until they arrived at Braxton's house.

When they arrived, Kate popped out and started a text, but Braxton came out of the house before she could even send it. He smiled and walked her way. Ellie was right about one thing. Kate wasn't about to talk to Ellie about her birth parents in front of Braxton. She'd have to put on an especially happy face for him so he wouldn't suspect anything.

After sharing a quick kiss, they sat in the back seat together, clicking their seat belts on. "Hey, Ellie."

"Hey." She pulled out of the driveway and only a few houses down, stopped again to pick up her most recent boy toy, Masters.

He slid into the front seat and put a kiss that was anything but soft and sweet onto Ellie's mouth. She gladly joined in on the assault. Kate squirmed in her seat.

Braxton cleared his throat. "Uh, yeah. School. Remember that thing we do five out of seven days a week? It's waiting for us." Kate snuggled into Braxton, and he put his arm around her shoulders.

Ellie laughed, pulling away from Masters. "Later." Masters pulled back and buckled his seatbelt.

***

Much to Ellie's chagrin, there was no time to talk in gym. They were in the throes of a basketball tournament. While Ellie ran willy nilly up and down the floor, Kate worked hard, making half her team's points.

Kate looked toward the showers, but knew it would be social suicide if she ventured in. No one ever showered. Ever. Instead, she grabbed her bag and headed into the bathroom where she pretended to pee. Instead, she took off her sweaty clothes and wiped her body down with wet wipes before washing her hands and face at the sink. She dressed quickly and fixed her makeup and hair. Her face was still hot and red from the game. The blasted changing room was too hot for her to cool down. She rushed into the gym, letting the fresh air cool her as she waited for Ellie.

Ellie walked out, and Kate moved to meet her for lunch. They made their way to their lockers, and Kate finally felt the heat leave her body. They pulled out their lunches and hurried to their regular spot to eat just down the hall. All their other friends had second lunch.

"Look," Ellie said around a mouthful of roast beef sandwich. "I want to believe your parents, too, but my family and I have seen too many betrayals to simply take things at face value."

"You mean you've seen too many betrayals on reality TV." Kate chomped on some chips.

"Same thing."

Kate turned her head away and rolled her eyes while she chewed.

"All right then—what's the first thing you can remember about your life? Like, actually remember?"

Kate stared at her friend like she was insane. "I don't know! Kissing Matt Gonzales in the first grade? What's yours?"

"My point exactly—you don't remember your life enough to corroborate your parents' story. Maybe you were adopted at one, or maybe you were older. *You* don't remember."

"Do you remember anything from when you were one?"

"No, but that's beside the point. The point is..." Ellie was scrambling for something, and Kate had to laugh at the look of slight desperation on her friend's face. She really wanted to create intrigue out of nothing. "The point is—are there pictures?"

Kate nearly choked on a chip. "What?"

"You know, the day you were adopted. All the cute little things you did when you were a little one-year-old baby. Are there pictures?"

"I..." Kate blinked at her friend in mild shock. What Ellie was suggesting was impossible. And yet—she couldn't remember ever seeing pictures of herself before age four. She didn't have a baby book, and all the family pictures on the walls were ones taken after Jori and Amelia joined the family. "I'm sure they're somewhere. I just never really asked."

Ellie wiggled her eyebrows. "Or maybe they don't exist because you weren't actually adopted when your parents say you were."

"I think you're just desperate to make life a little more like those shows you watch. Could you do me a favor and find some kind of scandal in your own life and leave mine alone?" Kate meant it teasingly, but the words came out in a more irritated tone than she'd intended.

Ellie's words were bugging her more than they should.

Ellie raised her hands defensively. "Look, I'm just trying to help you find the truth. All I'm saying is, we should check the stuff out. Prove that your parents' story is true. Wouldn't that make you feel better about it all?"

"I feel fine, Ellie. It's you that seems to have a problem with things."

"Yes, I do. And you're lucky to have a friend who is willing to stand up for you. Your family, it's like nothing I've ever seen. Everyone is so regulated. Level. They're hiding something, I know it."

This wasn't new; Ellie was always looking for trouble in paradise. "Just because our lives aren't full of chaos like yours doesn't mean something is off. Seriously. Maybe we've just figured it out."

Ellie huffed and held her hand out. "Give me that locket and cross, please." She was taking control, like she always did. Kate reached into her pocket and pulled the two articles out, handing them to Ellie. Ellie set the cross down on the carpeted floor and focused on the locket. She fumbled with opening it. Kate set her sandwich down to help her. "It catches right here." She pointed to a little piece of jutting metal and then flicked the locket open. Ellie stared at the picture, pulling it close and then letting it fall away to look Kate over. She bit her lip.

"Do you care if I take it out?"

"What? The picture?"

She gave Kate a *duh* look and then began to pry the picture out with her fingernail.

"Be careful, Ellie." Kate reached out for the locket.

Ellie turned away, blocking her and continuing to work on the picture. Kate stopped eating. "If you ruin that picture, I'm going to be so super mad."

"I won't. I'm a professional, remember?" She turned back, picture in one hand and the locket in the other. She turned it over in her hand. "Hey, check this out!" She held the photograph out to Kate. On the back of the heart-shaped paper, *Constanzie* was written in cursive in black pen. "Constanzie?" Kate questioned, eyes fixed on the word. Ellie handed the picture to her and typed the word into a search engine on her phone. It was obvious from the results that it was a name. An Italian name meaning constancy in English.

"So—the woman's name is Constance? And she's from Italy? How did a locket from Italy get into my attic?" Kate leaned back into the lockers.

"Well, it could be the baby's name. And there are a lot of countries that speak Italian. But we are definitely going to find out how it got in your attic, and I'm betting it's got something to do with you."

Ellie had that look in her eye. The look that told Kate she was thrilled beyond words at the challenge of uncovering something. "Can I hold onto these?" She held up the two necklaces.

Kate reached back and massaged her neck, her mouth going dry. "I was hoping to put them back tonight. What if my mom discovers they're gone?"

"She won't. I know how you feel and no worries. I've got this. I know how to take care of precious things."

"What exactly are you going to do with them?"

"I'm going to investigate. Find out everything I can about them. And you're going to help me."

Kate raised an eyebrow at her. "I am?"

"Yep." Ellie grinned. "I know it's hard to think that your parents might be lying to you, but you're going to face that because you're a very brave person, and more than anything in the whole world—you want the truth."

Kate stared at the locket in her hand. For some reason it was almost physically painful to think of handing it over to Ellie. But her friend was right—she did want the truth, more than anything.

"Fine. And here," she handed over the locket and cross, then dug in her pocket for the receipt she'd found. "That receipt I found. Maybe it can tell us something." Something niggled at her, but she ignored it. They sat back down and continued to eat again.

"You are one brave soul." She gave Kate a meaningful look. "You are braver than Maria was when her best friend outed her."

Nine times out of ten, Ellie used some connection to the reality shows she watched to make her points. Maria was on a reality TV show about dating. Kate didn't watch those shows unless she was with Ellie, but Ellie kept Kate up to speed, filling her in to what was happening on her favorites every day. And it wasn't only Ellie who was enamored. Her whole family lived to watch those shows. They went to great lengths to find out everything about the various players. They even worked with a publicist who sent in application after application for their family to get on a reality show. They planned their vacations around reality TV filming schedules.

"Well, that's a huge compliment." Kate raised her eyebrows and shook her head. "You're obsessed."

Ellie slugged her with her petite fist. Kate laughed. Ellie scowled. "I didn't see you complaining about my *obsession* when you were on the beach with me last year." Ellie's family planned all their vacations around the reality stars, hoping for any chance to see or mingle with them. And lucky her, Kate always got to go with them. Last year they went to California to stay near the filming location of *Getting Your Beach Body*. They'd seen eight of the ten stars on that show and talked to one. They considered that more than amazing.

"You know I like those shows, I just don't have the energy or time to focus on them like you guys do. And I loved the beach. Where are we going this year?" It wasn't like Kate was assuming too much. She'd vacationed with them for the last six years.

"Well, it's not set in stone yet." Ellie's eyes sparkled and she looked around as if telling Kate a secret she wanted no one else to hear. Her brown hair waved over her shoulders. "And it probably won't happen, but Max Trenton and Sally Foster are starting a new reality show, and our publicist thinks we have a real shot at making it on."

Kate had no idea who those two people were, but figured they were TV producers of some sort. "What? When?" A mix of excitement and dread filled her.

Kate Unmasked

"It's scheduled to start shooting right after school lets out. But how many times has our publicist told us we were shoo-ins for something and it never happened?" She grimaced. "My parents are betting on this one, though."

"I'm crossing my fingers for you. You're finally going to be on TV!" This had to have been in the works for a long time. Why hadn't she brought it up before now? Kate had a sinking feeling.

"Yeah. The bad part is that if we do get on, it's a minimum year-long gig, and that means no vacation this year." She tapped her fingers on the table and cleared her throat.

"It sounds amazing, except for the whole, no vacation with your best friend thing. So why are you so nervous? What's the show about?"

She swallowed hard. "It's not in the U.S."

Kate's head jerked back. "What?"

"It's in Italy." Ellie's eyes lit up with excitement that was obviously shadowed only by what she thought Kate's reaction would be.

Kate let that sink in. No wonder Ellie had kept it from her. She wanted to be excited for Ellie, but how could she be? "Italy?"

Ellie nodded and reached out for Kate's hands. Kate pulled them onto her lap. "Don't be upset," Ellie said.

Kate looked at her hands. This was not good. "Don't be upset? How long have you known about this?" Kate's eyes flashed.

"A while, but like I said, it's not a sure thing. I didn't want to worry you about it yet."

"You're going to leave me for a whole year? Our senior year?" Kate bit her lip.

"It wouldn't be forever, and I'm sure we'll be able to write it into the script somewhere that you could come for a visit. Italy, Kate. Seriously." Her eyes brightened again and her smile—she was over the moon about it.

Kate's stomach soured. What would she do without Ellie? "You don't think I could go with you the whole time? We could pretend to be fraternal twins or something." Kate clutched at her necklace.

Ellie shook her head. "The show chronicles families moving to foreign countries and the struggles associated with that. Colby and I would play the son and daughter who hate their parents for moving them away from the only life they'd known. It's a great angle actually. I'm sure you'll be able to come at some point." She leaned closer to Kate and exhaled while looking up. "It will be hard, Kate, but I need you on my side. I need you to be happy for me."

Kate couldn't handle all the feelings roiling inside her. She needed to get out of there. She stood up. The bell rang, and she ran down the hall.

She spent her last class of the day embroiled in a battle with herself. She wanted to be happy for Ellie. This was what her family had been working on for at least the last ten years. It was about time for their publicist to get them a show. But what about Kate? She would be alone. Sure, she had Braxton and other friends, but none were like Ellie. If Kate were to be honest with herself, she'd have to admit that it wasn't Italy that was the issue. It was the fact that Ellie had purposefully kept it from her. She told Ellie everything. She was her best friend. Ellie brought fun and excitement into Kate's life. Without Ellie, she would be left to live a very normal and predictable life, and that suddenly wasn't okay. She knew on some level that she was being selfish, but she didn't care. Maybe if Ellie had told her the second her family knew it was a real possibility she would have had time to accept it.

As it was, one minute she was willing to give Ellie the benefit of the doubt and accept that she was trying to protect her and the next, her stubborn side took over, and anger and betrayal filled her. The final bell rang. The moment she was dreading had arrived. Should she underline her disapproval of Ellie's late admission by not going on the shopping trip? If she went she most likely wouldn't have a good time. But if she went home she would definitely not have a good time. At least at the mall Kate would be with a whole group. And Braxton would probably show up at some point. It would be the ride to the mall that would be awful. She stood, still not knowing what her choice was going to be.

4

Kate stood outside the school doors, staring at the line of busses waiting to take kids home. In fifty feet she could be on her way home on one of those busses and show Ellie just how upset she was. Her stomach ached. She didn't want to be mad at Ellie.

"Kate!" She turned toward the voice. Amber, one of her good friends, ran down the school stairs and right up to her. "Ellie just texted me. She's waiting for us."

"Oh!" Kate said. "You're riding with us?" Ellie must've wanted some interference.

"Yeah. Melissa went home sick. Come on. Jessie and Stockton already left." Amber started down the steps.

Kate bit her lip. She'd hang back and let Amber sit shotgun. That would give her a good separation from Ellie and give Kate more time to figure out what she wanted to say to her. She texted Braxton, asking him if he was going to be able to come to the mall. He didn't answer so she figured he had baseball practice.

Amber must have anticipated that Kate would want to sit in the front, like always, because she sat in the back seat. Kate almost followed her, but at the last second wondered if Ellie would ever forgive her for that. Kate didn't want an all-out war.

Kate yanked the passenger side door open and sat with a huff. Ellie raised her eyebrow and offered a questioning gaze. Kate turned and stared out the front window, letting out a heavy breath.

"Are you two fighting or something?" Amber asked. "What happened?"

Neither of them responded. Ellie turned up the music for the five minute drive, the music relaxing some of the tension that abounded. And all Kate could think about was that she'd given Ellie the two necklaces. How could she have been so careless?

They lucked out with a close parking spot near the food court entrance. The three climbed out of the car, and Kate rushed forward, glancing back to see Amber give Ellie a concerned look. They met up with the others in the food court waiting in line to get shakes. Ellie held back, her hands twisting together as she rocked side to side on her feet. Kate forced herself not to go to her. Instead, she sidled up to Jessie near the front of the line. "What flavor are you going to get?"

They both ordered and went to find a table where they could all sit.

Colby, Ellie's older brother, showed up, making it easier for Kate to avoid Ellie. Colby was a senior, and Kate had had a crush on him since before she hit puberty. Ellie and he loved to hang out, so Kate spent a lot of time with him. He was a forward on the school soccer team and had enough charisma and good looks to make people stare without doing a darn thing. And while her knees went a bit wobbly and her mind a bit numb every time she saw him, in the end, a sweet big brother comfort swept over her by the time they left each other.

Awkwardness and dread vanished as Colby met them while waiting for their shakes to be prepared in the food court. Kate ran to him and gave him a huge hug. Colby swung her around.

"I thought you had soccer practice today." Kate caught a quick breath as he let her down.

"The field's too wet to play on, and other teams are using the gym, so we got a day off."

"Nice." She nodded at him. Would the baseball team be practicing in the gym?

"You getting a shake?" He motioned with his head toward the shake shop.

"Yep. Chocolate mint." She bounced on her toes.

"Typical. You really should branch out." His eyes flicked to Ellie, who was sullen. And while there was a twinge of regret, Kate thought that was as it should be—and then immediately felt bad for thinking that. Colby gave Kate a questioning look. He lowered his voice. "And you two?" He motioned toward Ellie. "It must've been bad; you two haven't squabbled for months."

"She told me about Italy at lunch today, for the *first* time." She growled.

"Oh!" His lips rounded and then pressed together. "I thought she was waiting until we knew for sure to tell you."

Kate pushed him back. "Thanks a lot. Maybe I should be pissed with you, too?"

"No. And you shouldn't be mad at Ellie, either. She wanted to tell you, but she didn't want you to react badly."

"I wouldn't have reacted badly if she had been open with me." She crossed her arms over her chest.

"You mean like you're acting now?" He shifted his weight to one side and raised his eyebrows.

Kate hung her head, her hands falling to her sides. "She should have told me before now. You could be leaving in less than two months."

"All the more reason to enjoy every moment until then." He smiled that perfect white smile.

Kate huffed.

"Right?"

"Right," she admitted. "But I want to be mad a little longer."

"Of course you do." He mussed up her hair.

"Hey!"

He pointed to the counter. "Your shake is ready."

Kate retrieved it. He motioned with his head toward Ellie. "Make up. You may as well do it now so that this trip is fun. I hate to see her all sad and dejected."

"Not yet," Kate said, shaking her head.

"Look. I'm going to go order and by the time I get my shake, I want you sitting with Ellie. No excuses." He broke away from Kate.

Kate looked at Ellie. Not yet. She couldn't forgive her yet. Maybe at the end of the shopping trip she'd feel differently, but not now. Kate never wanted Ellie to repeat this mistake. It hurt too much. She sat next to Amber.

"Man, that looks good, Kate. Trade?" Amber said, eyeing Kate's shake.

They each took a bite of each other's shakes. Amber's was cookie dough. It was good, but not great. Ellie's eyes flicked to Kate's, sorrow lining them. It took all of Kate's strength not to forgive her right then and there, but she told herself she had to in order to protect herself from future pain.

Colby sat next to Ellie and raised a brow, shaking his head.

Shame rushed through Kate, but she buried it deep. She would forgive Ellie, just not yet.

She got a text message from Braxton saying he would meet them in ten minutes at the information booth. Relief shot through her. Braxton would take her mind off Ellie and give her something else to think about.

As they passed the information booth, Kate couldn't help but notice the five grand pianos circling it. A piano dealer had brought the pianos in to sell them, but no one was even giving them a second look. She felt bad for the sales person and for herself and how badly things were going with Ellie. She needed her fix of peace, and one of those pianos would give it to her. It wasn't often that she got to play on such a beautiful instrument.

She hated playing in public, but she took a deep breath and headed over to the nicest one. She knew it would ease the sadness she felt. She'd do a quick number and then go. No one would even notice. And no one was forcing her to do it. It was her choice. While the group went into

Buckle, she sat down to play. She let herself get lost in the music, her tension and feelings of betrayal melting away. When she reached the end of the Piano Concerto by Grieg, she opened her eyes. All six of her friends were standing around the piano, and the piano guy finally had customers. Several people clapped. She stood in a quick burst and wanted nothing more than to get out of there fast.

Ellie said, "Look, you're famous."

"Seriously epic, Katiebug," Braxton said. "I have the most amazing girlfriend ever."

"Okay. Moving on," Kate said. The piano salesman smiled and winked at her, unwilling to leave the customers she'd helped to attract. Why couldn't she love playing for an audience? Why?

"I seriously don't get why you don't give concerts. They'd sell out." Maria said.

Kate's gut twisted. She had a very good reason for not playing for people, but she never talked about it to anyone. "I'm not that good. I'm much better at math, and it's by far the more useful talent." It was her pat answer, and she'd said it so many times, it flew out of her mouth automatically.

"Whatever," Maria said. "Seems that's more useful with all the stress people have these days than being able to work out a math problem."

"Ah, but using perfect equations to build buildings and roads and bridges, now that is useful." Kate smiled and looked sheepishly at Ellie who stood a bit behind everyone else, staring at her feet. Kate moved over to her. Ellie looked up. Kate shrugged, looked at Ellie and then hugged her. With all her stress gone, Kate was able to let go of the pain and hurt and forgive Ellie. Ellie melted into her. "I'm sorry," she whispered into Kate's hair. "I should have told you sooner."

"I was being stubborn. It was my fault. I can't believe you're going to Italy."

They laughed and everyone in the group seemed to let out a collective sigh of relief. All was as it should be in the universe. They walked to the next store, Braxton on one side holding her hand and Ellie on the other.

***

Kate stared at their family photos on the wall in the family room. Every one of them was from the time following Amelia's adoption. She'd never noticed that before. Ellie's earlier words about Kate's age at adoption were getting to her. This was an easy problem to solve. All she had to do was to get her mom to get her some pictures. She vaguely remembered bringing some to school and looking at picture books with her mom when she was younger, but it'd been a long time. There had to be a ton. Seriously, she was their first child.

She marched into the kitchen. "Hey Mom, could you get me some of my baby pictures?"

Her mom shut the cabinet she'd opened without getting anything out. "What do you need those for?"

"Nothing. I just wanted to look at them. I can't seem to find them."

"Uh. Well. Sure. I can get you some." She turned and opened the cupboard door again, pulling down some plates.

"Can you maybe do it now?" Kate shifted on her feet. She wasn't usually so demanding.

Her mom walked to the table and put the plates down. "Not right now. I'm getting dinner ready."

"Tell me where they are, and I'll get them." Kate forced a smile. "Are they in one of the two boxes in the attic that I didn't get to check?"

"No. It's too hot in the attic. I'm not exactly sure where they are. I'm going to have to look." She moved toward the stove and stirred the spaghetti.

"How about I finish dinner and you go get them?" She moved toward her mom. "I really need them right now."

Her mom tapped the wooden spoon she'd been using on the edge of the pot and laid it across the top. She turned in slow motion. "You *need* them, or you *want* them? You're going to need to exercise a bit of patience on this one, Kate. We can talk about it again tomorrow."

Kate Unmasked

"Tomorrow? But I really want them now. Let me finish dinner. It's not a big deal."

"I said, tomorrow." Her mom turned back to the stove, removed the spoon from the pot and poured the water and noodles into a colander in the sink.

"Ugh!" Kate said, throwing her arms into the air. "I don't see what the big deal is."

"Not that I need to give you further explanation, but I don't have time. Your dad and I are going to a movie right after dinner, and I'm already running late."

Her dad walked in at that very moment. "We're going to a movie?" he questioned.

Her mom whipped around. "Of course we are honey, did you forget?" There was something in the way she said it that told Kate her mom was hoping her dad would play along.

"Oh, yeah. Uh, huh. Sorry honey, I had a busy day at work today."

"It will be nice to forget it all and relax at the theater." Her mom sighed. Kate watched her parents with narrowed eyes.

"Whatever," Kate said under her breath.

"What was that?" her dad asked.

"Nothing. I'll tell everyone it's time for dinner." She hunched her shoulders forward as she walked away.

When she came back into the room followed by her siblings, her parents were whispering by the stove. Kate stared at them as they turned. Her dad rubbed at his chin and looked at his feet after his eyes briefly met Kate's. Her mom cleared her throat and shifted before announcing much more loudly than necessary, "Spaghetti and meatballs tonight. Who's ready?"

The boys were the first to holler out that they were ready and the girls said, "Sweet," in unison. Ellie was right. Her parents were hiding something about those pictures. Kate ate without speaking unless someone asked her a direct question. She then answered with as few words as possible, making sure not to allow a true conversation.

Feeling irritable again, Kate turned to the piano to find solace before heading to bed. She couldn't remember a time that she'd felt so out of sorts for so long. She lost herself in the piece and once done, she stood, feeling much better. She wasn't alone. Her dad sat on one of the sofas in the room. She forced herself to acknowledge him.

"Hi, Dad."

"Hi, Sweetie. That was beautiful."

She smiled, but inside, she wished he wasn't there. She didn't want anything to disturb her newly acquired calm.

"The office is having a dinner party at O'Shay's, and I'd like you to play during the time the guests arrive and when dinner is served. Something upbeat and interesting. How does that sound?"

Her body hunched forward, and her hands began to tremble. She wanted to say no, but knew that wasn't a possibility even though she would be sick, truly sick for the entire day before the performance. Her parents forced her into using her talent over and over again, believing that repeating the act would free her from the nerves they thought she suffered from. Kate knew it was more than that, though.

Ever since she'd started playing the piano, she'd been having a recurring dream of a faceless woman sitting with her on the piano bench, encouraging her, teaching her, and loving her. The dream usually filled her with comfort. Playing the piano brought the woman's presence to her side, and she always felt an incredible love and sense of joy. But a few years ago, the dream had changed. Now, instead of just the woman, she also dreamed of an audience. When she had those dreams, she woke in cold sweats, terror and loss coursing through her. She could never remember the details, but the fear she felt when she awoke was undeniable. Ever since she'd started seeing the audience, playing in public always brought the same cold dread to her heart.

She didn't understand how one thing could cause her so much pain and so much joy at the same time. And who was the faceless woman? It wasn't any of the professors her parents had her work with. It wasn't anyone in her immediate family. And she knew it wasn't a stranger. She swallowed hard a few times before croaking out, "When?" She bit on her inner cheek, trying to control the panic that flooded her.

"Next week on Friday. And your mom has arranged for you to perform at Mr. and Mrs. Conrad's fiftieth anniversary next month. She thought a few nice pieces by Mozart and Beethoven would be just the ticket."

"Okay." She rubbed and twisted her hands together.

"Excellent." He stood and pulled her into a hug.

Her heartbeat seemed to slow, and she took a deep breath. She could do this. She always did. Her parents were doing their best, and she knew they had her future in mind. While they did get a jolt of praise for her playing, she knew deep down that they only wanted her to use her talents to the fullest and share them whenever possible. And they couldn't be held accountable for repeatedly causing her so much anguish, because she never shared with them the root cause.

5

When she got back to her room, she noticed a text from Ellie waiting for her on her phone. *I have news. Can you come over?* It was nine now, and her parents would never let her go out so late on a school night. Ellie'd sent the text an hour ago.

Kate wanted to call Ellie, but *The King's Court* was on TV from nine to ten and she knew it'd be better to text. Ellie could decide when to read and answer back that way.

Sorry. I was practicing. What's up? She didn't want to tell Ellie about the confrontation with her parents about the baby pictures. It would just feed into Ellie's crazy theories. Kate got ready for bed, glancing at the phone every five seconds to see if there'd been a response. It took Ellie five minutes to respond, which wasn't unusual when she was watching a reality TV show. It did give Kate just enough time to pull out her search journal and flip through some of the pages, which wasn't the best idea. Her moroseness returned.

Ellie called and speed talked, giving Kate the information as fast as she could. "Guess what? I ran a picture of you and the one in the locket through a facial recognition app. It's a 95% match. That picture is definitely of you. Oh, the show's back on. I'll call you back." She hung up, leaving Kate with an open mouth and saucers for eyes. Her heart plunged into an erratic beat, and she started breathing fast and shallow.

Bile rose up in her throat. It couldn't be. If that was true, even the little she thought she knew about herself was a lie. She wanted to deny it, but her heart told her that what Ellie had said was true. She'd known from the moment she'd found the locket in the attic—her parents were hiding something. She just hadn't wanted to face it.

The phone in her hand vibrated, bringing her out of her stupor. She looked at it. Ellie's name showed on the screen. Like she was moving in slow motion, she pressed the answer button. "Ellie?" Ellie didn't answer. Maybe Ellie had been right all along. Maybe her parents had been keeping things from her. The call ended, but Ellie tried again. Kate didn't answer it this time. She closed her search journal, curled up into a ball on her bed, and fell asleep.

The next thing she knew, Ellie was shaking her awake. "Kate," Ellie whispered. Kate blinked pushing sleep from her. "Ellie?"

"I'm here. What happened? I was so worried. I sneaked in your back door. I was so glad it was open. I thought something terrible happened. Did you just fall asleep?"

That's when the tears came. Ellie held Kate, rocking and shushing her. Once the majority of the tears had fallen, Ellie said, "Now. Tell me what happened. I thought you'd be excited about what I found out and now you're crying."

"My parents knew all along."

"They knew what?"

Her words poured out in an angry tirade. "They've had that picture the whole time. They let me search for years—*years*—for any scrap of information, and all along they've had this! They let me hire a private investigator—oh holy crap—" she stared at Ellie's shocked face. "They gave me a flippin' fake onesie! That outfit I gave the P.I. wasn't even mine—he followed fake clues. Oh, no. Oh, no, I am so dumb. He didn't follow any clues at all. He just told me what they wanted me to think, and I fell for it. This is— I just— I can't—" Her head filled with a rushing sound, and she suddenly felt too hot. She couldn't catch her breath. "I think I'm going to faint."

Ellie put a hand on her back and pushed down hard, forcing Kate's head between her knees. "Breathe, Kate. In and out, in and out." Ellie coached her through slow breaths until the whooshing sound in her head subsided and she could finally sit up without feeling dizzy.

"Wow," she said breathily. "How'd you know to do that?"

"Saw it on *My Not So Normal Life on the Jersey Shore*." Ellie tried to smile, but it came out as kind of a weak grimace. "Jace was panicking about a lunch date with his parents and Susan had him do it. Are you all right?"

"You were right. My parents have been lying to me my whole life. I hate it when you're right."

Ellie sat next to her in uncomfortable silence for a while. "I'm sorry."

"What for?"

"I got kinda wrapped up in proving to you that your parents were lying liars, and I didn't stop to think how that knowledge might affect you. It was kind of like a game to me. I should have realized this wasn't going to be, like, super awesome news for you."

Kate chuckled wryly. "No kidding."

"But hey—now you know."

"And knowing is half the battle?"

Ellie smiled. "Exactly." She bumped Kate with her shoulder. "Seriously, though. Now you have some actual clues—real leads to finding your birth parents."

"Yeah—all I have to do is ask the lying liars I live with." Kate scowled. She knew there was basically no chance of getting the truth out of her parents. She tapped her fingers on the search journal.

"Or..." Ellie waggled her eyebrows suggestively. "We could do our own investigation. Follow the leads."

"My parents would never—"

"Find out? Great plan!" Ellie's grin was infectious, and Kate found herself smiling, too, despite the churning in her stomach.

"You really think we can find them?"

"Bet on it."

Something occurred to Kate. Her shoulders slumped, and her smile disappeared. "Before you go to Italy? How am I ever supposed to do any of this without you?"

Ellie shook her head. "Don't think about that now. It's not even a sure thing, yet. And if it happens, it's still a few weeks away. Let's just focus on following these leads." She rubbed her hands together in cartoonish excitement.

Kate snorted. "You really should have your own reality show. Ellie Lambert—Girl Detective." She'd have to move away to get enough material for the show, though. Nothing ever happened here.

"Oh, that's an awesome idea!" Ellie's face was completely sincere. "I'll have to run that one by our publicist."

Kate laughed and hugged her friend, holding on a little tighter than normal. Ellie smelled like cotton candy; her newest cologne fit her personality perfectly. Kate picked up the thick journal and said, "And to commemorate this new search, I hereby archive this journal."

"Archive it? Didn't you say it was full of lies? We should burn it."

Kate rubbed her hand over the slick surface. "It's been such a big part of my life the last three years." She grimaced and then patted it. "But you're right. The information in it can't be trusted. We'll burn it, and I'll start a fresh one to put the truth in."

"That's the way. We're going to figure this out."

"Thanks for coming."

"Any time."

***

Kate trudged into the kitchen the next morning. She wasn't sure she'd ever be able to smile again. The initial sadness she'd felt at her parents' betrayal had turned to potent anger as she tossed and turned before falling into a fitful sleep. She ignored the hot breakfast her mom had prepared and made a noisy commotion of getting a bowl, spoon, and frosted flakes. She wore workout pants, an over-large hoodie, and Chucks, and had pulled her dark brown hair into a low ponytail. It snaked down her back, long and straight.

"Someone didn't get her requisite ten hours of sleep last night," Jori said.

Her mom cleared her throat like she always did when someone in the family wasn't kind to someone. It was her warning that their behavior was not acceptable.

"Kate." She paused, waiting for Kate to acknowledge her.

Kate ignored her. She would not play the good daughter today.

Amelia tapped Kate on the leg. Kate didn't stop shoveling her cereal into her mouth, chewing loudly.

"Kate."

Kate continued to eat. She knew she was pressing her mom's buttons, but her feelings of betrayal made her bold. Inside her, a tornado raged. Ellie had warned her not to say a word to her parents about what she'd discovered. Her words echoed in Kate's mind. "They've kept the information from you this long. Your mom will cut you off from the information if she discovers you know. If you want to uncover who your birth parents are, then you're going to have to fake it."

Kate thought she was right, but it didn't make it any easier for her to control her emotions. The moment stretched on. If her mom had to say her name once more, she'd take Kate out of the room and talk to her one on one. Maybe Ellie was wrong and she should have it out with her mom. Maybe now that Kate knew her mom had lied, she'd feel bad and tell Kate everything. She looked up at her mom, who was stirring something on the stove. No. Kate's mom was stubborn, and she would dig in her heels and not tell her anything. Shoot, she'd probably take everything Kate had found and get rid of it. Her mom wouldn't allow her perfect world to be disrupted. She'd have to put it back into order as fast as she could. She was an expert at sweeping problems into oblivion. Normally Kate liked the calm normality, but not now. Not when it had to do with her birth parents. Not when it had to do with her parents' deception.

"Yes," Kate finally spoke.

"Are you having a hard day today?" Her mom's back was still to her.

"Yes, ma'am." She clenched her teeth.

"Would you like to talk about it?" Her mom twisted and looked at Kate.

"No, ma'am." She clutched her spoon so hard it dug into her skin.

"I'll be here when you're ready. In the meantime, I'd appreciate you using your words in an appropriate manner to express your feelings instead of stomping and creating all kinds of havoc."

"Yes, ma'am." She took a few more bites of her food, tasting nothing. She washed out her bowl, feeling her sisters' stares burn into her. They'd never seen her act that way. She was always the picture of cooperation and consideration. She left the room and stomped to the hallway to get her backpack to go to school.

Her mother hurried down the hall after her, carrying her lunch. "Sweetie, you almost forgot your lunch." She held it out for Kate to take. Kate wanted nothing more than to reject the lunch, but thinking of Ellie, she gave her mom a pressed smile and took it. "Just remember," her mom said, "that nothing is really as bad as it first appears." She pulled Kate into a hug. Kate squirmed out of it.

"I'd appreciate you going upstairs and putting on a pair of jeans. The pants you have on are not appropriate attire for school."

She'd waited until Kate was out of sight of her sisters to admonish her. Heaven forbid any correction occurred in front of others. And why did she never raise her voice? Everything about her was so fake. Kate gritted her teeth.

"But I'm late. I'm sure Ellie is already outside waiting."

"It's important that we present ourselves appropriately for the activity we will be participating in." She smiled.

Kate wanted to yell in her perfectly calm face.

"Fine, Mom." She ran upstairs and pulled on a pair of jeans, feeling a touch triumphant that her mom hadn't noticed she wasn't wearing a shirt under her thin hoodie. She ran downstairs. Her mom waited for her at the bottom.

"Bye, Mom." The word felt sour in her mouth, and she decided at that moment, this woman she called Mom was not her mom, and she wouldn't address her as such ever again. She wanted nothing more at that moment than to disappear out the front door, never to return.

***

Kate was in a funk all day until meeting Ellie at lunch. Ellie didn't try to cajole her or get her to look at things from her parents' perspective. Instead, she offered Kate exactly what she needed—a plan for how she was going to find out the truth. She laid out the three items Kate had found in the attic—the locket, the gold cross, and the receipt.

"Okay, our first step is to find out everything we can about each of these items. I think we're safe to assume that these things—along with the clothes and shoes you found—were on you at the time you were adopted. Oooh—or maybe abducted?"

Kate's heart did a flip-flop. "You think I was kidnapped? Like Tom and Abrie stole me?"

"I think we can't rule anything out right now." Ellie's face was deadly serious. "We know they have been lying to you, and so they are 100% suspicious at this point."

Kate pressed her lips together but didn't argue.

"Also," Ellie continued. "We need to get back in that attic so I can look at the other items."

"What? Are you crazy?"

"There's no way I can investigate this without seeing all the evidence."

Kate thought Ellie was taking the detective thing a bit far, but she knew it was probably futile to argue. "I'll see what I can do."

"Okay, for now, let's see what we can learn about the evidence we have in front of us." She picked up the gold cross and turned it around in her hands. Her eyebrows knit together, and she held the cross out for Kate to see. "Hey, did you notice this?" She pointed to some small lettering that was stamped into the bottom part of the T.

Kate Unmasked

"I didn't really look at the cross," Kate admitted. "I was paying more attention to the locket." She examined the lettering. It read, St. Catharine of Siena. She dug into her messenger bag and pulled out her new search journal. "What do you think?"

Ellie took it from her. Kate had decorated the front with various pink crafting papers and in the very middle on a piece of baby pink paper was written *The Truth About Me.*

"Very nice. I love it."

"Turn it over."

On the back was white paper with a flowery pink print and down at the bottom was a picture of Kate and Ellie together with the words, *Ellie and Kate—Girl Detectives.*

"Love the logo, Kate. Great job."

The two huddled in their spot near their lockers and used their phones to research St. Catherine. Lots of churches and colleges were named after her. There were many St. Catherines, but not as many results for St. Catherine of Siena.

Kate scribbled the information down and after reading it over said, "Well, that led us nowhere."

"Not nowhere. We have more information than we had before. And if we get another piece of information and cross it with the information we have about her, we could get very different results." Ellie had learned all her snooping skills from her parents as they researched and sought out information about people on TV. Together with Colby, the four of them made a formidable team when it came to uncovering everything there was to know about someone. Ellie continued. "For example, let's put Italy plus St. Catherine and see what comes up. You use the default search engine, and I'll use another."

They both put the words in. "You see, now we've narrowed the information down. Siena is a city in Italy, and there are only a few results that come up this way. Man, she gave herself to God when she was so young." After many moments of reading, Ellie continued. "Totally gross. They took her head and put it in a bronze bust. Grosso.

Such violence after a person's dead. Ick. I don't get this Catholic thing. What does it mean to you?"

Kate continued to read and then spoke aloud about what she read. "Catholics consider her one of six patron saints of Europe. She had a truly adventurous life. She basically died of starvation."

"Mine says she died of a stroke." Ellie stared intently at the little screen.

"Hmm."

"How do you get those crosses?" Ellie gazed at Kate, focusing on her.

Kate frowned. "You can buy them at churches, and people can give them to you. My grandma gave me one of St. Christopher before our trip to Rome a couple years ago. He's the patron saint of travel. She wanted me to be safe."

"Interesting and kinda sweet. The question is where did the owner of the diaper bag get the cross?"

The bell rang, signaling the end of lunch. Kate gathered up the necklaces and her journal and placed them carefully in her bag. She paused a second, then pulled the locket back out and put it around her neck.

"Okay, we'll follow up on this tonight." Ellie said. "I can come over—maybe get a look at the attic?"

Kate ignored the nervous, guilty feeling in the pit of her stomach and nodded. "Sounds like a plan."

***

After school, Kate hurried to the car, hoping Ellie would, too. She'd only have a few minutes to chat before the boys arrived. Kate couldn't use her phone in her last class—Mr. Duffin was a nazi when it came to unauthorized use of cell phones. And she wanted to keep her phone. Braxton was already leaning on the mini-cooper when she arrived. She hated that she didn't have a single class with him all day. She never got to see him while at school unless there was an assembly or something. She felt a stab of regret that she wouldn't be able to spend time with him today.

"Hey, Cutie. I missed you." Kate's insides melted when he talked to her with that deep, gravelly voice. She hurried into his arms. His solid warmth calmed her. She wished she had more time to spend with him, but with her parents not allowing boyfriends, she had to settle for more quality time than quantity. Braxton was one of the best things in her life. Kate would have found him perfect but for one thing, his dislike of Kate looking for her birth parents.

"Can you go to the play tonight?"

She started to say yes but then thought better of it; she wanted to spend time with Ellie investigating the things from the attic. "I don't think I can. You know my parents." She didn't want to outright refuse him; she wanted him to know she'd like to go.

"They usually like you to go to the cultural things, though. Play it up. I want some private time with you."

"And a play with hundreds of people is private?"

"You know what I mean." He grinned.

"I do, but I don't think it's going to work out tonight, sorry." Kate frowned. She wished she could tell him everything that was going on, but she knew he'd just get upset.

Braxton shrugged and pulled her in for a light kiss. "All right. I just wish I got to spend a little more time with you."

"I know. Only another month and it'll be summer, and we won't have to worry about my parents as much. I'll be a free agent."

"I can't wait."

Ellie and Masters arrived hand in hand. She let them in the car, and they drove home. After the boys got out of the car and walked away, Ellie asked, "We're still on for tonight, right?"

Kate nodded. "Of course." She felt a little bad about blowing Braxton off, but the excitement she felt at finally learning about her birth parents overrode the guilt.

6

That night Kate let Ellie into the house at ten thirty. To Kate's knowledge, everyone was sleeping away. Kate retrieved the attic key from the spring cleaning folder, and they tiptoed their way into the attic, flashlights in hand. "We have to use our quietest whispers, okay?"

Ellie nodded. Kate pulled up on the panel, and Ellie climbed in. Ellie then pushed out on the panel to help Kate climb in. They crouch-walked over to the back of the crawl-space, where the two boxes waited in exactly the same state Kate had left them. She carefully peeled back the tape on each box. First she pulled out the outfit and shoes for Ellie to examine.

"Maybe we can learn something about these clothes from the tags," Ellie explained as she snapped pictures of the clothing with her phone. "If you were kidnapped, maybe your real parents put out a description of what you were wearing. We should look for that on the Internet. There might be a copy of it in a newspaper archive or something."

Kate grimaced and whispered back. "I really don't think Tom and Abrie stole me." Her parents might have lied to her, but they weren't actually bad people—not criminals anyway. The idea made her insides squirm. "I don't think it's really a likely explanation."

Ellie pressed her lips together. "If it's too painful for you, I'll follow that line of investigation for you. Don't worry about it." She finished taking pictures and folded the clothes up neatly and placed them back in the box. "Okay, now the bag. It might have a tag, too." Ellie pushed the little box of clothes back toward the wall to give them more room.

Kate complied, feeling a little silly. She had a hard time believing they were going to learn anything useful from tags. She pulled out the dusty pink bag and handed it over to Ellie, who examined it meticulously, looking into each section and feeling for a tag. When she didn't find one, she looked at the strap. Her brow creased as she ran her fingers over it.

"What is this?"

Kate leaned in. "What's what?"

"This brown stuff?"

"No idea," Kate said. "Chocolate?"

Ellie scrapped a fingernail over it and it flaked off. She dropped it.

"What?" Kate asked, alarmed.

"It's blood, Kate."

"No. Why would blood be on it?"

"It's blood. I'd bet my life on it." She picked it back up and took a picture of it.

Kate ran her hand over her forehead and through her hair.

"That cross didn't do much to protect the person carrying this bag."

Kate's hand went to the locket around her neck. Her mother had been wounded? Bleeding? The implications swirled around in her head.

"She didn't want to give me up," she whispered, almost to herself. "She was in some kind of danger, and that's why she had to." She scooted toward Ellie to get a better look, her hand landing on a piece of paper on the floor where the box had been only moments earlier.

Ellie squeezed her arm. "Let's not leap to any conclusions. But I have a bad feeling about this, Katiekins. A really bad feeling."

Kate took hold of the paper and shined the flashlight on it. It was a faded lime green sheet of notepaper. "Where'd this come from?"

Ellie moved over to look at it. She read the words out loud.

"Savino—Here is the information you requested. Constanzie.

Southern Ocean County Hospital. A date, but I can't read it. And a signature. It starts with an A, but I can't read the rest and the last name starts with M-a-r-c, but the rest is too sloppy to make out. A man must've signed this. Terrible handwriting. Another clue. The same name from the back of the picture, Constanzie."

"I was thinking Constanzie had to be my mom's name, but you were right, it could be my given name, but what are these other names?" She rubbed at her forehead and blinked several times. She couldn't think, couldn't make any connections that made sense. Heat enveloped her and she had to get out of there. She scrambled out, breathing hard and fast.

***

Kate and Ellie spent the next few days speculating about the source of the blood, uncovering what the green note was all about, and trying to learn more about St. Catherine's of Siena. She kept meticulous notes in her new journal. Ellie got prints of all the pictures she'd taken on her cell, and they dedicated a page to each picture, keeping them in groups determined by where and when they were found.

Ellie Googled and Googled. "OMG, Kate. You've got to see this. There is a church in Seaside, New Jersey called St. Catharine's. It's spelled differently than the others. Quick. Look at the picture we took of the stamp on the cross. This could be the clue we've been waiting for."

"What?"

"Just read me what is stamped on the back of the cross. Spell St. Catherine's."

Kate opened the page in the journal that had the picture of the cross. "C-A-T-H-A-R-I-N-E."

Ellie squealed. "How did we miss this? St. Catharine's with an *a* is in Seaside, New Jersey. The same place that pizzeria is. I bet you anything you're from Seaside."

"You think?"

"Yes. You most likely attended that church with your parents."

"I was probably christened there." She lay back on the bed and kicked her feet in the air. She didn't care that it made her look hyper or immature. A lightness filled her chest. She was from Seaside, New Jersey. Her parents, if alive, lived there.

"Most likely."

The name Savino hadn't turned up anything, but the hospital in question was near the church and the pizzeria, too. "I can't believe we know what hospital I was born in. Today just keeps getting better and better."

They couldn't figure out the signature. They had come up with ten different possibilities, none of which could be found with a Google search—at least none in or around Seaside, New Jersey, which seemed to be the nexus of the clues and most likely her birth place as well as place of residence until she was adopted.

Kate was so wound up, she had a hard time concentrating on anything, including Braxton. Ever since they'd gotten together, she'd split her time up between Ellie and him, or they all hung out together. Now, because so much was going on that Kate wanted to keep from Braxton, she'd been avoiding him. It was hard, but she thought it was the only way. She had too much on her mind to add Braxton nagging her that she should stop looking for her birth parents. She texted him a ton and called him whenever the opportunity arose, but Braxton was getting a bit peeved.

"How about I come help you with the yard work?" Braxton said during one of their rushed phone calls. "It'd get done so much faster, and we'd have time together." Kate's spring cleaning yard work only took her about half an hour a day, but she used that as an excuse for why they couldn't hang out.

"Yeah, like you coming over and working wouldn't send up a huge red flag? They'd know we were seeing each other for sure. Don't worry, after next week, the chores will be done." She hoped they'd have some more answers before then, but she thought she better give herself a little cushion of time.

"I guess I can wait, but seeing you before school and after school only on the drive home is killing me."

"Me, too," she said. She did miss him, and wished she didn't have to keep what she was doing secret, but it couldn't be any other way at the moment.

"Braxton?" Ellie said.

"Yep." Kate slumped in her chair.

"You need to give him some attention or you're going to lose him. And you don't want to lose him. He's hot. Kind. Adores you. Puts up with all your crap and your parents' crap and and and. I know I don't need to go on. And don't be mad, but I think you should tell him what you've been up to."

Kate sat up straight in her chair. "No way. I have to have found my birth parents before I tell him. He gets so upset whenever I tell him about my search."

"Well, I'm going to do you a favor. You are not allowed to come over here to work on sleuthing until you've spent some quality time with Braxton."

"Please. You don't mean it. You want to find my parents as much as I do. The mystery is killing you."

"I do want to find them. For you. Not for the mystery of it. Although I do love a good intrigue. I'll compromise. You spend half of your time with Braxton, as usual, and I won't cut you off.

***

"Are you sure your parents don't mind me crashing dinner again?" Kate asked Ellie as they ran down the stairs to eat. Ellie'd been acting a little sullen today, and Kate wondered if she was tired of her being around so much. They'd spent the afternoon brainstorming ideas. They'd decided to write the hospital, but quickly found the hospital was no more. It had been demolished five years previous. They tried to figure out where the records were now, but had been unsuccessful. "Let's write to the church," Kate had suggested, but Ellie had said, "I think it would be better if we could look the priest in the eye when we ask. If something did happen to your mom, he might not want to tell us about it. But if we're there, we'll be able to see all the non-verbal clues and tell if he's lying or something." Colby had come up to tell them dinner had arrived.

"Of course not. You know my parents. It's take-out around the TV. The more the merrier, as far as they're concerned." But Ellie didn't act excited about it. Kate thought about confronting her and getting everything out in the open, but the thought of going home kept her from saying anything. Hanging with an irritated Ellie was better than being with the lying liars for sure.

The Lamberts, while hard workers, spent most of their free time watching one reality TV show after another or researching their favorite ones and the characters on them. TV wasn't a simple hobby for them, but more of a second job. They not only got caught up in the characters, but what they had to do in order to land a spot on such a show.

As Kate and Ellie entered the family room, Ellie's mom said, "Do we get to have you for dinner again, Kate? It's Chinese today." She looked like she'd come from a TV set. No one would ever guess she was nearly forty and had two teenagers. She and Ellie were often mistaken for sisters, and looking at them at that moment, Kate could understand why. Both had flawless makeup and clothes straight out of a magazine, were tan and had thin bodies with curves in all the right places. Their big, clear eyes and voluminous sleek hair made men's hearts fail. And Ellie's mom had no pesky signs of aging at all.

"If that's all right with you?" Kate said, following Ellie to the other end of the couch.

"You know you're always welcome here," Ellie's dad said. He could have been a model, too. "I hope you like spicy. I felt like going hot today."

"I can take the heat," Kate said. This had been her third time eating at Ellie's this week. She used every excuse in the book to stay as far away from her parents as she could. It was becoming easier and easier to lie to them.

Since it was spring, a lot of the TV shows were ending segments, preparing for a month of break before summer taping started, which meant the action and drama had been ramped up to make sure to keep the audience raging for the next segment. Despite that, Kate couldn't get into the show. All she could think about was Seaside, New Jersey and what it had to offer her. She remained in a state of extreme excitement tempered with a good dose of fear.

"I can't believe they'd end it like that. It makes me not want to watch the next season." Colby stood in frustration.

"Yeah. I want to know who did it. It's not like they don't know," Ellie said, huffing.

"No luck on breaking into the emails of the producer, huh?" her mom said to her dad.

"No. Not yet, but one of my programmers is creating a line of code that might get us in as long as they actually open the email we send. Once they do, the code will embed itself into his email account, and we'll have him."

The Lamberts had created an international computer programming and assessment business. They'd sold it for millions after only ten years in business. Mr. Lambert still sat on the board and had some sway with some programmers he'd hired on at the birth of the business.

Ellie's parents stood and began to clean up.

"I've got that today," Kate said. "Thanks for dinner. My mouth's still on fire, but it was worth it."

Mr. Lambert patted Kate on the head. "Thanks for your help, but we love having you."

"We'll be at the gym if you need us," her mom called back.

"Okay, but we won't. Have a good workout."

"Yep!" The girls heard her mom and dad go through the kitchen to their room to change and listened to Colby run up the stairs to his room.

"By the way, I have news." Ellie let out a big breath.

"I'm not sure I want to hear it. Your tone tells me it isn't good news." Kate closed her eyes and sighed before leaning back hard into the soft sofa.

"It's sad news for me, but good news for you. Very good news."

Ellie pressed her lips together.

"What are you talking about?" So Ellie was finally going to spill the reason for her strange behavior all day. Kate was glad she hadn't needed to bring it up.

"Italy is off." Ellie frowned.

"What?" No wonder Ellie had been sad.

"No more Italy."

Kate couldn't help gasping with joy. "Oh, Ellie. I'm sorry," she said, but she was grinning. "No, I mean it, I really am. I know how much you wanted that. I'm heartbroken for you." She couldn't convince her face to stop smiling, even though her words were true.

"Well, I know you mean it, despite your stupid face. So, thanks."

"What happened?"

"We were in the final five apparently, but didn't cut it. Not this time, anyway."

Kate hugged her. "I really am sorry. Why did you say it was good for me?"

"Because, my dear. I'm pushing for New Jersey."

Kate's hand flew to the locket. "New Jersey?"

Ellie nodded, an excited glint in her eye. "We've learned everything we can sitting on our butts and Googling. If we are going to move forward in this search, we have to go there—talk to people, ask questions, track down leads."

She was right—the clothing tags hadn't told them anything, and the blood on the bag wasn't exactly screaming answers either. All they had was a church, the name of a pizzeria, and the name of a demolished hospital—all in Seaside, New Jersey.

"Yeah, but there's no way your parents and Colby are going to want to go to New Jersey."

"Are you kidding me? Of course they will. *My Not So Normal Life on the Jersey Shore* is filmed there, remember? I asked our publicist to uncover their schedule so I can present a good case to my parents. I don't think it will be hard. Sandy beaches, hot guys, celebrities. Yeah.

Easy sell. My mom loves Grant on the show, and if we have even a glimmer of hope of seeing him in real life, my mom will be all over that. And shoot, if I could meet Jace or Milton. Yum."

"I hope that happens. And if the choice comes down to Jace or Milton, go for Milton."

"But he's so vanilla."

"Yeah, but Jace, he's like a mash up of every flavor there is and in the end, that makes a pretty muddy brown."

"Don't tell me that if you had the chance to spend the weekend with Jace that you'd refuse it."

"Well..."

"I thought so."

***

Kate was going crazy waiting for Ellie's parents to make their decision about New Jersey. Those few days went by like a snail crossing the sidewalk. She couldn't talk about or think about anything else while with Ellie, so Ellie banished her, making her hang out with Braxton, which wasn't bad, it only took a bit of coordination to hide it from her parents, as always. With Braxton, she couldn't talk about the search, so she actually enjoyed herself at the school play.

"I'd always heard of *Noises Off*, but never thought I'd enjoy it as much as I did." Kate smiled up at Braxton as they left the school auditorium.

"Yeah. Super funny. My gut hurts from laughing so much." The outdoor lights cast harsh shadows across his face. Braxton was attractive, but even more so when he smiled and laughed.

"Laughing looks good on you."

"You think so?" He gave her a crooked smile in response.

She bit her lip. He grabbed her hand, and they rushed down the outside steps to the car, where he opened her door for her. Kate climbed in and sighed. She was one lucky girl to have a guy like Braxton. Smart, funny, and loving. He climbed in and gave her a quick, soft kiss that left her wanting more. But he was too much of a gentleman to give her more there in the parking lot of the school.

He pulled out of his spot, and they joined the throng of cars leaving the parking lot. They stopped for some ice cream and walked to a nearby park. The moonlight flickered through the leaves on the trees, dappling the sidewalk with intermittent light. His warm hand in hers made her feel safe and sure. After swallowing a lick of ice cream, she said, "I'm so lucky to have you."

"I'm the lucky one." He swung their held hands behind them and grinned down at her. "Sometimes I wonder why you're with me." His nose bunched up in question before he took another lick. His towering mound of ice cream was now almost level with the cone.

"How do I love you? Let me count the ways." Kate tugged on his hand, and they stopped. "No one makes me laugh the way you do. No one is as patient as you are. No boy I know is as thoughtful. Those notes you write are pure poetry. I've saved every last one. I can't think of a better pitcher anywhere. And at the risk of sounding too superficial, there's no one as good looking as you are. Yep!" she quipped. "You are hot."

He tossed his cone into a nearby trashcan. He raised an eyebrow at her, and she gave him hers. He tossed it too. After looking around to make sure they were alone, he pulled her into a soft hug and planted tender, warm kisses on her lips, sending a tingling sensation throughout her body.

7

Ellie didn't even bother to text or call, she simply showed up at Kate's house and rang the doorbell after dinner. "Ellie? Why didn't you tell me you were coming?" Her eyes bored into Kate.

"I was too excited." She looked around Kate. "Are we alone?"

Kate looked back, too. "No. Full house."

"Then let's go up to your room."

"Okay." They hurried up the stairs, and after Kate shut the door, they plopped down on her little sofa. Ellie whispered, an excited, breathy whisper, even though they were behind closed doors. "It's done. My family's in. The itinerary is amazing, and I convinced my parents to fly three days before the TV show arrives so that we can get acclimated to the area before we actually run into the stars."

"Seriously?"

She nodded. "We have two full days to use to find your parents. With some planning, it will be more than enough time, don't you think?"

Kate nodded and grabbed her into a hug. "You're the best. It's really happening."

"We're going to New Jersey! It turns out the show is planning on doing a special weeklong filming at a resort in Seaside, and our publicist is working to get us to be in the right place at the right time. She's sure she can get us on the screen at some point during the week."

"Wow! I can't believe this is really happening."

"It is. And you're going to have to get used to it fast. We leave the day after school gets out."

"No way!"

"Yep. In two weeks we're going to be on the sandy beaches of Seaside, New Jersey with the cast and crew of *My Not So Normal Life on the Jersey Shore.*"

The next day on their way to school, Kate thought about everything that was happening. The trip with the Lamberts was too good to be true. Kate thought of her recent behavior at home—how distant she'd been around Tom and Abrie—and knew she'd need to change her attitude if she wanted them to allow her to go on such short notice. Lost in her thoughts, she didn't even realize it when Braxton jumped in to sit next to her in the back seat. Ellie drove on to Masters' house and hopped out, wanting to surprise Masters when he opened the door.

"Earth to Kate."

She jerked out of her reverie. "Braxton!" She lunged at him and planted a huge kiss on his lips, and she didn't stop kissing him until he pulled back.

"Whoa! What was that for? I mean, I liked it. No, I loved it, but…"

Kate scrunched up her shoulders and grinned. "Italy is out, and the beaches are in."

He blinked several times. "Uh, it would seem to me that Italy would be the coveted destination."

Then the truth gushed out. "Not when my birth parents are there!" She slapped her hands over her mouth.

Braxton reared back like a snake about to strike. "Your birth parents?"

There was no taking back what she'd said, and by her own actions she condemned herself.

Kate's hands fell to her lap. "Well…"

"Tell me it isn't true, Kate. Tell me you haven't started looking for your birth parents again."

Her head wobbled from side to side, and she pushed air out her nose. Her leg jumped with anxiety. "It is true. And guess what? We have a pretty great lead. We know they're in—"

Braxton cut her off. "You know?"

"Well, we found a cross in my baby bag and it came from a church there and there was this receipt in the bag and—"

He cut her off again. "Do your parents know?" He hadn't heard a word she'd said. His cheeks turned pink, and the angles of his face appeared sharper.

"No!" she said a bit louder than she'd intended. "And they're not going to." She crossed her arms in front of her chest and scowled at him. "This is exactly why I didn't tell you I was searching again. You should be happy for me."

Dimly, Kate was aware of Ellie and Masters getting into the car and Ellie driving on to school.

"Happy for you?" he hissed. "Happy that some nut job is going to play on your desire for a father or mother and then do something horrible to you? Happy that you're setting yourself up to get your heart broken? I don't think so. You already hired a private detective to track them down. If he found nothing, you won't either." He huffed.

"Well, this won't be a dead end, and it's important to me. You should see that. You should know that, and you can either support me or get out of my life."

"You can't be serious. You'd rather go on a wild goose chase than stay with me and be happy?"

Kate didn't respond. They pulled into the school parking lot and as soon as Ellie parked the car, Kate dashed to the school.

8

Kate didn't have to deal with Braxton on the ride home, because he had texted Ellie that he had an appointment and wouldn't need a ride. Kate felt both relief and anxiety. She needed to apologize to him. She hadn't been fair, and she didn't mean what she'd said.

Kate yelled, "Mom!" the second she walked into the house. She wouldn't call her Abrie to her face just yet. She'd come up with an excuse for her recent behavior and everything. She had to convince her parents to let her go on the trip.

Abrie's voice played over the intercom when Kate entered the kitchen. "We're in the living room, sweetheart." To her surprise, Braxton walked from the direction of the living room into the kitchen, directly up to her.

"Don't be mad." He took one of her hands in his and kissed her on the cheek. "I only want you to be safe. I did this to keep you safe."

A hard, dark cold shifted inside her, growing large and painful. "What did you do, Braxton?" Her eyes narrowed.

"Only what had to be done, Kate. Just remember how much I love you." He stepped back and gave a quick nod of his head before leaving.

"Kate?" Tom's voice came over the intercom. "You coming?"

The idea of Braxton interfering was too heinous to consider. She wouldn't let him take her off her game. She looked at herself in the mirror, fixing a fake smile on her face and removing the locket and telling herself that her boyfriend could not have ratted her out. She stuffed the locket into her pocket. She'd have to be smart about this. She didn't know what Braxton told them. Before she said anything, she needed to discover what he'd said. Kate turned and went straight into the room.

She froze, unable to keep her pretend focus.

"Come on in and have a seat," Tom said, indicating a chair across from him.

She did. Abrie closed the door behind her.

"Kate," Tom said. "Your *friend* Braxton was here. Nice boy."

What she wanted to say was he used to be a nice boy. Sweat trickled down her spine, and she forgot to breathe.

"He told us some interesting things. We thought it important that you corroborate or negate what he said. " Tom's expression was one of forced pleasantness, and she knew it would be anything but pleasant to stay and chat. She clenched her teeth and gripped the arms of the chair. "We asked him to leave while we discuss what he told us."

Kate swallowed hard. She'd have to be very careful with what she said. "Okay." The word came out as a squeak.

"He claims to be your boyfriend."

Relief swept through her. Is that why he had come here? He wanted to out them? A smile crept on her lips.

"Yes. He is. I'm sorry. I know it's against the rules, but he's such a nice boy, and he does all good things. I mean he's better than I am—he couldn't bear the idea of keeping this from you. He had to come tell you. He's super smart and would never do anything to hurt me."

"We don't really understand how this could have happened," Abrie said. "We don't forbid you from hanging out with boys in groups. Why did you want to be alone with him so badly?"

"We're almost never by ourselves."

"It's the almost that scares us. We thought we could trust you. Why didn't you come to us when the decision presented itself?" Abrie squeezed her hands tightly together.

"Because I knew what you'd say."

"Yes. We would have told you to wait to single date and have a boyfriend until you were in college. This rule is for your protection. You are too young to be serious with anyone. You should be dating a lot of different guys to see what you like and don't like. You are limiting yourself by having a boyfriend."

"We hang out with a lot of different people. I'm exposed to all kinds of people."

"We don't doubt that, but seeing someone romantically is very different than hanging out as friends. It's not smart to single date while in high school."

"Fine! Did you tell him we had to break up?"

"No. That's for you to tell him." Tom's even voice irritated Kate.

"I told Braxton we couldn't trust you. His idea of honor ended our relationship." She spit the words at them.

"Oh, that's not the whole reason he came. Before we could agree to talk to him, we really needed to know the nature of your relationship. He's very worried about you."

In other words, they'd pried it out of him. It hadn't been the reason for his visit. "Worried about me?" She rubbed at her gut, hoping to alleviate some of the burning.

"Yes. It's a good thing to have people who care about you worry about you occasionally when you go off the path of safety."

She couldn't get mad yet. She had to find out what he told them. "I don't know what you're talking about."

"Well, he claims that you think you've found your birth parents. And that you and Ellie intend to find them while on vacation."

She didn't answer immediately. She had to find a way out of this one. What exactly had she told Braxton about the vacation? Her mind whirred trying to recall the details of their conversation. Her dad had the upper hand, and she needed to regain control. She needed to be clever. Telling them the whole truth would not be a smart thing at the moment.

She'd be vague.

"You have part of that right. Ellie and I do think we found a strong link to my parents."

"He said this year's trip with the Lamberts is all about you finding your birth parents. Is that true?" Abrie asked.

"And you felt a need to keep that from us? Haven't we done everything we could to help you locate them?" Tom said.

Heat pushed out from her face and swept down her neck. She fought hard to keep from screaming at them. They had done everything they could to keep her from her birth parents, but she couldn't let on that she knew.

She'd have to tell them she and Ellie had just discovered the information or she'd be toast. "We found out yesterday. I was planning to tell you, but I was trying to figure out the best timing. I didn't want to tell you guys and then have it be a dead end again. I know you're exhausted with my search."

"We're not exhausted with your search. Have we ever forbidden you from continuing?" Tom asked, his face scrunched up.

Kate bit her tongue and managed to shake her head. Having it out with her parents at that moment was not a good idea. She needed to go on this trip. She needed to keep her temper in check or they might forbid it. She wished she could call Ellie but knew it was impossible. She was on her own.

"How does your trip play into this? Where are you headed?"

The Jersey Shore flashed through Kate's mind and fell on her lips, but she didn't speak. If she told her parents that, they'd never let her go. She'd be too close to finding the truth about her birth parents, but she needed to tell them something close to the truth or it would be too hard to remember.

"They decided they wanted another beach trip, so Mexico it is."

"Mexico?" They said in unison. This was not what they were expecting to hear. They leaned back and visibly relaxed. She took this as a good sign.

"Yep. Where did you think we were going?" Had she told Braxton the Jersey Shore? She couldn't recall exactly what had been said.

Abrie crossed her legs and said, "Well, I'm sure there'll be a lot of educational experiences for you there."

"And fun. Don't forget the fun."

"Of course not," she said.

"What information did you find out about your birth parents that has you so excited about Mexico?" Tom gave Abrie a significant look.

Kate's mind searched for the answers. What could she say that would be believable and lead to Mexico? "You've always known that I would never give up on finding my birth parents, so it shouldn't come as a shock to you that I've found something," she hedged.

"What did you find?" Tom asked.

His kind demeanor was throwing Kate off. She never dreamed the conversation would go into this depth. She didn't know what to say. She started babbling. "Well, Ellie was watching the news and heard how kids are stolen and taken to Mexico where they are sold and—" she continued to elaborate, the lie growing out of control and exposing her deception.

Tom interrupted her. "For some reason, I feel like that wasn't the truth. Is there a reason you want to keep it from us?"

The ugly beast she'd kept hidden the last month woke as she looked into their smug, smiling faces and there was no stopping it.

"Yes, there is. Because you have lied to me all these years." She reached into her pocket and with an angry jerk, she pulled the locket out and dangled it in front of her parents.

Abrie looked immediately ashen. "Where did you get that?"

"In the attic. Where you left it with my baby bag and clothes. How dare you keep this from me?" Her voice shook. "You knew how much I wanted to know what my mom looked like. That I wanted any little tidbit from my previous life. You had no right to keep me from it. You are so selfish." Tears, angry and sad, poured from her eyes.

"Kate," Tom said. "That's enough. You may not talk to us that way." His voice was strained.

Kate refused to be intimidated, stayed at the edge of her seat, and pressed her lips together. Now she'd done it. She'd have to find a way to soften the blow so that they would let her go on the trip despite her outburst.

"We need to discuss this like adults." Tom said. "Your mother and I made a decision when we adopted you to keep certain information from you until you were mature enough to understand it for what it was. We are sorry if you disagree with that decision, but we thought it was the right one at the time. We wanted to protect you. You can believe that or not. That is up to you. Now, what is it about that locket that leads you to Mexico?"

Kate took a deep breath trying to focus on her goal of being able to go on the trip instead of blowing up and telling her parents what awful people she thought they were. An episode of one of Ellie's TV shows popped into her head, giving her an idea. Her heart hammered in her chest. She had to play this cool. A dull ache sat at the back of her neck.

"The locket was handmade in Italy. No two are exactly alike. A shipment that was intended for the US got sent to Mexico instead. This locket was one of them. My birth parents had to have bought it there. We might be able to find a record. A name." The hurt rose up in her again. "But you knew that, didn't you?"

"Calm yourself. We did not know this."

"You've always said I should tell the truth, and you've been lying to me my whole life. You said you had no idea what my mom looked like." She held the locket out. "A picture of her was in our attic all this time. And surprise, I'm older in this picture. At least two. That's why you were all whispery yesterday after I asked for some baby pictures."

"What good is it going to do you anyway to find them? They gave you up. They didn't want you. We did."

"How dare you say that? You have no idea what the circumstances behind them giving me up were. Or do you?"

They shook their heads, and she thought she recognized truth in their faces, but who was she to make that judgment when she hadn't been able to spot any of their earlier lies.

"Let me see the locket," Tom said.

"No." She shoved it into her pocket. "It's mine. It was always meant to be mine. Why? Why did you keep this from me?"

"We never thought you'd be able to use those things to find your birth parents. We were planning to give you all of those things when you were older, when you were more capable of handling them."

"And you don't think I'm capable now?" She clasped her hands in her lap in an effort not to fidget.

"We wanted to wait for a less volatile time in your life when you were more mature. That's all." Tom held out his hands in supplication.

Kate huffed. "You made me into a crazy person by withholding this information. And all I've learned from all this is that you two can't be trusted." She stood and stomped toward the door.

"Don't you dare walk out of here!" Tom yelled.

She turned around just inside the door.

"We are your parents, and we deserve respect whether you want to give it or not. We have reasons for the things we do, and we're sorry that you feel we've lied to you. We felt we were doing what was best for you. You need to accept that."

"I don't. And while I'm in Mexico, I'm going to find them."

"Please stop searching, Kate," Abrie's voice came out as a small whisper. She'd been silent this whole time. "Kate. I think someone was after you. I don't know for sure, but it's the feeling I got when the man delivered you. He was nervous, unsettled. I don't want you walking into the very danger someone was protecting you from."

"Please," Kate snapped.

"I said that was enough!" Tom yelled. "You listen here. You will give us respect. You're out of control, and I don't believe we can allow an out of control daughter to vacation anywhere with anyone."

"You can't forbid me from going."

"But we can."

"You can't keep me from the truth." She stood up, her fisted hands straight at her sides. Her body shook and perspiration dotted her brow.

"You forget that you've been keeping secrets, too. A boyfriend? Really? We can't trust you."

"I guess there's a lot of that going around now." Kate's lip twitched, her defiant words hurting her in ways she never knew possible. A month ago, she never would have dreamed of treating her parents this way.

"I think we need to perhaps remind you of who you are and what proper behavior looks like. You're grounded."

"What? For how long? School's out in two weeks and then there's the trip."

"We'll monitor your behavior closely, and if we feel like it has improved we'll give you that last week of school. And dependent on your behavior those two weeks, we'll decide about Mexico."

"That's not fair. They already bought my ticket."

"Then I suggest you behave properly. Should you choose not to, you will pay them back for their very generous offer."

"Or *you* can, with the money I paid that private investigator who did nothing but lie to me on your instructions." Kate spat.

After a short pause, he said, "Do you need a crash course in proper behavior?"

He didn't deny it. They had diverted the P.I. from doing what Kate needed him to do. Her parents were that bad. That was unforgiveable, but she couldn't show her disappointment, her anger. She squared her shoulders, took a deep breath in and said, "No. I got it. May I be excused?" Her blood rushed double time through her body, but she refused to allow herself another outburst.

"Grounded. That means no activities outside this house until next Wednesday. You may, however, use your phone."

Thank heaven for small favors. "You mean no Ellie either?"

"No. One week of stellar behavior or it will grow to two and no trip." His voice was icicle sharp.

She squeezed the locket hard as she went to her room, and while her feet ached to stomp up the stairs, she reined them in.

She immediately texted Ellie. *Call me. 911.*

To her credit, Ellie called immediately. "What's the 911?"

"Braxton ratted me out to my parents."

"What? Ratted what out?"

In extreme detail, Kate recounted the ambush.

"It was so bad, Ellie. I wanted to stomp out and never return. I should have been really belligerent so that they kicked me out. Then I could have gone and lived with you."

"At least they didn't take your phone. You lucked out big on that one."

"Yeah. I would've died without it."

"Oh, wait. It could be a trap. I saw it on one of my shows that parents can use this gps to track you. They'll be able to see you're not in Mexico."

"Good point. I'll tell them we won't have good service there with it being international and all and that I'm going to leave my phone home and use your parents' phone to contact them. But I won't tell them that until the day of so they can't do anything about it."

"And the parents read all their kids' texts. Maybe your dad let you keep your phone so he could keep tabs on you and me and what we find out. No texting from now on, only calling."

"Are you sure they can't listen in on our calls too?" Kate chuckled.

"Don't joke, Kate. We've got to be careful if you want to get to New Jersey to find your parents."

"You're so suspicious." Kate rolled onto her stomach and crossed and uncrossed her legs, waving them in the air.

"Like I don't have reason to be." Kate could imagine Ellie raising her perfectly plucked eyebrows.

"I know. I have to joke. There's too much tension around here. We'll talk. No texting. I'd want to call you anyway since I'll barely see you at all. Abrie is even going to drive me to school. I'm going to play the perfect daughter, though. I'm not letting anything get in the way of our trip."

"That's what I like to hear."

"What am I going to do about Braxton?"

"You are going to dump him on his ratty butt, that's what. Any boyfriend who would rat his girlfriend out to her parents doesn't deserve any consideration. I still can't believe he did that."

"Yeah. It's a good thing he didn't give me a chance to give him all the details." Her phone vibrated. She had twenty texts from Braxton.

"All right. What now?"

"We need to plan our two days. What do we need to know?"

"My birth parents' names and address." A thrill of excitement rushed through her at the prospect, and she took in a deep breath.

"So, we go to St. Catharine's first thing Saturday morning and talk to the priest."

"By the way, the whole Mexico angle was brilliant. Where did you get that idea?" Before Kate could tell her, she figured it out. "Oh, my heck! You stole it from *Who's Baby Am I Anyway?*"

"Yep!"

"That's awesome. I told you watching reality TV was a good thing. And your parents will never know since they won't watch such *drivel.* It's like someone's helping you get what you need."

"Yeah. Somebody. And if God is helping me, that must mean my birth parents are good people."

"I hope so. With that said, I guess it's a good thing that our link in Jersey is at a church. He's a man of God right? He has to speak the truth and all that, right?"

"Says the girl who watches reality TV and witnesses one betrayal after another by the very people who are supposed to be the best and most trusted people. Hello, boyfriend betrayal."

"True. But we can hope. My show's on. Gotta go. I'll see you at school tomorrow. Remember, no texting."

***

The next week was full of tension . The first several days, Kate was busy with family things: extra chores, a cousin's birthday party, planning their family's summer vacation, and lots of piano practicing which was really her stress relief. She tried not to think about playing for Mr. and Mrs. Conrad's fiftieth, but she had a lot of time on her hands and couldn't help it. She'd woken up the last two nights in a cold sweat from the dream. It seemed to be getting worse. She'd played for Tom's office party at O'Shay's last month and had only been sick the day of the performance. Would she have the dreams again that night and be sick the next day, too? Maybe she'd have to start refusing her parents' "help."

Abrie drove her to and from school and had chores for her to do if Kate looked the least bit bored or contrary. Kate wanted to sneak out and meet up with Ellie until Ellie told her that her parents couldn't officially take her to New Jersey without her parents' consent because that would be considered kidnapping, so she better play it straight.

Kate had avoided Braxton like the plague, which wasn't really that hard considering she didn't have lunch or any classes with him. He'd texted her and left messages explaining he had done it for her own good and she shouldn't be mad and that he was sorry. To her it was all blah, blah, blah. She'd texted him that it all came down to trust and she didn't trust him anymore and therefore she couldn't be his girlfriend. It hurt to spend the last weeks of school without him, but she was determined not to let her feelings of being alone send her back into his arms. She would never forgive him for what he'd done.

After a good two hour practice to calm her nerves on Thursday, she went to bed hoping she wouldn't dream in her relaxed state. She was wrong. She bolted upright, a scream rushing out of her as she did. Loud, shallow, anxiety ridden breaths met Tom and Abrie as they rushed into her room.

"Sweetie. Are you okay? What in the world is going on? This is the third night in a row!"

Kate shook her head and closed her eyes. It surprised her when she felt comfort as Tom's arms wrapped around her.

"Do you remember the dream?"

She shook her head, even though it was a lie. She remembered every detail, even the new ones.

"Would you like to sleep in our room?" Abrie asked.

"No. I'll be fine. I just need a drink of water."

"I'll get that for you." Abrie left the room.

"Are you sure I can't do anything for you?" Tom continued to hold her tight. He kissed her forehead.

"No."

Kate drank the water Abrie brought back for her and then she lay back down, hoping they would leave quickly. She couldn't think straight while they were there. After they'd gone, she looked at the clock. Three A.M. She'd wait until morning to tell Ellie. Maybe she'd have it sorted out by then. She'd seen more of the audience this time, and they'd been screaming, looks of horror on their faces as they stared at her. The rest of the dream was the same. Remembering the looks on the faces of the people in the audience made a fear creep through her toes and weave its way around her legs and up over her torso until it landed in her heart.

***

"Does your stomach still hurt?" Ellie asked as they hurried to their last class of the day. "I don't understand why pills don't work on you on performance days."

"I don't understand it, either. I wish I knew why the change in the dream all of a sudden."

"It's seriously creepy. All I can think is that something terrible happened when you were playing or perhaps it's how you felt the first time you had to perform. Have you thought of that? Maybe you've always had performance anxiety."

"Maybe," Kate said, but that didn't feel right. She clutched at her stomach as a strong cramp attacked it. "But why don't I freeze up at the performance if that's the case? Why am I still able to play? If it was performance anxiety wouldn't I freak out while playing, not before?"

Ellie shook her head and pulled her to the side of the hall near their class. "Only the weekend and then you're free. We'll go get you a burner phone on Monday."

"I can't wait. This will be a long three days."

"Well, after your performance, maybe you should do a bit of research. We still don't know anything about that Savino guy. Maybe spend your time looking into him. That should take your mind off being grounded."

"I'll do it."

***

The performance went as planned except when the audience clapped the image from her dream superimposed over those nice old people, and she almost fainted. She'd had a stroke of luck that Tom had been next to her and caught her before she could fall.

She called Ellie when she got home and told her about it.

"I'm really sorry that happened. I wish I had answers."

"Being able to tell you is all I need. I don't expect you to fix my broken butt."

"Let's focus on what we can fix. I'm going out to a movie with Masters, but then I'll see if I can find where the records of the demolished hospital ended up. You work on Savino."

"Have fun on your date."

"Masters is getting on my nerves lately."

"You've been saying that for weeks now."

"Yeah. Too bad he's so hot."

"Like I said, have fun."

Kate moved to her desk and opened her computer. At first glance, the first twenty pages of Google searches for Savino were in Italian. "I can't let this stop me," she said to herself. "I'll look at every page and see if I can find anything." She slogged through the first five pages of results before shutting the laptop and falling asleep.

She woke to a bright sun shining in her room. She realized she hadn't had the dream again. A part of her sort of wished she had so she could hopefully see even more. After taking care of all her family duties, she started on her search for Savino again. It took until that evening after dinner to find something. The articles didn't even have to be translated. They were in English originally. The third document turned out to be what she needed. The title of the piece was An Angel for Children. It was all about a man named Savino Cremashci, a priest at a Catholic church. She looked at the location stamp, Seaside, New Jersey. Her hand flew to her mouth.

She read the whole article again. Savino was being honored for his efforts with easing children's burdens. He held fundraisers and hosted free carnivals to help needy children. The article even called him the savior of children. It was claimed that he had helped over a thousand children improve their lives by providing food, jobs, and a place to go and be safe. She looked at the picture of him. He was seated on a bench surrounded by children. He looked about fifty or so, a face of happiness displayed for all to see. She checked the date. The article said he had been the pastor for almost twenty years already. That would mean he would have been the pastor when she had been there. Could he be the Savino mentioned on the green notepaper? She printed the article and taped it into her journal. She texted Ellie. *Call me.*

Instead of calling, Ellie showed up on Kate's doorstep. They rushed to her room where Kate showed Ellie the article.

"You know, Kate. That article really plays into the idea that you were in danger. I mean why else would he have the information about your birth?"

"Maybe he visited everyone who had babies in his parish. He loved children. Maybe he brought a basket of goodies to all new mothers or something."

"That could be, but this seems like something else. Moms usually know crazy stuff about their kids, and your mom had a feeling you'd been in danger. We should be careful."

"Yeah, it makes me feel a slight twinge of guilt for how I treated Abrie and Tom. But only a twinge."

"Don't go getting all soft on me now, Kate. Don't go spilling your guts to your parents. They'll never let you go on the trip."

"I'm not going to spill my guts. No way."

"On the matter of the hospital records, it's like a terrible maze that can never be pieced together. I'm giving up on that angle for now. If we need to revisit it when we get to Jersey, we will."

"I don't think we'll need it, Ellie. I'm putting my bets on Savino. He has our answers. He has to. I was a child then, and he saved kids."

"I hope so. I really hope so. But the article says stuff about food and shelter and such, not adoptions."

"I know, but it isn't that big of a stretch in my mind. Now we definitely have to start our search at the church. If we find Father Cremashci, we'll find my parents. I can feel it."

"You're the boss, and I'll follow your lead on this one." Ellie grinned. "I still can't believe you're going against your parents in such a huge way. Girl, you do have a rebellious bone in your body, and it's huge."

They giggled as quietly as they could.

"And guess what?"

"What?"

"I broke up with Masters."

"Why?"

"Girl solidarity, I guess. This way we are both boyfriend free while in Jersey. That way we can totally live it up. I want to see you let loose while there. You are a gorgeous unattached female, and you should celebrate that. Live more than a little on this vacation. Don't let anything hold you back."

"I don't know. That stuff is easy for you. Not for me."

"Look how you're breaking free of your little regulated, planned cell here. Don't let all your effort go to waste by being a party pooper." She bumped Kate's elbow. "Okay? Promise you'll let go."

"I can promise you I'll try."

***

Kate sat in plane, the locket and cross hung from her neck and the search journal was tucked neatly away in her messenger bag. Tom and

Abrie had said goodbye at the house, blissfully ignorant that their obedient daughter was headed in exactly the opposite direction she claimed. She'd done her job so well in the two weeks of her probation that they'd even apologized to her before she left and told her they hoped she'd have a good time. She wanted to be exuberant and ever so smug about her deceit, but she couldn't make herself be. She knew that this adventure would change things forever.

9

Kate and Ellie flung themselves onto the fluffy white comforter on the queen sized bed of their own room, a part of the three-bedroom suite. It was always the first thing they did when arriving at the different hotels each year, and there was nothing like honoring tradition. The day of travel had been draining, but the thought that they were finally in Seaside, New Jersey energized them. They'd pulled it off. Colby and Ellie's parents had headed straight for their rooms to unpack. They always unpacked their luggage, putting the contents away in the closets and drawers in their respective rooms to help make them as comfortable as possible. The first night of vacation for their family was dedicated to relaxation. They would also go to the fanciest restaurant in town, and they would pump and bribe the servers for information on the famous people in the area.

It would be strange not to be constantly posting on Twitter, Instagram, and Facebook while on this vacation. They couldn't risk Kate's family somehow hearing the truth of her whereabouts. Besides, it would be nice not to have that social connection with home. Without her phone, she wouldn't have to worry about the constant bombardment of messages and texts from Braxton. An ache settled in her gut thinking about him being out of her life, but it wasn't nearly enough to make her seek him out and forgive him. She didn't know if forgiveness would ever come, no matter his motivations.

The Lamberts' publicist, Sally Foster, had given the family the taping schedule of the show, and it started on Monday. The place was buzzing with excitement even though none of the stars would arrive for two more days.

The girls sat up, slid off the luxury bed, and slipped into their swimsuits to hit the beach. Kate carried the beach bag with towels, sunscreen, and her notebook, pen attached. Only seconds after stepping outside, she had to run her forearm over her forehead to stop sweat from going into her eyes. They claimed a cabana and were about to rush down the beach to the water to get some relief from the heat, but Ellie stopped Kate.

"Uh, you'll want to take those precious necklaces off before we jump in the water. Can you imagine what would happen to that picture in the locket if it got wet?"

Kate's hand flew to the locket. "I'm so glad you thought of that. I forget I'm wearing them. It's like they're a part of me now."

Kate put both necklaces into the beach bag. She looked longingly back at the bag before stepping into the sand. "What if Tom and Abrie find out we're not in Mexico? What if they find out where I am before I have a chance to find my birth parents?"

"It won't happen. Put that from your mind. You took all the precautions you needed to in order to keep your location from them. My whole family agreed not to post anything online about the trip until we're home. Your idea of telling them it wasn't smart to post things that would show we weren't at home was a brilliant one. It'll be like we get to re-live our vacation again when we do post."

The briny smell of ocean felt heavy in the heat. After a quick dip, they found their way back to the cabana, where they ordered cabana service from a tan, tall server boy. Dinner wouldn't be until around eight thirty, and fancy restaurant food was never in abundance.

"We are so in hot guy heaven—and did you hear his accent? He sounds just like the cast of the show."

Kate Unmasked

"Funny how when you live somewhere you speak like the people there." Kate laughed through her sarcasm.

"Shut up! It's different hearing it in real life." Ellie lay down on a lounger, and Kate did too, but only after grabbing the beach bag with her notebook. She rarely let herself be parted from it since she created it.

"Looks to me like Jersey boys are a bit rough. I'm not sure about the longer hair yet."

"Rough around the edges is maybe not good for a full time boyfriend, but perfect for vacay." Ellie pumped her eyebrows.

Kate pulled out the notebook and set it on the side table next to her. She wanted to grab the journal out and look over everything again, but she refrained, trying to be fun for Ellie. Ten minutes later, when both girls were dry of ocean water, but starting to sweat, their food arrived. After taking a big bite of her cheeseburger, Kate opened the notebook and turned to the page the two had used to plan their time while in Jersey. Tomorrow would be here before they knew it. She couldn't wait a second longer. She needed to do something to stop her mind from going in circles about the possibilities tomorrow.

"Today we relax. Tomorrow we start bright and early." Kate grinned and then frowned. "The church opens at ten on Saturdays. We'll need to get up at seven in order to make it there by then."

"Got it. But listen, when we get to the church—we need to be a bit strategic about what we say. We can't just come right out about who you are and what you want."

"Why not?" Kate asked.

"Um, hello? The blood, the intrigue? Your mom's feelings—"

"Oh, she was just saying that to scare me off."

"We can't know for sure. I think we need to approach this carefully," Ellie insisted. "Just follow my lead."

Kate couldn't help but laugh. "Okay, whatever you say." She grinned at her best friend, "The next two days are going to be epic. Thank you for sacrificing them for me." Kate couldn't help but be grateful that no celebrities were at the hotel yet. She knew that once they arrived, she'd be on her own no matter what Ellie promised.

Ellie took a dainty bite of her veggie burger. Once she swallowed, she said, "It's not a sacrifice actually. I think you're the one that's going to be sacrificing on this trip if you don't find your parents."

"Nah. I'm sure hanging around the celebs will be a constant party. It'll be fun." She tapped her fingers on the open page of the journal and pulled the locket out of the bag.

"Yes, it will," Ellie said, her eyes twinkling. "I want you to let loose this time, okay? Fall in love for a day or two. See how awesome it is."

"I don't know. Pain isn't my thing." She sipped her smoothie and turned to the page in the book with the results from the face recognition app Ellie had used to compare the baby picture, the woman, and Kate. She ran her fingers over the numbers. 95%. Her stomach churned, and she set the smoothie down, trying to concentrate on Ellie's words.

"It will be good practice for you. See if you can tell if the guy is a winner or not. Work on noticing everything."

"I'll try. I'm nervous about tomorrow and what this priest is going to say."

"I have to admit the suspense of it all is killing me." Ellie squealed. "What if he tells you exactly where your parents are? Are you going to be brave enough to go right to them? You're going to have to dress with that in mind. Once the priest tells us their names, we'll go straight to their house."

Kate shook her head. "I don't know what I'll do. Seriously. This is unbelievable really. I never thought…" she stopped, a golf ball filling her throat. Swallowing wouldn't dislodge it.

"Ah, Katiekins. It's going to work out. You'll see."

Colby walked in. "Drama? Cute guy got you down?"

"No, Colby," Ellie said with an exasperated huff. "She could find her birth parents tomorrow. That's like the best and worst thing ever."

He nodded and said, "You know, Katiebug, even if they aren't there for you, it doesn't change how we feel about you. You are loved, and it would be their loss."

Kate Unmasked

How did he know that's what had upset her? How did he know her greatest fear was of rejection? She was finally able to swallow the lump, and he nodded. He really was like the perfect big brother.

"What if they don't want me? What if they have other kids? What if we don't find them at all?" She stood up and started to pace.

"They will want you, and having more brothers and sisters wouldn't be a bad thing. We will find them."

"But they gave me up. Maybe they thought I was defective in some way. And why would they keep other kids and not me? What does that say about me?" She scrunched up her nose and looked to the top of the cabana in hopes of staving off tears.

"I know you're scared, but dwelling on all the bad possibilities won't help." Kate could feel Colby's sincerity, and she appreciated it, but he'd never understand. Not really. "If you want me to come with tomorrow, I'm happy to. I can be the muscle forcing the priest to give us the information." He flexed his muscles.

"It's okay. Ellie and I can handle it, I think."

"Okay, but if anyone gets up in your grill, call me. I'll set them straight."

"I keep telling her she needs to stay optimistic. Things are falling into place." Ellie put her hand on Kate's sweaty back. "You are strong and brave."

"Keep me in the loop, though, really." Colby grabbed her hand. Kate sniffed and, not wanting to bring a cloud over the evening, said, "You're right. There's no use in worrying."

"I'm dying of the heat," Colby said. "Last one into the water is a dead sea lion." He dashed out. After a quick breath, Ellie ran after him. Kate opened the locket and stared at the picture. "Are you here, Mom? Have you been looking for me?"

***

Blame it on all the sun or the late dinner the day previous, but Kate slept like a rock and when her alarm sounded, she immediately turned it off without really waking up. Two hours later and a bit sunburned, she startled awake. She stared around the room in a frantic search for the familiar. When her eyes lit on a still-sleeping Ellie, she was able to catch her breath and relax. A second wave of hysterics pushed through her when she realized it was really light outside. She snatched her charging phone off the side table and moaned when she saw it was already nine. She shook Ellie. "Ellie, we slept through the alarm. It's already nine."

"What?" Ellie said, rolling over and snuggling deeper into the covers.

"Get up!" Kate hit Ellie with her pillow. "We've lost two hours already. We'll have to skip the beach run. There's no time for breakfast. I'm getting in the shower. Maybe you can use Colby's?"

Ellie grunted, and Kate sent another pillow her way as she plopped onto the floor. She took the fastest shower possible. She'd have to dry her hair and straighten it. It was the fastest style she knew how to do. With a towel wrapped around her, she did her makeup. Once her hair was dry, Ellie opened the bathroom door and joined her. She picked up the straightener and started on Kate's hair. "I think you should wear that cute purple flower dress. It'll show them you're classy but have a fun, flirty side, too. If you wear those nude strappy shoes you brought, it will make your legs look like they never end. Are we leaving your hair down?"

"Yeah. I think so."

"I'll add a little wave okay?"

"Sure." Kate watched their reflection as Ellie ran the straightener over her hair. It was so surreal—going through these motions as if it were any normal day. Kate felt like she might throw up. "I don't know if I can do this. My heart is going to jump out of my chest. What if the priest tells me my parents are dead? What if they're alive and do have other kids and don't want anything to do with me?"

"Deep breaths. You're working yourself into a frenzy for nothing. You can't change the past. And if they have other kids that they kept, there will be a good reason why they didn't keep you. Maybe it's like your mom thought. Maybe you and your parents were in danger somehow and they had to give you up to save you? Focus on the positive and no more *what ifs*."

Kate took deep breaths and stared at herself in the mirror, telling herself to be calm, that it would all work out.

"I love your hair. It's amazing. The sun already made it lighter." Ellie stopped and looked into the mirror. "Is mine lighter too?"

Kate snorted, trying to calm the hope and anxiety having a battle inside her gut. "You crack me up." Ellie was not the patient type. Kate knew her hair wasn't lighter, and Ellie's wasn't either.

The conversation turned to what they needed to find out. "The first item of business is going to St. Catharine's and finding Father Cremashci."

"And you're going to let me talk," Ellie admonished.

"And I'm going to let you do the talking," Kate said. She continued to breathe deeply

"We'll find out what he knows, and we'll deal with it when it comes."

"*If* he knows anything." Kate's shoulders slouched forward, and she rubbed her achy jaw. Had she been clenching her teeth again?

"That wasn't a *what if*, but no more *ifs* either."

"I want to be ready for anything and not get my hopes too high. That's all." Kate felt a headache coming on.

"Fine, but keep those thoughts to yourself. They are going to make you depressed. Once he tells us your parents' names and possibly addresses, we'll go visit them."

Kate pulled on the front of her blouse, back and forth. "Is it hot in here or what?"

"You're nervous. Don't worry, we'll get a smoothie for the cab ride. There. I'm done. You look picture perfect. Your parents are going to love you." She smiled, and her eyes danced. She wanted this just as badly as Kate did. Kate put the locket around her neck and then stuffed the cross into her pocket along with the green note. Maybe the priest could tell her what the note meant.

Ellie snapped photos of the church as they climbed out of the taxi. The white stucco shone bright in the sunlight. A large tower held a shiny silver bell inside. "I wonder when that rings."

Kate knew the answer. It rang before church started on Sundays and on religious holidays, but she was too nervous to say anything. The church was not the largest Kate had ever seen, but it held its own. They walked up the steps to the large wooden doors. Ellie pointed at a sign to the left of the door that listed the hours of operation. Her eyes lit on *Sat. 10:00.* "We made it."

Kate turned around and started back down the steps.

Ellie grabbed her arm and stopped her before she reached the bottom. "Kate. We are going inside that church. We are talking to Cremashci, and we will hear one of two things. Number one, your parents are alive and well. Number two, they aren't. Either way, we are getting the answer, and we will deal with it."

"There are so many things that could happen. Maybe I'm not ready."

Ellie grabbed her into a hug. "You are ready."

The bell rang, and the doors to the church suddenly popped open. Both Kate and Ellie jumped. A mass of people poured out, all in suits and dresses, looking like they owned the place. Two large men held the doors open for the rush. Ellie and Kate stepped to the side to allow the group to pass. Out of the fifty or so passing, only one set of eyes lit on the girls—and they were dark brown and brooding and belonged to a boy about their age. Some of the mass of his tousled dark brown hair hung into his eyes. He popped large sunglasses onto his scruffy tanned face.

Ellie grabbed Kate's forearm as she openly stared at him. The corners of his mouth tugged up before he looked away, following the crowd down the sidewalk. Kate continued to stare as he walked away. A line of fancy cars took the churchgoers away. The two men holding doors open remained, and Ellie and Kate gave each other a curious look before stepping forward to go inside. The man closest them put out an arm, preventing them from entering. An elegantly dressed older man and woman exited the building. One of the men acting as guards walked out in front of them and the other behind them, letting the door shut as he followed.

The girls gaped. "Who was that?" Kate whispered, an ominous feeling filling her chest.

"Were those two massive guys guards?" Ellie whispered. That's when Kate noticed Ellie had been using her phone to snap pictures. Her secret stalker talents were paying off in a big way at the moment. She must've thought they had to be someone important. They watched the couple climb into a white Cadillac, the two guards sweeping the area for—for what? After the car drove away, they turned to each other and Ellie held up her phone. "Don't worry. I'll find out who they were. I can't believe I was so close to so many important people." Kate rolled her eyes. Ellie hoped she'd seen a bunch of celebs. "And did you see that boy stare at you, Kate? He definitely will need to go to confession for the thoughts he was having about you."

"Very funny." Kate opened one of the massive church doors, and they went inside.

"I'm serious. He was totally crushing on you."

Lit candles seemed to be in every nook and cranny of the church and, mixed with the bright sunlight coming through the myriad of stained glass windows, they created harsh areas of dark and light. Their shoes clicked on the stone floor and for the first time since arriving in New Jersey, Kate felt cold. She rubbed her hands up and down her arms. She may have even held her breath for several seconds.

A man dressed in full ceremonial vestments, obviously the priest, was using something to put the candles near the altar out, his back to them. The interior was modeled after the massive cathedrals in Europe with small areas dedicated to various saints for worshippers to pray to. They walked up the long aisle in silence, passing the rich toned wooden benches. At about twenty feet from the altar, the priest turned their direction.

He startled, clutching at his chest. "Sorry, I thought I was alone."

"Oh, are you not open, yet?" Kate said, eyes wide.

"No, we are. Sorry. I was cleaning up after a baptism." Two young boys walked out of a back room. They must have been the helpers for the baptism.

"Father," the taller of the two said. "We finished in the back. May we leave?"

He nodded and waved them away. They wasted no time in disappearing out the door.

He turned to the girls. "What may I do for you today?"

"Are you Father Cremashci?" Ellie asked even though she knew he wasn't. This man didn't look anything like the picture they'd seen.

"Father Cremashci is no longer here."

The girls looked at each other. "Is he at a new church now? Do you know where he is?" Ellie asked.

His head bobbed in the affirmative. "I do, but perhaps I can help you."

"Actually," Ellie said, taking a step closer. "He's the only one who can help us. Kate here is looking for information about her dad. Her dad wrote about Father Cremashci in his journals, and Kate was hoping to find out more about him. He died when she was really little."

Ellie was lying in a church. This was not good. Did she have any respect at all?

"Well, I'm afraid he won't be able to help you. He's at a care center. Alzheimers. I'd be surprised if he even knew your father anymore." His kind and yet hard eyes lit on Kate. "Was your father a part of this congregation?"

Kate opened her mouth to speak, but Ellie charged on. "Could you maybe tell us what center he's in? We'd like to visit him. It's the least we could do to hopefully repay some of his kindness to Kate's dad. He'd like that, wouldn't he?"

"Oh, I'm sure he would, but I'm telling you, if it's information you're after, you will be sorely disappointed." He tilted his head to the side and peered at Ellie. Curiosity glowed in his eyes. "If you give me his name, I could look through the records. Perhaps Father Cremashci mentioned your father in *his* journals." His eyes flicked back to Kate's. It was like he was fishing for information. Why would he do that? When Kate said nothing, he said, "Let me get you the name of the care center." He walked away and through a doorway to the left. Kate began to follow. Ellie grabbed her arm. "Whatever you do, don't give him any names. Don't tell him anything. I don't trust this guy."

"But what if Father Cremashci did keep some kind of a record, and my parents and I are mentioned in there?"

"We don't even know your birth dad's name."

"No. But we do know my birth mom's, Constanzie."

"Not a word, Kate. "

Kate wanted desperately to give her mom's name, but Ellie was right, without her dad's name, it meant nothing. The Father returned, holding out a slip of paper. "I wish you luck on your journey..." He paused, waiting for Kate to tell him her name, and she almost did, but Ellie jumped in and snatched the paper from his hand and said, "Thank you, Father." She took Kate by the arm again and pulled her down the aisle. When Kate looked back, the priest was still looking their way. He raised a palm in farewell.

Kate shrugged Ellie off. "What are you playing at? He might have had information."

She kept going to the curb. The cab, parked in the lot now, had noticed them and was heading back to pick them up. Kate, not knowing what to do, followed her. "He said he has the priest's journals."

"But you don't have your father's name, and that was weird. There was something off with that guy."

"You just don't like religion or guys that are helpful."

The cab pulled up. "Yeah. I don't like religion, but that guy was being anything but helpful. Trust me. We did the right thing in leaving." They piled into the back seat, and Ellie gave the driver the address on the paper. "We'll get information on your birth parents. Don't worry. We won't, however, be using that priest to get the information. I just hope this Cremashci isn't a shady guy like that one was."

"He wasn't bad, Ellie. Seriously."

"You mean to tell me you didn't get this ache in your gut every time he spoke?"

"No," Kate blurted, but she couldn't deny the ominous feeling she'd had as she looked at the man.

Ellie waved her hand in the air. "Don't worry about it. We don't need him, but you really need to start tuning into your feelings. I always listen to what my gut tells me. And when I do what it tells me to do, I don't lose. Start paying attention to your feelings, Okay?"

Kate nodded, still unwilling to admit that the guy had given her the creeps, too. She let a cautious wave of hope roll through her, thinking Father Cremashci might still be able to tell her about her parents and who she was.

10

Ellie did her duty and snapped pictures of the care center. It was a mansion, not a sterile clinic built to house those with mental illness. She hoped the interior was as inviting as the stately exterior. In order to save money, Ellie sent the cab away. They had no idea how long they'd be inside. Kate took a deep breath. Ellie held Kate's hand in hers. "It's going to be okay. If he can't help us, we'll find another way." She spoke like a mother to a small child. "Now, let's do this. And let me do the talking."

Kate nodded. Heat raced up her spine. This was it. Ellie could talk about different ways all she wanted, but Kate knew this was the only solid lead she'd come on in three years, and it was likely the only break she'd ever get. Ellie pulled open the front door and walked in, Kate following close behind. She wasn't disappointed once inside. She felt right at home. The rich colors and textures made her feel cozy and warm. The luxury of it surprised Kate. How could a man, a servant of God, pay for such opulence? Did St. Catharine's have an excellent health care and retirement plan or what? Kate found that hard to believe. The green acres of lawn, shrubs, and trees seemed to go on forever. If Kate ended up in a care center one day, she hoped it would be half as nice. It felt great to think the church gave such good care to its ailing priests.

They stepped up to the reception desk, where a smile met them. "Welcome to McArthur's. May I help you?"

"You sure can," Ellie said. "We're here to visit Father Cremashci." Kate looked up, admiring the fresco painted on the high ceilings.

"Sign in here, please, and I'll find out where he is." She pushed a clipboard toward them. They signed their names while the receptionist talked on the phone.

"You're in luck. Father Cremashci is out back in the gardens right now. He so loves to be out in the gardens. Thank you for coming to visit." She pulled out a map and showed them where to go. As they walked down a wide hallway, Kate stopped to get a drink from the fountain and overheard the receptionist say, "Yes. They are here. Yes. Their names are Kate and Ellie. I'll have someone close, Father."

Kate hurried to catch up with Ellie. She leaned in close to tell her what she'd overheard, but noticed a camera peering down at them and decided to wait. They passed a bathroom, and Kate pulled Ellie back toward the bathroom door.

"I'll wait outside, thank you very much," Ellie said, tugging away.

Kate shook her head. "No. I need you." Kate sincerely hoped no cameras were in the bathrooms. She scanned the room. None were apparent, but she still turned on the faucet and pulled Ellie close. Ellie narrowed her eyes, but played along. "I overheard the receptionist as we left telling someone that we were here and we'd be watched. She gave the person on the phone our names."

Ellie turned her head and whispered. "Bathroom faucet. Nice touch. You're learning." She gave Kate a meaningful glance, before continuing to whisper. "I told you that priest was up to no good."

Kate's head flinched back. "No. You don't think?" But even as she said it, she knew it was true. The receptionist had called him Father. "If that priest who took Cremashci's place is somehow dirty, what does that say about Cremashci?"

"You mean Cremashci, the 'children's father?' The man whose defining purpose was to save the children? No way was he dirty. You read the article. Stay strong. I'll play interference so you have time with Cremashci and can get what you need."

Kate nodded. "Maybe he thought we were bad people. We were really vague. Maybe he wanted to make sure Cremashci was safe."

"Maybe. I think we should be careful, though."

Kate flushed a toilet for good measure and then turned off the faucet. Kate threaded her arm through Ellie's as they walked out of the restroom and down the long hallway. They opened the large wooden door at the end of it and found themselves on a flower-rich patio that stretched the entire length of the center. Tables, chairs, and loungers dotted the shady, welcoming space, and various people, young and old, occupied a good portion of them. It was Saturday, probably the best day for most family and friends to visit.

They stepped off the patio into the wide expanse of grass surrounded by terraced hedges and climbing roses. Several older men sat alone or with a care center worker on benches or in wheelchairs. Small children ran and played with siblings in the gardens, entering and exiting from the various openings around the hedges. A strong scent of roses filled the air. The girls stopped almost at the same time. "We should've asked what he looked like now," Kate said. "I had no idea there would be so many people out here. The picture we saw showed a man in his fifties or so. Cremashci must be in his eighties now."

"No joke, but it's probably best if we don't let on that we don't actually know him. I mean if we knew him, we'd be able to recognize him, right?" Ellie gave Kate a meaningful look.

"But how will we find him in this mass of people?"

"Leave it to me." Kate watched Ellie work her magic, walking from table to table and talking to the people. Ellie was smart. When she and her family went to visit their grandma they couldn't help but get to know the other residents. Not all, but most of the friendly ones. The sixth person pointed out to the garden to an old man, hunched over and holding a black cane with an ornate, carved handle between his legs. A worker sat beside him on the bench, reading a book.

Ellie came back to Kate and said, "I'm going to get rid of the worker. You go in and work your magic once I lead her away." She started to walk away, but Kate grabbed her arm.

"My magic? What are you talking about?"

"Go get the information you need and then leave. Be quick about it." Ellie walked away.

"But…" Kate's mind seemed to fill with mud. Didn't Ellie realize she needed to practice what she was going to say? Her heart raced. Kate couldn't remember why she'd come. What information did she need? What was she supposed to do again? Kate watched as Ellie spoke with the worker and led her away through an opening in the hedges. Kate stood frozen for several seconds until she reminded herself of what was at stake. She could work through her anxiety and do this. It was easier to talk to this man than lead that worker away. She willed her feet to move. Once she started walking, it was easy to continue. The grass tickled her toes through her sandals as she walked. As she neared the old man, he looked up and smiled at her. "Do I know you?"

She nodded and pushed her phone recorder on, a lump forming in her throat. The anticipation of discovering who she really was slammed into her, and she bit back tears as she sat next to the man. Hope filled her, and she took a deep breath to calm herself, her eyes closing momentarily.

"I do? Who are you?"

"I think you knew my mother. I think my mom and dad were part of your congregation."

He seemed to be waiting for her to continue, his eyes placid and unfocused. Kate wasn't sure, though—he might not even have heard her. Her hands trembling, she pulled out her journal and flipped to the page where she'd taped in the lime green note. She held it out to him, and he took it in an automatic gesture, but he didn't look down.

Kate swallowed hard. "That's you, isn't it?" She tapped the page, pointing to the name *Savino*. She searched his eyes, hoping for a spark of recognition or even just awareness of what was going on.

Finally, his eyes drifted down to the paper. Kate thought she saw a flash of understanding, but still, he didn't speak. She clutched the locket around her neck and held it out to him, her fingers fumbling with the latch. "Look, Father Cremashci—this is my mother. You helped her, didn't you?" She held the photo out for him to examine.

He looked at her face, awe and disbelief making his jaw tremble, "Carmela? You're alive?" His voice was a shaky whisper.

"Who? Carmela?" Despair rose in Kate's throat. This man was in a totally different reality. "No, listen. I think her name was Constanzie. She was in danger—and you helped her."

His eyes flicked behind her, and he grabbed her hand. "You can't stay here, they're watching me. I hide here." He cut off and looked down at his hands as a few people passed them.

She grabbed at the locket again. His hand shot out and settled on her knee. "Carmela. You must go. It is not safe."

She started to sob.

"They will find you. Go." His eyes darted about. She wasn't going to get any answers out of this man. He was too far gone.

"But Constanzie…" Her voice trailed at the end of her mother's name.

He did not look up. "Safe and loved. Marconi safe."

"Where?" Was he even responding to her, or was he reliving the memory of a conversation from long ago?

He shook his head and squeezed her knee. "Let her be. You only bring her danger. It's not safe, child. Go, now. Never return. They watch me, they will know you were here."

"Please, try to remember. You're the only one who can help me."

"Carmela, do not return. I can tell you nothing more." His head tilted up, and he looked around. His hands shook, holding them fast to the cane. "Do I know you?" Fear danced across his face. "No," he said, his eyes suddenly seemed sharp with intellect. "I do not know you."

Kate's head jerked up. "No. You have to remember. Please. Anything you can tell me would mean so much. Do you remember them? My parents' names." She rubbed the cross at her neck. He stared at it. The old priest's eyes were bright.

"Go. Quickly now." But she wanted, no needed, more.

He had nothing. His eyes once again dulled, and he started rocking. "Forgive me, Lord." Then he whispered, "A Marconi comes. Danger. Go." Then he went on to recite something, but he was mumbling, and she couldn't make anything out.

She pressed on his hand. "Father Cremashci. No. Please. Come back. You knew them. You did." The tears fell freely and she knew, no matter what she did, she would not get more out of this man. His mind was broken. She sobbed, not caring who might see or hear. Her head fell into her open palms and tears leaked around and through her fingers. She was so close.

A hand lit on her shoulder. The lady from the front desk. She looked at her name tag. Lenora Marconi. "I'm sorry," she said. "It can be hard to see someone like this when you were accustomed to seeing him differently. How did you know him, again?"

Kate was about to spill the beans in her weakened state, but a chill rose slowly up her spine as she looked into the woman's face. What had Ellie said? Divert when needed. "Yeah. It's terrible. He just keeps asking the same questions over and over. I can't even have a conversation with him."

"I'm sorry, honey. It can be very jarring if you're not used to it. Alzheimers can really mess up a person's mind—so many of their memories are just gone, and the memories they do have can even be false. I'm so sorry." While her words said one thing, her eyes said another. She was glad Kate hadn't gotten anything out of him and was trying to tell her anything she did get was not reliable.

Kate blinked several times and brushed the heels of her hands over her eyes, wiping away any remaining dampness. She had to be careful what she revealed. She had to lie to this lady. She channeled Ellie as much as she could, visualizing herself "working her magic."

"I think hearing anything from him, even if it was a lie would be better than this." Cremashci hummed a tune now. "Is he ever lucid?"

"No," the receptionist blurted, much too quickly. "I'm sorry."

Kate Unmasked

Kate looked at Father Cremashci and put her hand on his once again. "It was nice visiting with you, Father. Enjoy your time in this lovely place." Kate patted his hand and then stood, looking about, wondering where Ellie had gone.

"Where did your friend go?" Something about the way the receptionist looked at her told her she knew exactly where Ellie was and that's why she was there.

"I'm not sure. She doesn't tell me anything."

The receptionist made a slight puff out of her mouth. "She's a wild one, huh?"

"Can be. Well, I think I'll look around for her."

The receptionist gave a small nod, and Kate rushed away. As she walked past a large hedge, she noticed the woman on a cell phone, staring after her. A twitch started in her right eyebrow as she wove her way out of the hedge garden and into the expanse beyond. She turned off the recorder. Ellie was headed her way with a very irritated worker. "Oh, there she is," Ellie said, pointing in Kate's direction. "Kate! Where have you been? This nice lady and I have been looking all over for you." They were now only a few feet from her.

"From the way you talked, I thought she was a small child. This girl's a teenager."

Ellie leaned in and whispered loudly, "She is a teen, but she is mentally challenged."

The worker raised her head slightly and then said, "Oh, I understand," as her head came back down and her eyes lit on Kate.

Kate had no words after that, she simply stared at Ellie, waiting for her next clue as to what she should do.

"You had us worried, Kate. We're going to have to go home and not see Grandpa after all." Ellie turned slightly and winked.

"But I—"

Ellie interrupted Kate. "No buts. You know the rules and when you don't obey them there are consequences."

The worker nodded in approval.

Cindy M. Hogan

Ellie took Kate by the arm and said, "Come on, let's go." Ellie turned to the worker and said, "Thank you for helping me look."

"No problem. Mr. Cremashci is one of the easiest patients here during the day. It's night that's the problem, and I'm gone by then."

"Oh. Is he a wanderer?"

"Sometimes. But the real issue is his nightmares. He screams out about saving the children all the time, and it wakes the other residents. They've had to move him to a pretty secluded spot to keep the quiet."

"Save the children, huh?" Ellie raised one eyebrow.

"Yeah. It's surprising because he's very happy all day every day even though no one ever visits him."

"I guess being a priest really put a lot of weight on his shoulders, but if he saved so many children, shouldn't he feel good about that?"

"That's the thing, right? Perhaps he is tortured by the idea of the ones he couldn't save." The worker tilted her head to the side. "It's so sad, because by all accounts, he did such wonderful work and helped so many. It's so tragic that he can't remember." She looked back at him sadly for a moment, then turned to the girls with a sigh. "Do you know the way, then? I really should get back."

"We'll be fine, thanks."

Kate and Ellie watched her walk away and the second Ellie thought the worker was out of earshot, she said, "Did you get it?"

Kate shook her head. "No, he's too far gone. I got nothing."

"Come on Kate. I gave you plenty of time."

"Hey, you listen to this and tell me if I didn't try my best." She pushed the recording and as she listened, it was as if she was hearing something completely different than before. At least the meaning was different. Kate thought about the way the man looked at her, and now she got the feeling that he was more lucid than she'd realized. They stopped walking, both totally engrossed in the recording.

"I'm Constanzie." Kate met Ellie's eyes. "He answered my question, but I didn't understand because I thought he was talking about my mom—but when I asked about Constanzie, he said 'safe and loved.' He

99

was talking about the baby. Me."

"Yeah, and he thought you were your birth mom."

"He thought my birth mom was dead."

"You're in serious danger." Ellie grabbed at Kate's phone. "Turn that off. Let's get out of here."

11

The new cab pulled up shortly after they got to the front of the estate. The cabbie's face was covered with a black beard and a mustache that curled at the ends. His eyes were covered with large mirrored glasses. "Welcome to my cab," he said as they climbed in. The W on *welcome* sounded like a V. *Velcome.*

Kate pulled out her phone as soon as they were in the cab and looked up Marconi.

"Are you a Marconi, then, or are they the bad guys?"

"I don't know." Kate pulled out her search journal from her messenger bag and turned to the page with the green note. She ran her fingers over the signature at the bottom. Whoever had signed it was probably the one who'd given her to Father Cremashci—and Father Cremashci had placed her with Tom and Abrie Hamilton. She couldn't help thinking that signature belonged to her father. She stared at it and then held it up for Ellie to see. "Does the last name look like *Marconi* to you?"

"Could be." Ellie grabbed Kate's phone and rambled off information from the search results. "Nobel Prize for physics, inventor. Died in 1937. Nope. Mafia boss. Uh, no." She kept scrolling. "Hopefully you're related to this Nobel Prize Marconi. Info on him goes on for pages. All kinds of things, including parts of universities, wireless stations, clubs, and even a holiday were named after him." Ellie brushed some loose hair behind her ear and checked her makeup.

"We should narrow the search. Put in Marconi plus New Jersey. That poor man. They put him there. And he's faking Alzheimers. These people are that evil that he'd rather be considered out of his mind rather than be out in the open?"

"A good man trapped in a bad place—lovely to look at, but truly a jail for this man—but by whom? There's more in here about the same Marconis and a bagel shop owned by some Marconis."

"Add in Catholic."

"All results are Catholic now. Nothing useful." Ellie tapped her fingers on her knee.

"Hmm." While they were stopped at a light, Kate noticed a large bagel painted on the side of a truck. The name Marconi was painted through the center of it. "Look Ellie!"

Ellie leaned over Kate and looked out her side window. The bagel truck moved forward through the intersection. They watched it, and then Ellie blurted, "Follow that bagel truck."

"Ellie, he can't. We're not in the turn lane. We can drive to the shop."

The light turned green and lo and behold, their cabbie didn't move. Cars honked behind them, and the two girls lowered in their seat, heads below the rear window. The driver suddenly jerked the car to the side as he began to drive, and they turned the corner. Kate and Ellie inched back up. "You like?" the cabbie said, aiming to please.

Ellie grinned and said, "Heck, yeah!" She bounced a couple times in the seat, and the cabbie smiled. He was obviously gunning for a big tip. He wove through the cars until they had the truck in their sights. Next thing they knew, it pulled off the road and stopped.

"I stop?" The driver asked, flipping his glasses up over his eyebrows to look at them in the rearview mirror.

"Yes." Kate leaned forward. "Definitely."

Kate couldn't believe how much money they already owed.

"Wait here," Ellie said, like this was a normal thing for her to do. Kate wanted to tell him to go, her pockets only went so deep.

"I wait," he said.

Of course he would wait. If he didn't, he'd be out a ton of money. By the time they walked the short distance to the truck, the driver had put blocks behind the wheels and was now putting up an awning out front, getting ready to sell bagels.

Ellie continued to walk with complete confidence right up to him as he anchored the last of four posts holding the awning up.

"Hey there," Ellie said. "Your bagels any good?" She let her Texas drawl come out more than usual and flashed him a flirtatious smile.

The guy looked up and grinned. "The best." He stood straight and pushed his trendy sunglasses up over his moderately long, shaggy hair. He looked nothing like the guys on the Jersey Shore show—what was it the girls on the show called them? Guidos? Most of them had short, spiked hair and overly tanned skin. This guy looked mostly like the guys back home, except for his beefy arms, perhaps. With a jolt, Kate realized he looked familiar. His hair was pinned back from his forehead now, under the glasses. His big brown eyes peered over at Ellie. Kate realized how she knew him. He'd been at the church.

"Great. How long until we can get some?" Ellie said, leaning on a post nearby.

Had Ellie not recognized him?

"Give me ten minutes, and I'll have you some nice hot ones."

"Perfect." Ellie nudged Kate, but realizing he'd been at the church freaked her out too much to react.

He pulled a rope into a loop on the side of the truck and tied it off. It was impossible not to stare at the toned, deep muscles of his arms. He wasn't the sort of boy Kate was usually attracted to, but he did look fine setting the truck up. "Where are you two lovely ladies from?"

"Texas." Ellie flashed a grin. "Can't you tell?"

He grinned back. "I thought I heard something of an accent. I never met a real Southern girl before." He kept working, but he seemed to be enjoying the attention.

"Where's your accent?" Ellie teased, and Kate had to fight not to roll her eyes. "I thought you Jersey boys were all 'Hey yo, yous guys,'" She lowered her voice and made a ridiculous duck face as she spoke, and the guy snorted with laughter.

"Oh, you watch too much TV," he chuckled. "We talk normal around here. Those guys you see on Jersey Shore and that crap aren't even from around here. They're from New York."

Ellie sidled up to him and touched his muscled arms. "Well, you may not have the accent, but you do have the body. Look at those babies. You are so strong."

He grinned, and a dimple appeared on his tanned cheek. "Thanks. I try to stay fit. So, Texas, huh? That's a long way from here." He glanced at Kate, who quickly looked away.

"This your truck?"

"Naw. It's my cousin's. He's sick. I'm helping him out today." He smiled at Ellie.

"This is a family business then?" She smiled right back.

"Yup."

He moved near Kate, his arm brushing hers and his eyes fixing on hers as he grabbed a stack of chairs and started to set them around. She drew in a quick breath before stepping back. "You the quiet one?"

"No," Ellie said. "She usually talks your ear off!" She gave Kate a death glare.

"Sorry," Kate blurted, wringing her hands out in front of her. "But—I think I saw you earlier today, at that Catholic church."

"No!" Ellie said, running over to the two of them and staring at his face. "It's the guy that undressed you with his eyes."

Kate slugged Ellie in the arm, her face burning furiously. "Ouch." Ellie rubbed at her arm.

The boy raised an eyebrow. "Is that what you thought I was doing?" He gave them a devilish smile.

"Don't deny it, big boy. Here," she moved closer to him, "have a napkin for that drool." She tapped at the corner of her mouth.

One corner of his mouth went up into a smile. "I appreciate beauty when I see it." He gave Kate a meaningful look and disappeared around the truck before reappearing inside the truck.

Kate shot daggers at Ellie, but Ellie just waggled her eyebrows. His back was to them, and he washed his hands and put an apron over his t-shirt and jeans, tying it in the back. "Ya know, there are much better places for tourists to go around here."

"Really? Where?" Ellie asked as if she hadn't thoroughly research everything about Seaside.

"I could show you some places later if you wanted." He turned and smiled at Ellie before glancing at Kate.

Ellie put her arm through Kate's and said, "We'd love that."

"Which flavor would you like?"

"Blueberry with strawberry schmear, please." Ellie bit her lip.

Shameless. Ellie was shameless with her lip biting. "And you?" he asked, his deep voice echoing off the truck walls. He smiled, and it made him look even better.

"She's Kate. I'm Ellie." Ellie twisted side to side.

"Well, Kate, what will it be?"

Her pulse was galloping. She gulped. "The best you've got."

"Coming up." He set to work.

Ellie turned to Kate and giggled. Kate rolled her eyes. She didn't get the thrill Ellie did from flirting with hot guys. Kate felt stupid and awkward. Nine times out of ten she never saw the boy again, anyway. It seemed like a bunch of trouble for nothing. Ellie leaned in and whispered, "Oh, my goodness, he is hot and he totally wants you."

"He is. He definitely is. But he doesn't want me." Kate couldn't deny the obvious. She wanted to ask Ellie what she thought would happen with this guy. Did she want Kate to join him in the truck and make out on the dirty floor, right then? Blech.

Kate had to get it together. There would be no making out. He was a means to an end. She had to get answers. "Marconi Bagels? Like

Marconi, the scientist and Nobel Prize winner?"

He chuckled. "I guess these bagels should win my uncle the Nobel Prize. They truly are that good."

"Your cousin's lucky to have you talking up the goods."

"Tito. My cousin's name." The signature at the bottom of the green notepaper popped into Kate's mind. Tito Marconi. Not the Marconi that signed the notepaper. That name started with an A.

"So you're a Marconi?" Kate asked, determined to get more answers.

"No." He laughed.

"If you're not a Marconi, then who are you?" His laugh was too sexy.

"I'm Lino Bellini."

"Do all your relatives' names end with an *I*?" Ellie giggled.

"Italian names, you know."

"Is that why you have such fantastic skin or do you have to work at that tan?" Ellie giggled again. Kate tugged on her arm. She was going too far.

"You're full of questions."

"Yeah. I like to know stuff. Do you mind?"

"I guess not." His eyes flicked to Kate and back to Ellie. The timer rang on the toaster, and he turned.

"So if this isn't your real job, what is?" Ellie was like a freight train without a conductor with her questions.

He handed them their schmeared bagels and when Ellie held out money to pay, he waved it off. "Those are on me."

Kate examined the bagel and took a bite. Crunchy and chewy with all kinds of flavors running through her mouth. An everything bagel with a caramel schmear.

"Oh, my gosh, this is amazing," Kate gave him an appreciative nod.

"Thanks. That's my favorite, too. I work at my other uncle's store on the other side of town. Bellini Bagels. Tito watches out for me, and I watch out for him."

"That's cool. Do you all live together or something?" Ellie asked.

He laughed again. "No."

She was making a mess out of this. He would cut her off soon.

"Oh. I thought since you were so close maybe you lived together."

"We do both live in Jersey, but not in the same house or block or anything."

"The Marconis are good people, then?" Kate thought Ellie was asking all the wrong questions.

"Of course."

"I've never known a Bellini or a Marconi, being from Texas and all."

"You're looking at a Bellini right here."

"Besides you, I mean. And I do have to say I like what I see. Do you have a girlfriend?" Ellie was out of control.

"Sorry," Kate said. "Ellie doesn't know how to keep her mouth from places it shouldn't go."

"It's okay. I'll answer. No." His eyes lit on Kate. She forced herself not to look away. As they stood bantering, people started trekking up to the truck, interrupting the conversation as they ordered and paid for their food.

Kate stepped back, wanting to strangle Ellie. She was flirting when she should have been working hard to find out about the Marconis. They should leave. Lino loved the attention, she could tell. He had to be a player. Perhaps she shouldn't feel bad for playing him. Soon Kate couldn't even hear what was being said. Instead, she people-watched and worried about not finding her parents on this trip. Ellie needed to stay on point and stop thinking of herself. They only had today and tomorrow to find her parents, and things weren't looking very good. She punched more words into the search bar of her phone, hoping to find all the Marconis in Jersey.

Again the Nobel Prize winner and all his accolades filled the screen. She tried with New Jersey zip codes, and the screen populated with the names of hundreds of Marconis. How could she narrow them down? She pulled up the names. She used a birthdate range to narrow the results. Now she was down to only a hundred names. She glanced up at Ellie and over to the cab. Seriously, they should get going. She could flirt at the hotel and not have to pay a driver to wait on them.

Kate pushed through the crowds and gave Ellie a look that said they should go.

"So, you really want to show us around?"

Kate's face flashed hot as the bagel boy stared down at her. "Maybe." She couldn't understand why she was reacting this way. "If it's both of you."

"Give me your number, and I'll call you." Ellie bit her lip again. Argh! Kate shifted her feet.

He scribbled on a napkin and handed it to her. Crazy. Kate felt her jaw slacken, and she clacked her teeth together. Lino smiled at her before turning to the next customer.

"Toodles," Ellie said, giving a flirty wave.

"Bye, Kate," he called after them.

Kate pulled Ellie close. "Bye!" she called back.

Ellie said, "He's in love with you, and I was the one doing all the talking."

"What the heck was that?" Kate asked.

"That was me getting the information we need." She looked smug.

"And what information was that? The color of his underwear?"

"Didn't you hear? His uncle could be your dad."

Kate stopped in her tracks, taking a quick glance back at Lino. "How did you get that from that conversation?"

"It's not like you can jump into personal questions. You have to take time with all kinds of questions and sprinkle the important ones in here and there. Then the conversation feels natural and not contrived. There are a lot of Marconis in the East, but only six families near the Jersey Shore. And they're all close. All have children but one. And there's one whose wife and child were killed in an accident."

Kate raised her eyebrows.

"You. You are that child. He's never remarried and—"

"I didn't hear any of that."

"You walked away too soon. He really started spilling once he got busy with the other customers. He had to drop his guard and couldn't pay close attention to me. Most of the Marconis live right by the beach."

They climbed into the cab, and Ellie pulled out her phone. "To the beach please. Seaside."

Ellie's fingers flew over the buttons on the phone, and she pulled up some addresses of Marconis and even some pictures. "We need to find one that has your nose."

"Very funny." Acid bubbled up in Kate's gut.

"We'll go to the area they live and ask around until we find him." She pulled up some pictures. "Whoa. Hold on."

Kate leaned in. "What? What did you find?"

"A picture of that fancy dude at the church, I think." She pulled up both pictures side by side and sure enough, they matched. "I knew he was someone important. It says his name is Rinaldo Marconi. He was arrested for embezzling. Great." She continued to read. "But it says he got off. Sounds like he gets himself into trouble quite often, but he's always innocent. I can't wait to get to the beach and check these guys out."

"Hold on," Kate hissed. "You've got to take a step back."

"What? Why? We're so close."

"The priest said I was in danger. We can't go asking around about my parents. What if it puts us in danger? They were hiding me, remember?" She pulled out the journal and looked at the signature on the notepaper.

"That sounds like the ramblings of an old senile man. Besides, it's been forever."

"I don't think Father Cremashci was senile at all—he was faking it. You told me to start listening to my gut, and that's exactly what I'm doing. Something is not right. We need to be careful. And we can't go badgering everyone in the neighborhood for information."

Ellie sat in silence staring at Kate, but also through her. "You've got a point, but what if you are a Marconi, and all we need to do is ask the right person?"

"Let's be strategic about this. It won't do us any good to stumble upon the wrong person and end up dead."

"Dramatic much?" She gave Kate a whimsical look. "Fine. Tell me what to do."

"I think we hang out down there, get a feel for things, and then call our new friend to show us around, maybe even introduce us to his family."

"Scary."

Kate paid the cab fare when they got to the beach. "Cabs are so freaking expensive."

Ellie pushed on her, indicating that she should get out of the cab. "It'll be worth it in the end." Kate did know that, but it made her feel uncomfortable to blow that much money and not even get a receipt.

They looked out over the boardwalk to the beach. People milled about everywhere. There were no high rise buildings or big apartment buildings that they could see. Small businesses and large amusement park rides lined the boardwalk. Kate turned to Ellie, whose eyes were wide.

"Uh," Ellie said, "We definitely better call Lino."

12

"We found ourselves out on the Seaside Boardwalk. You should join us." Ellie said to Lino over the phone.

"Kate and I. Uh, huh. It's pretty incredible, but maybe you could give us the insider's view. Sure. We can wait. We'll kick it on the beach or something."

Ellie squealed. "He'll be here in half an hour."

"I can't believe you pulled that off. I bow to your brilliance."

She bowed to Ellie, but a fire lit in her gut and she wondered if she'd be able to keep her cool around Lino. "Our hotel is about half a mile down that way. We don't want him to take us that way. I'll let him know we came from that direction."

Kate nodded and hugged herself, trying to calm her nerves. "Let's get a drink."

They sat on a bench, watching the waves and sipping on sodas while they waited. It seemed like the half hour only took a few minutes to tick by. Lino walked up, and Kate felt like she was on a movie set. He wore a slightly rumpled, deep blue button up, unbuttoned to the second button, his sleeves pushed up past his elbows. His shirt was tucked into khakis with a dark brown belt. His flip flops smacked as he walked toward them. She took in a sharp breath, her heart pounding wildly.

Kate Unmasked

"Yo."

"Hey."

Kate couldn't help it, she said, "You look great." Heat prickled up the back of her neck.

He chuckled and stroked his scruffy chin. "Thanks. You do too. I should have told you that earlier." He looked at Kate for an extra beat before turning to Ellie. "You, too. What do you want to see?"

Ellie shook her drink cup, the ice crunching inside. She turned and tossed it into the trash. "You grew up here. Take us on a trip down memory lane. We could start at your house and work out."

"My place is kinda far, but we could start at my uncle's. I was there a lot after school."

"Perfect." They were going to a Marconi house.

"You're going to have to fill Kate in on the whole family tree. She didn't hear most of that, and I couldn't remember it all."

He nodded. "We're going to my uncle Rinaldo's house, he's the head of the family. He has five brothers, Benito, Antonio, Armand, Andre, and Stefano. They all live near here. They're always together. Work and play. Family is super important to us."

Kate's mind automatically pulled up the signature in the journal. It could have been any of those A names: Antonio, Armand, Andre. Certainly, one of those names had to be the right length. As soon as she got the chance, she'd check the names against the signature.

"What do they do? Does each brother own a bagel shop or something?" Ellie asked.

"Uh," he looked away. "No. There's only one Marconi bagel shop, but they also own a few clubs and do stuff with the market."

"Hard workers, huh?" Kate asked, lips pressed together.

"Yup. Anyway, they're the nicest people you'll ever meet. Seriously." He didn't say anything else, and Kate didn't know what else to ask.

They walked several blocks until they came upon a house that took up almost half of the block. Its sun-bleached tan exterior screamed money. "No way!" Kate said. "This is your uncle's house? It's huge."

"Big family. Lots of kids."

"So he's not the brother that lost his wife?"

"No. That's Andre. He and my cousin Tito moved in here, though. Family isn't just wife and kids for us, you know? We don't lose track of our extended family like the rest of America. We care for our own."

She nodded, imagining Andre's name on the green notepaper. Was the name long enough to fit there? If so, he could be her dad—and the person who had saved her as a baby. Lino's family sounded nice, but a bit creepy too, like the mafia. She wouldn't say that though. Kate laughed instead and said, "Must be nice to have someone always have your back." His eyes widened, but then he looked at his feet and chuckled while kicking at a piece of wood.

"Can we go inside?" Ellie asked.

"Uh," he looked at Kate. "Not sure that would be a great idea. They had a baptism today, and they're probably still celebrating."

Kate's head shot up. "Wait a minute. That was a baptism at St. Catharine's church?"

He frowned. "Yes."

The memory of the serious processional raced across her mind. "We wondered what was going on."

"Yeah," Ellie broke in. "A baptism is supposed to be a celebration. That seemed like more of a funeral."

He clasped and unclasped his hands. "Well, the baby's mom, uh, she, uh, well, she died in child birth, so while it should have been happy and all, it was a bit sad, too, being reminded about her mom's absence and all."

Kate nodded. "Sorry. I didn't know."

"It's okay, there was no way for you to know." He sucked in his top lip.

"Who were those goons at the door? They wouldn't let us go inside until this woman and man came out." Ellie had to ask.

"My uncle Rinaldo and my aunt Patrizia. They own this house. One of the guys at the door was my uncle Andre and the other was Tito, his son. The Marconis are a bit more formal than the Bellinis, but they're still great people. They loosen up when they're home."

"Really? I can't picture it," Ellie said. "I thought those guys were body guards."

Kate tried to remember details about the two men. All she could remember was that they seemed to scowl, were tan, tall, and bulky. Not fat, but totally beefy strong. Her father and brother? Andre and Tito?

"Well," Lino started, but didn't finish because people started filing out of the house laughing. A man with dark grey hair combed back from his face with a couple-day-old beard with patches of white, turned their way and smiled. He wore his blue and white checkered shirt with the arms pushed up to his elbows just like Lino. He lifted his shiny sunglasses up to his forehead and squinted in their direction. "Lino? Is that you?"

They were at the opposite end of the house, but Kate thought Lino looked nothing like him, even though he was quite handsome.

"Hey, Uncle Vinny. I finished with the truck and returned it. I met these nice girls from Texas, and I'm showing them around town."

"Lucky them. I hope you have fun. There's no better guide than Lino. But Lino, don't take too long, your aunt's expecting us for dinner at seven."

"Where you going?" Lino asked the guy.

"I've got some things to take care of. I'll be back." There was a gentle roar in the tone of his voice. Kate liked him immediately.

"Okay. See you after a while." Lino raised a hand goodbye.

"Who was that?" Kate asked.

"That was Vincenzo."

"Let me guess," Ellie said. "Your uncle."

He laughed loudly and took a step back. "Yup. My uncle."

"Another Marconi?"

"No. Bellini. I work at his shop. Come on, I'll show you around town."

For the next hour they went up one street and down another with him telling them all about how it used to be while they explored interesting places and met some of his friends. When they got back to the beach, he took them straight for the roller coaster.

"Are you sure that thing's safe?" The coaster was half in the water on stilts. Kate's stomach did flip flops thinking about getting near it.

"I've been on this beast over 100 times, and I'm still here. The idea of it hanging out there over the water without much support makes it more fun. Kinda scary even."

"Yeah, uh, maybe you two should ride it and tell me about all about it," Kate said, stopping in her tracks. "I'll watch from here."

"No way. I'm not letting you miss this, you'll regret it. I'll hold your hand the whole time, and you won't even have to watch. But it's better when you do."

"Yeah, Kate, you're not missing this one. It's going to be epic. I'll take pics while we're flying around the track. It'll be awesome." Ellie grabbed Kate's hand and hurried to the short line. Lino paid for the tickets and joined them. Ellie and Lino chatted about great rollercoasters while they waited their turn, and Kate tried to regulate her breathing so she wouldn't pass out.

Lino helped Kate into her seat and then took her hand. It was warm, on the brink of being hot, and her chest swelled with what felt like tiny birds twittering away. "The first time I rode this baby was when I was five. I'd wanted to ride it before then, but I wasn't tall enough. I wouldn't let my dad hold my hand. I told him I was a big boy and wasn't scared at all. Sure, I screamed as we went down the hill. . ." Kate knew Lino was trying to get her mind off what was about to happen, but as soon as the car began to move, sheer terror filled her mind, and she didn't hear the rest of the story. She didn't even see Ellie turning and taking pictures of her terror.

Ellie laughed with delight as they exited the ride and started showing them pictures. Kate couldn't focus quite yet. Lino tugged on her hand, and she realized he was still holding it. "You okay?"

Kate Unmasked

"Look at your face, Kate! You looked like you were being chased by a thousand human-sized spiders."

She took a couple of deep breaths. "Yeah. I'm okay." She looked at Lino's concerned face. "You were right, it was great with my eyes open."

He busted up laughing, swinging their held hands behind them and then back to the front a couple of times. "You hated it. Admit it."

"Well, I might like the dentist more than that."

"Aw, I'm sorry." He turned to her, a goofy smile on his face. "Just because I love the ride doesn't mean everyone will. You deserve a treat. Ice cream on me."

"Yeah, I think she needs the pick-me-up."

It was close to six, and Ellie ramped up the assault as they walked on the boardwalk eating their cones. "I don't get your family tree. How exactly are the Marconis and Bellinis related? By marriage?"

He snorted. "They aren't, but that doesn't mean they can't be family."

She gave him a what-the-heck look.

"It's like this. The Marconis and the Bellinis came to America at the same time. Things were different way back then. It wasn't easy to survive. The two heads of the houses came together and made it work. They became successful together. Ever since then, the families have been inseparable. Yeah, they have their moments, but what family doesn't? To be totally honest, I'm not actually a true Bellini, either."

That was shocking news. "What does that mean?" Kate asked.

"My folks, they were murdered, and I was alone."

Kate and Ellie stopped walking at the same time and openly stared at him. He moved off to the side of the boardwalk, and the girls followed him, weaving through the crowds of people.

"It's okay. It was a long time ago, and I have a new family now."

"I'm so sorry about your parents. That must've been awful."

"It was, but the harder part was living on the streets. I didn't have any other family."

"You had to live on the streets?" Ellie asked, still staring, mouth

116

agape. "That would never happen where we live. It's totally safe there."

"That sounds nice."

"So how did you end up with the Bellinis?" Kate asked, curiosity getting the better of her.

"Vincenzo caught me stealing one day, and he told me I had to come work for him to pay off the debt."

"That's like child slavery." Ellie gasped.

"Naw. He had me do easy stuff like delivering things, you know errands for the business and all. I'd collect stuff for him, too. Lots of people don't like doing the errands, but I thought it was fun. I owe him everything."

Kate shook her head back and forth, trying to understand the story.

"As I got older, Vincenzo told me I needed to find a way to start earning. That wasn't for me, so he put me to work at the bagel shop and had me go to school. Said I was too smart to stay out of school. I'm saving to get to college. Vinny's gonna pay half my tuition as soon as I can pay the other half as long as I spend some of my time learning the market."

"That's pretty incredible," Kate said. "Not every story like yours ends well."

"Yeah, I was found by a great guy. Vinny's the best. Let's ride the sky ride to the other end," Lino suggested. "It'll put us about where we started, and you can see for a really long ways."

They made their way there. Ellie jumped in the first seat that came around, elbowing Kate out of position and not allowing her to ride with. Kate knew Ellie was trying to get Kate to ride with Lino, but it felt too contrived, so she quickly stepped in front of the next seat with the intention of also going solo, but before the safety rail could be locked into place, Lino slid in with a smile. "Whew! I almost missed it," he said. His light brown eyes laughed down at Kate, sending a tender tingle to her gut. Ellie had conquered again. A skyride with a hot guy couldn't help but be romantic. A feeling of awkwardness settled over her, and he must've felt it because he looked away at the same instant she did. Then she felt silly. She should be enjoying herself, so she turned back to ask him something. She jerked back and her forehead hit into Lino's with a smack.

They both cried out and rubbed their heads, laughing. "That hurt," Kate said. "Sorry." He said the words at the same time. "Too close." She nodded and after a quick glance at each other, the awkwardness returned and she looked away. She forced herself not to look back at him, but instead look out over the city. Lino started peppering her with descriptions of places in the direction she was looking. She grabbed onto the safety bar and tried to relax. He seemed to be talking so loud. She was sure Ellie could hear every last word, but she didn't turn around, no doubt to give Kate and Lino the opportunity to steal a kiss without prying eyes. Kate's stomach was a bundle of squawking birds. Could things be any more uncomfortable? She didn't want that. She had so many questions for Lino, but was unsure how to ask them. They were about three-fourths the way through when she put her hand on his arm, getting the courage she needed, but feeling totally dumb. "I'm nervous, too."

He sighed. "Sorry, I was babbling, wasn't I?" She thought he'd described the entire city already.

"Yeah, but that's okay. Did Vinny adopt you?" She no longer looked out over the city, but directly into his curious eyes.

"No, but we don't need a paper to tell us we're family."

"I'm adopted," she blurted, shocking herself. "But sometimes I wonder if I belong with my adoptive family. You're lucky to know where you belong."

"Do you know who your real parents are?"

She shook her head. She had this irrational desire to tell him everything. "I wish I did. Maybe then I'd know where I belonged."

"Do you like your adoptive family?"

She nodded, knowing she couldn't get into those problems with him.

"Well that's good at least."

Despite her feelings, she said, "Ellie told me you have an uncle whose wife and daughter were killed."

He nodded. "Really sad."

"Which uncle again?"

"Andre. Almost fifteen years ago."

"And he's never remarried?"

"Says his heart couldn't take it. He's done amazing stuff with the bagel shop, though. He puts his whole world into it."

Andre Marconi had to be her dad. Someone had targeted them and killed her mom. Whoever it was must've wanted to kill Kate too, so Andre made it impossible to find her. The blood on the baby bag at home was most likely hers. She took a deep breath in. She'd found her parents.

13

Kate and Ellie returned to the hotel, exhausted and ready to relax. It had been an emotionally draining day. Her mom was most likely dead, and her dad had never moved on. She grabbed her journal and took note of everything she'd learned. The Marconis and Bellinis were family. The Bellinis saved Lino. Andre Marconi lost his wife and daughter around fifteen years ago. Kate was seventeen, and if she was adopted at two, then Andre Marconi could very well be her dad. Tomorrow she'd go see if there was a way to confirm it.

When they walked into the hotel suite, they were surprised to find it empty. On the table was a note that read, "We're at the bistro on 37th. Some cast members may show up there tonight."

"What?" Ellie shouted. "They went without me?" She immediately texted her family and then ran into the bathroom to freshen up. She came out ten minutes later in a bright blue dress with a slit that almost came to her waist. Her three-inch, sparkly heels played off her sleek, shiny necklace and earrings. "What are you doing? Hurry, get ready. I don't want to miss a thing."

"I'm bushed. Go without me." Kate plopped onto the sofa for emphasis.

Ellie narrowed her eyes but only for a split second. She obviously changed her mind about something in that moment in time. "Are you sure? Tomorrow we'll see your dad, and he's going to be ecstatic about finding you. You'll see."

"I need a little time to myself. I'll be okay. And who wouldn't want to meet their kid, right? Especially one that you thought was dead or lost forever?"

"That's the spirit!" She smiled at Kate, but Kate could see in her eyes that she was already gone. Already at the bistro.

"Have a good time."

Ellie raised a hand in the air and gave a loose wave. "You know I will," she said, as she walked out the door.

Kate got up and flung herself on the bed, letting her thoughts run wild about the possibility that her mom was dead and that she would only be a sour memory in her dad's life. She wrote the words *hopeful* and *sour* in the journal. She scribbled out the sour and circled the hopeful. Then she wrote, *Birth mom still living? Maybe. Who saved me? My dad?? Andre Marconi?* Her head spun, and she got up to get some aspirin. She stood at the large window overlooking the boardwalk and beach and found herself longing to go for a walk along it in the dark. She hoped the fresh sea air would clear her head of all its conjecture. She changed into some sweats, a hoodie, and flip-flops.

Even though the hotel said they had security at night on the portion of the beach that lay directly in the path of the hotel, she grabbed her little purse that had pepper spray in it, tucking her keycard inside as well. As she made her way to the back of the hotel to go to the beach, she noticed a white grand piano in a room off to her left. The room was not well lit, but the piano lights for the music were on as well as some indirect lighting on the edges of the room.

She couldn't help herself, she tugged on the door. The beach might have helped her to feel better, but the piano was sure to. She slipped through the partially open door and after checking for people and finding none, she shut the door and made her way to the piano.

As her fingers hit the keys, she forgot all her troubles, and there was only music and peace and happiness. As she finished, she thought she could feel the presence of the woman in her dreams next to her. She tried to uncover the woman's identity in her mind's eye as she played, but her face was completely blank. She tried to see the freaked-out audience, but it didn't show itself. As she was about to start playing her next song, the presence next to her clapped. It was real. She turned abruptly, her eyes popping open in fright as she reached for her bag that held the pepper spray. When her panic cleared, she had the pepper spray in her hand, ready to spray the guy who only seconds earlier was sitting next to her. At the moment, he was scrambling away from her. "Who are you?" she demanded.

He held up his hands and waved them in front of him. "Please don't spray me. That stuff is no fun."

"So you've been sprayed before?" She raised an eyebrow and stood up.

He nodded once and bit his cheek. He looked familiar somehow.

Kate repeated her question. "Who are you?"

"I'm Jace. I'm sorry I scared you. I promise I have no bad intentions." He held his hands up in an innocent gesture, and there was laughter in his eyes.

It finally clicked, and she realized who it was she was talking to. He was one of the reality stars on *My Not so Normal Life on the Jersey Shore*. Her breath hitched. She had almost pepper-sprayed Jace McCollum, one of the hottest guys on the show. The most brooding and angry of the bunch, but still. He was a guy Ellie would die to meet in person. She looked around. "What, no cameras?"

"You do know who I am, then." A corner of his mouth tugged up into a smile.

"I only now realized it." She reached for her phone to take a picture with him so that Ellie would believe her—or even to have Ellie hurry back—but there was no phone. She'd left it in her jean pocket when she changed into sweats. The realization made her blush furiously. She was in sweats in the presence of Jace McCollum. A strange squeak sounded from her mouth, and she slapped her hand over it.

Cindy M. Hogan

"Are you okay? Do you need help?"

She shook her head and reached out to him, making him shrink back even more as he tried to avoid the can of pepper spray. She rolled her eyes. "Sorry." She put the spray back down and said, "No. I don't need help."

"Look, I don't want things to be weird. Can you pretend that I'm just another guy and that I'm not on TV, and you don't know who I am?"

She needed to pull it together. Could she treat him like a normal guy? If she wanted to spend time with him, she'd have to. "I'll try my best. If I start giggling like a crazy girl in the presence of an unearthly hot guy, feel free to throw me down the laundry chute."

"It's a deal. It's hard to be the real me, ya know? The show makes me out to be one way and that's what people expect, but it's not who I am. Not really."

She stared at him a moment longer, thinking about his request. Maybe she'd underestimated this guy. Maybe the fame thing wasn't working for him and he needed a break from the guy the TV portrayed. Maybe, just maybe, he wasn't an egotistical jerk after all. "I can imagine how hard it must be to be two different people all the time." She thought about who she was at home with her family and the person she was with Ellie. She could relate.

"Yeah. It gets confusing, and I hate it. I wish people could see that the show is just that, a show, and despite the fact that they call it a reality show, it's about as far from reality as it could be. And the worst is being used by so many people. I wish there wasn't a reason for people using me."

"If it were me, I'd probably get the two mixed up sometimes."

"Yeah. That does happen, and I hate that too."

"Well, I can tell you this," Kate pushed her hair over her shoulder. "I like the boy who's in front of me right now."

There was a moment of awkward silence until he grinned. "What you played, that was beautiful."

123

"I didn't know anyone was listening."

"I heard the music as I passed to go out to the beach."

"And I found the piano as I was going out to the beach."

"It was fate, then. Lucky me." He pushed his hand through his scruffy blond hair. He sat back down on the bench. "Do you mind?" She shook her head as he placed his hands on the keys and began to play. She tried to remember a time when he played on the show, but couldn't. She was sure Ellie would be able to tell her. He played the morose song quite well, and Kate found herself enjoying his enthusiasm.

"That was really great," she said as he started another sad piece. She put her hands on the keys and created a duet. What she added made the song light and airy instead of heavy and sorrowful.

"Be careful, you threaten to change my mood."

"That wouldn't be so bad, would it?"

He chuckled and continued to play, their hands grazing each other's as they learned to move together. He had obviously had extensive training, and she was having fun. Real fun.

"Just try to change this one." He had a glint in his eye and flashed a wicked smile. It was difficult, but she was able to lighten the mood of the piece, if only a little.

He cocked his head to the side when they finished. "You surprised me. I thought you'd massacre it with joyful playing. You held back. Why?"

"The souls of some songs are meant to stay heart wrenching." She gave him a sheepish smile.

"Good answer." They stared at each other for several beats too long. He cleared his throat and said, "Why don't you pick a song, and I'll try to change its soul to one that better matches mine than yours."

"Are you saying your soul is dark and brooding or what?"

"Life is a dark place, Miss Sunshine. You've yet to discover it."

She thought of her parents' betrayals and the most likely fate of her mother. "You'd be surprised at what I've overcome. Happiness is a choice. Despite all the crap life throws at me, I choose joy."

His eyebrows pulled together, and she expected him to ask what terrible things had happened to her, but he didn't.

"Maybe you can teach me a thing or two about joy." He took in a deep breath and took her hands out of her lap. "You're really talented. I haven't had so much fun playing in a long time. Your hands are a thing of beauty." He lifted them to his lips and kissed them. Heat spread through Kate's chest. To her surprise, he then set her hands on the keyboard and said, "Now play something sickly sweet, and I'll destroy it."

She laughed, her heart slamming against her ribs. She played, and he destroyed.

After several songs, they began to mimic their piano teachers, especially the ones that drove them crazy.

"Yeah, my parents quickly discovered that if they didn't get me a new instructor, I'd never play again," Jace said.

"I love my instructor at the university. He totally gets me." She realized she'd played with this guy without the memory of her dreams making it a painful experience. That's when the big doors leading into the room opened and a security guard walked in, her gun belt hanging loose on her thin hips. Her hair was pulled back so severely that her eyes were pulled to sharp corners. She walked right up to the piano. "I've actually enjoyed hearing you play, but it's past the time I'm supposed to lock up, and I really like my job." She grinned, a toothpick sticking out from between her lips.

Kate grabbed her keycard and shoved it back into her bag and did the same with her pepper spray. "Thanks for playing with me. That was a lot of fun." She never thought Jace McCollum would be so fun. As she moved toward the door, the security guard rushed ahead and held it open. Jace's hand landed on Kate's arm. "Weren't you planning on a walk on the beach?"

She nodded and bit her lip. She actually bit her lip. No. This was not happening, and yet it was. She didn't want to act this way, but couldn't seem to help it. She felt all jelly like and silly.

"We could go together."

"All right." She parted her lips slightly and took a deep drag to get as much oxygen into her lungs as possible without taking an obvious deep breath. Ellie would not believe this. How she wished she had her phone.

The security guard locked the door behind them, and it felt as if a little piece of her was left behind.

"I'm Kate, by the way."

They turned down the hall leading to the beach. "Where are you from, Kate?"

"Texas, if you can believe that."

"I thought I detected a slight accent."

"My parents couldn't beat it out of me." She chuckled.

His eyebrows spiked up.

"Kidding," Kate said.

"Good, cause I was gonna have to go and learn them a thing or two."

She laughed.

The sounds of the ocean greeted them as they opened the exit door. The moon shone brightly on the water, the sand, and the boardwalk. It almost seemed like it was dawn. The smell of the sea drifted on the wind as they rushed over the boardwalk. Kate took her flip flops off and went running through the cool sand. She was vaguely aware of Jace setting his bag down on the sand. A gentle breeze blew strands of her dark hair across her face, tickling her chin. He came up behind her and took her hand in his. For the briefest of moments, they looked at each other, then continued to run and laugh.

She thought of Ellie, and a little ache played in her gut. She should go up to her room and get her phone and tell Ellie what was happening. She glanced over to Jace, and he must've felt her gaze because he looked at her again. She didn't want the spell to be broken by returning to the resort. No. It was Ellie, after all, who'd said she should let everything go while here. Wasn't she doing that?

Jace turned them toward the ocean and before she knew it, waves lapped up over her feet. She let go of his hand and rolled her sweats up past her knees. He'd taken his pants off and stood further in the water with only his boxers on. He beckoned her to join him. The water lapped at his waist. She looked down at her bulky sweats and bemoaned the fact that all she had on under them was her undies. *Live with abandon,* she thought, and ran out to him, her sweats getting heavy as they soaked up the water. Goosebumps rose on her skin. They walked until they couldn't walk any longer and then they swam. The waves were slow, languid, as if they were taking a much needed rest. They lay back and floated, his hand reaching out to hers. The warmth of his hand seemed to counteract the coolness of the water to soothe her and relax her instead of causing her to shiver.

After some time relaxing, bobbing in the water on their backs, he pulled her to him and moved vertical. She followed suit, her legs kicking to help her remain upright. "I think you're pretty awesome," he said, his voice husky. The moon left a streak of light across his hair and face. Her heart fluttered, a soft whisper of a shiver that emanated out through her body. He stroked her chin with light fingertips, his touch continuing up her jawline to the back of her neck. His face moved closer, slowly, smoothly. She wanted him to kiss her. Wanted to feel his lips on hers. And he didn't disappoint. He kissed her with experienced lips that made her heart whip hard against her ribs and heat sweep up her neck. The waves moved them slowly toward shore and all at once, he had her in his arms, his feet having found the sandy bottom. Their wet bodies molded into each other's, and she melted into his soft, slow kisses.

14

A voice called to them over the wind. Kate and Jace ignored it, but it persisted and grew louder. It was calling Jace's name. Kate snuggled her head in the crook of his neck as he turned and called out, "What is it, Tim?"

"The paparazzi got wind of your early arrival. They're at the front of the hotel getting ready to start scouring the area for you."

"Crap!" Jace said.

"We need to get you into the hotel now."

Jace looked down at her, and she looked up. "Want to come up to my room?" For the first time since she'd been with him, a shiver rushed through her.

She knew what that meant and while she loved being with him, making out with him, she wasn't ready for that. "I better not." It seemed like more of an explanation would only make it harder to leave him. Excuses could always be worked around.

"Are you sure? We can just hang out." It was too dark to see the expression in his eyes, and she was glad. She wasn't sure if she'd be able to refuse him.

"Nah. My friends will freak if I don't show up soon."

He nodded, and they walked out of the water and onto dry beach. "See you tomorrow?"

For some reason, this caught her off guard. Kate wanted to see him again, but how could that possibly be arranged? "Sure."

He let go of her and ran up the beach. She watched him go. Realization struck her and her eyes fell to her feet, the water lapping over them. He'd only said that to be nice. He had no way of finding her. No way of contacting her. She sighed, determined not to let anything ruin the evening. She'd had fun and that had to be enough. She looked up and Jace stood there, phone in hand. A smile tickled at her lips as he held the phone out to her. She took it and added her name and number before handing it back. "You know, you'll have to call me, because I'm phone-less right now." Fear rushed through her. What if he never called? She shivered, and he put his arm around her.

"You don't have to worry about that. Tonight was incredible." He leaned in and put a light kiss on her lips, warming them again. "Come on. I don't want you out here alone." They picked up her little bag with pepper spray and keycard, and he put his towel around her shoulders. She snuggled into it and took his hand. They left the beach and walked through the hotel kitchen and took a service elevator up to her floor. "I'm sorry about this. It's like I don't have my own life anymore. It's awful," Jace said.

So he did hate his TV life. "I can only imagine."

The guy who found them stood in the corner of the elevator, like a fly on the wall, and it felt weird to have a personal discussion in front of him. The door opened. "This is you, I guess."

"Yep. Number 804."

"You're sure you don't want to come up?" He kept his eyes fixed on her. "It's still early. We could sit in the hot tub and warm up. We could grab a bite to eat."

She put a hand on his arm and interrupted him. "See you tomorrow. The proverbial ball is in your court." She walked out, taking a quick look back as the elevator doors closed. She skipped to her room and inserted the key, expecting to find everyone back, excited to tell Ellie about what happened, but the space was dark. She flipped on the lights and found her phone. As she typed the words about Jace, she wondered if Ellie would believe her. She had no proof after all. She snorted. This wasn't something to tell over text. She needed to tell Ellie in person. She erased what she'd written and then wrote, *I have news. Wake me up if I'm asleep when you get here.*

Will do. Still no one, but we're hopeful. You could join us. Smiley face.

No thanks. I'm so tired.

***

The next morning, Kate snuggled into her pillow, but then remembered and sat up. She pushed on Ellie, but she didn't even move. She was practically dead. Kate would wake her after she showered. She was going to reveal herself to her dad today. A surge of excitement brought a deep smile to her lips. A note with her name on it was taped to the mirror. She yanked it off and glanced back at Ellie on the bed.

We didn't get in until three. Six isn't going to work today. Go do your stuff and meet back up with me at noon. She had drawn several hearts across the bottom of the paper and underneath wrote, *P.S. They never came.*

Great. Kate was on her own. She should have known she wouldn't be able to count on Ellie. Not when the chance of running into a star was on the table. She bit the side of her lip. She could do this. She'd have to channel Ellie, but she could. Taking a deep breath, she jumped into the shower and after getting out, took great care in her choice of what to wear.

***

She met a cab in front of the hotel and asked him to drive to the Marconi Bagelry. She hoped both her dad and brother would be there. She had another sibling. She hoped he'd like her. She put the number of the cab company into her phone so that she could call them when she needed a ride back to the hotel. She stood on the sidewalk, her legs feeling a bit like jello. After a few seconds of internal persuasion, she walked in and ordered a bagel. She could take it slow. She didn't need to

130

storm in there asking for her father. She looked around for Lino, but didn't see him. He had said he worked at the other bagel shop, Bellini's. She longed for something familiar, but there was nothing.

The long, shiny glass case full of bagels looked unnaturally clean. She could hear the clanging of metal dishes being washed somewhere behind the wall from which t-shirts, baseball caps, and a big Marconi Bagels sign hung, along with the painted phrase, *Take everything you can from life. You deserve it*, with a signature line of *Andre Marconi* under it. She narrowed her eyes. Her mantra had always been *Give everything in life, for therein lies joy.* Would she find she and her father were complete opposites?

Cold air filled the room, and she shivered and tinkered with the locket around her neck. A long hall led to the right of the sales counter. This was it. It should be an amazing moment, so why did her stomach ache? Perhaps it had to do with the priest's warning. Someone had wanted her dead, and someone had saved her. She still wasn't 100 percent sure it was Andre's signature at the bottom of that paper. Could be too short. She watched the man she believed to be her father walk out of a back room and go even further into the back of the shop. She only saw his profile, but that mixed with the memory of seeing him at the church gave her a pretty good idea of what he looked like. He wasn't as bulky as she'd originally thought. It was obvious from the way his suit fit perfectly to his body that he was buff, though. And he was tall. His hair was cropped short around his ears, but longer on top. He had a perfectly shaped, very short beard. She watched him walk with a sure gait and a stiff bearing. She couldn't wait to talk to him, hear his voice.

Had he come from his office? She tried to swallow a chunk of bagel, but it stuck in her throat. She coughed a few times before taking a swig of her water to help wash it down. A prickling sensation ran over her scalp. She knew if she didn't go for it now, she'd just feel sicker and sicker. She'd walk over to his office and sit in a chair and wait for him to come back. Then she'd lay it on the line. His eyes would fill with tears, and he'd grab her up in a hug and want her to move here with him. She focused on that possibility and stood, walked stiff as a soldier to the room. Sure enough, it was an office.

She sat in the first chair she came to and, after letting out a deep breath, she perused the room. It was bare except for a few pictures on the desk. She reached out and looked at one. It was a picture of Andre Marconi when he was much younger. His face, while stern looking, had a kindness about it. He wore no beard. Next to him sat a beautiful raven-haired woman with expressive eyes. In her arms was a baby. Kate's mouth pinched. This baby's hair was blond and stood up in feathery tufts all over. She squinted and looked more closely. Kate had dark brown hair. She took the locket from around her neck and opened it, comparing the woman and the baby in the picture with the photos on the desk. The woman was not the same. The baby was not the same. She clutched the locket tight. Another dead end.

"Can I help you?" A man's voice asked. She turned abruptly, almost dropping the picture as she did, but saving it at the last second.

"Oh, sorry," she said, setting the picture back to right on the desk. "Your family?" she choked out.

"Yes." Pain crossed his face. "Did we have an appointment?"

She swallowed hard, trying to dislodge the lump in her throat. She had no idea what to say. Her eyes lit on an application on his desk. "Actually, I heard you were hiring and wanted to meet you and get an application." She stood up and put out her hand to shake his as an acquaintance, and not her father.

He nodded. "That shows a lot of gumption. I like gumption, but I'm only hiring managers right now. You look a bit too young to have three years' experience in the food industry."

She couldn't deny that his nose and cheekbones did resemble hers. But that baby was not her. "Oh, too bad. I think I would have liked it here." She pushed away the disappointment bubbling through her.

"You could leave your name, and I'll contact you when we're hiring again." The lines of wrinkles on his forehead told her he had a lot of things to stress about. She would not be one of them.

"That would be great," she lied.

He moved behind his desk, pulled out a pad of paper, and handed it to her. She caught a whiff of his cologne. Earthy and yet spicy. She started to write her real name, but she thought better of it and put down a fake one with a fake number. He took it and read off her name. "Well, Gabby Fontana, I'll be in touch."

"Thank you." Molten lava bubbled in her gut, and she thought she might be sick, but she reminded herself that she only needed to hold on for a few more minutes. She rushed out of the store and, once around a street corner, she bent over and repeatedly gasped for air. Andre Marconi was not her father, and she had almost exposed herself to him. What if he was one of the men the priest was talking about, and that she was supposed to avoid? Perhaps the death of his wife and child had hardened him.

She stood and caught her breath, leaning against the wall of the building. Varying emotions filled her. On the one hand, she was relieved that she didn't expose herself and her thoughts to this man who could have been a very bad man. On the other, she felt a deepening despair that he wasn't her father. She wrapped her arms around her middle, heat pricking at her eyes. She yanked her journal out and violently scratched out the words that gave hope Andre was her dad. She growled and then threw the notebook into the trashcan only a few feet from her. She put her face in her hands and quietly cried out before rushing back to the trashcan and pulling the journal back out and clutching it to her chest.

She peeked around the corner. People flowed in and out of the bagel shop. She decided to avoid the store all together by walking down the street behind the shop. She heard yelling down an alley right behind Marconi's shop as she passed. Her curiosity got the better of her and she paused to listen.

"Why not?" She heard a smack. "Get up and tell me why not." Was that Andre Marconi's voice? Was that whimpering she was hearing? "You do what I tell you. Understand? You are a gopher. You wanted this." The whimpering continued, and it sounded like something was being kicked or punched. Someone screamed out. "Now, get outta here, and get it done."

She stayed where she was, frozen. A boy shot out of the alley. He couldn't have been more than twelve. He limped and whimpered, leaving a dripping blood trail behind him. She peaked around the corner. A door with the words Marconi Bagels stood thirty yards away, straight down the alley. She could see half of the length of a man in a suit. The very suit Andre Marconi had been wearing when she talked to him. The alley made a T at the end and the edge of the brick building she hid behind also partially hid him. He was on the phone now. "I took care of it…No…he won't do it again. He's learned his lesson." There was a long pause. "Well, if he didn't, we'll take care of him. No. Antonio's here. Yeah. We'll see." Several minutes passed while Kate tried to digest what was going on.

"You ready?" Andre Marconi's voice again. He spoke to the man in the alley and was off the phone.

"Yeah, I got it. Rocco's really turning out to be a great earner behind a desk. Who would've ever thought it would be so easy?"

"Yeah." His voice lowered, and she had to strain to hear. "…another matter. It's Gino's time. He exposed the family."

"You want me to do it?"

"I don't care how it gets done, but I want it done tonight."

"Consider it done, boss."

Footsteps pounded her way. A part of her wanted to run away while the other wanted to see who Andre Marconi had been talking to. She decided to do something in the middle. She walked leisurely down the sidewalk like she didn't have a care in the world. Antonio Marconi passed her, climbing into a car parked on the street.

There was something not right with this family for sure. Did Andre order a hit on Gino? She was suddenly glad she was not Andre's daughter.

15

She walked quickly and could barely touch the right buttons on her phone to call the cab company, her hands were shaking so badly. The words of Father Cremashci, telling her she was in danger, seemed truer now than ever before. The cab met her a few blocks down. While driving, they passed the Marconi bagel truck. Lino leaned out of the truck service window and took money from a customer. He smiled and laughed with the man as he gave a receipt and change. A flicker of guilt for what had happened with Jace the night before rushed over her. The line of customers kept growing as Kate drove past. Her heart jumped in her chest. She looked back and asked the driver to pull over. "I'll get out here, thanks."

The cabbie pulled over without a word. She handed him money from her dwindling pile to pay for the ride and then got out, receipt in hand. She shoved it into her pocket and made her way back to the truck. The line was still long, but no one new was getting in it. She sat on a bench and watched cars pass. She had questions for Lino.

Once the line dwindled to only a few, she got up and made her way to the line. Lino's eyes lit on her, and a grin formed on his face. She noticed a dimple in his right cheek for the first time. He winked at her and continued to help the others. A flash of heat hit her face, and she looked at her shoes. He had such a strange effect on her. She thought of Jace and their kisses and a whisper of guilt filled her heart. She couldn't allow Lino to affect her. Nothing could happen between them, and yet she felt a bond with him, one that made her feel she could trust him. She looked at her phone. It was already two and no text or call from Jace. Perhaps she was expecting too much from a celebrity. She'd only been with him for one night, but that night had been the most amazing and thrilling night ever.

Lino cleared his throat, and she looked up. She'd also had a thrilling time with Lino. No one was in front of her, and he held out a bagel for her to take. She smiled when she saw it was an everything bagel with a caramel schmear. She glanced behind her and sure enough, no one else had joined the queue, and the crowd had thinned considerably.

"You're back."

She nodded, still not sure what to say or how to say it. How did you ask someone if their family was mafia? Instead, she said, "Your cousin's still sick?"

"Yup. But he'll be good to go tomorrow. You have plans?" He was moving quickly through the truck wiping things down and putting stuff away.

All her plans were in the toilet. She had no plan. She would never learn who her parents were. It was too painful to sift through everything to find them. And if they had anything to do with the mafia, she didn't want to have anything to do with them. "You mean now?"

"Yeah. I've got to hurry and pack up. I've got to be to work in one hour."

"Oh, sorry. I'll go." All her fervor had left her, replaced with doubt and fear.

"No." He stopped and peered down at Kate. "I was asking because I thought you might want to ride in this sleek, hot truck with me. I could show you where my real job is."

She chuckled. Maybe she was making too much out of everything. Maybe she hadn't understood the scene in the alley. Hadn't Giuliani put an end to the mafia? She was being irrational. She needed to talk it out with Ellie. They'd figure it out together. If Ellie ever texted her. "Okay."

"Great!" He finished a few things in the truck and then came out to put the awning, tables, and chairs up. "What have you been up to today, besides looking for me and my truck?"

"Very funny. I happened upon you. Seriously." She shifted from foot to foot.

"Sure you did." He laughed as he twisted a bunch of rope and put it in a compartment at the bottom of the truck. "And what exactly were you doing to bring you to me?"

"I was looking into my birth parents." A sour rumble tumbled through her gut.

"Find anything interesting?"

"I ruled some people out." She pushed air through her nose.

"That's good at least."

He bustled to the other side of the truck and cranked the awning. It rolled up tight against the truck roof. "Before Vinny, I thought I understood the importance of family, but in truth, he's taught me so much. Family first. Always. Maybe I can help you search." He collected the chairs and tables and put them with the rope in the bottom compartment. He scanned the area for any last items and shut and locked the compartment.

"Maybe I'm destined never to know."

He let the metal flap to the concession window down and bolted it in place. "Sometimes you have to find someone besides your biological parents to be your family. Someone who will always be there for you. Someone you will always be there for, too. Maybe you have everything you need with your adoptive parents, like I do."

"You could be right." Her parents had been so great. Yeah, they'd kept a colossal secret from her, but it was for a good reason, right? Perhaps she should just be happy with what she had.

"You ready to get going?" His smile shot a jolt of electricity through her. He was amazing.

She followed him to the front of the truck. He opened the passenger side door, and she climbed in. When he climbed in the driver side, he said, "I learned a long time ago that sometimes we can't choose our circumstances, but we certainly can choose our attitude about them." He backed up and headed out onto the main street.

"Such wise words coming from a Jersey boy. Who knew?"

"There aren't many truly bad people in the world. Most are doing their best, and sometimes their best leads them down paths not normally accepted." He paused and smiled down at her. "I'd love to meet your family. I'm assuming they're here on vacation with you?" Sincerity oozed off him. He was definitely the knight in shining armor type.

"Actually, I'm here with Ellie's family. Mine's back home." And they had no idea where she was and what she was doing. A sharp ache settled in her chest. "You'd like them, though."

"I'm sure I would. There's one thing I know for sure, family should come first and if there's a problem, most of the time it can be solved." He looked up at the sky. "Looks like rain later today." Dark storm clouds hung over the ocean, rolling over the beach. They drove in companionable silence for several blocks while Kate stewed over what he'd said.

"Your family life sounds perfect."

"It is pretty great, but nothing is perfect. I love my family. The Bellinis are amazing."

"Does it make you sad to think Vinny never adopted you?"

"No. Not at all. He calls me his son. He loves me, and that's all I need. They're not perfect, and sure, sometimes they do things I don't like, but still, I would do anything for them, and they would do anything for me."

Kate could feel his resolve and thought about her family in Texas. If she were honest with herself, she would have to admit that she felt the same way about them. She thought about Vinny and seeing him at the Marconis' yesterday. He seemed so different from them. Kind and loving, even.

They pulled the truck into an alley, and he parked. This alley was a bit wider, but shorter than the one at Marconi Bagels. She shivered, thinking about how similar it was. She stared at the metal door that read, Bellini Bagels. "We're here. Maybe I should take you around front so that you can enter through there instead of the back."

"No. It's okay. No biggie." Thunder clapped somewhere in the distance.

He hopped out of the truck and was by Kate's side fast enough that he was able to close the truck door for her. They walked the few steps to the door. He swiped a keycard across a pad, and the metal door clicked open. "Ever been in the guts of a bagel shop before?"

"No."

"Great. It'll be fun showing you something new." His eyes sparkled with excitement. He loved it here. They walked into the building, past a few shut doors and also some that were open, revealing storage rooms of one type or another. The hallway opened up to a large work area set up with oversized mixers, ovens, racks, and refrigerators. The clean and sterile feel of the room told her the work for that section of the business ended earlier in the day.

"This is where all the magic happens. The crew comes in at two in the morning to start the bagels so that they're ready by six when the shop opens."

"That's so early." Kate yawned. "Oh, sorry. I don't feel tired. I wonder why I yawned."

"It's your body's normal reaction to thinking of getting up at two A.M. I hate it when I'm on morning duty. Luckily, I mostly work late morning duty, which starts at six thirty."

They passed some other rooms. A quick peek told her they were offices. Out of the corner of her eye, she saw a painting in one of them that made her stop. It was of a woman who looked eerily familiar. She stepped closer to the open door to get a better look. It was the woman from the locket, only in oil paints. She stared, zooming in on a title plate at the bottom which read, "My Carmela." Kate's mouth went dry.

"Kate?"

"Who is that?" She pointed at the picture, feeling unsteady on her feet.

"It's a stunning painting, isn't it?"

She nodded and turned to him. "The plate says Carmela. Do you know her?" Maybe he'd met her mom.

"No. She was gone before I came here, but whoever she is, she definitely left a big impression on Vincenzo."

"Your boss?"

"Yeah. Remember? You saw him at my Uncle Rinaldo's. He mostly goes by Vinny, but I think he likes it when I call him by his full name." His chest puffed out a bit.

"You mean that isn't his wife?" She stared at the painting again.

"I doubt it. I've never known him to have a girlfriend, let alone a wife. I asked him about the painting one time, and he said his greatest sorrows were connected with that woman." Kate could see herself in that painting. She recognized the shape of her face and her tiny ears in the woman on the wall. Her heart thudded in her chest. She was looking at her mother. She knew it. Her mind, body, and soul told her it was true at that very moment. She clutched at the locket.

"We better get out front. Vincenzo is a bit funny about his space and people getting in it." He shifted on his feet.

She took one last look before following Lino to the front of the store. Her body buzzed. Was she about to meet her dad? Really meet him? If Vincenzo, Vinny, was there, the answer had to be yes. She clasped her hands together to stop the trembling. The room opened up to a bright sales counter with a display of bagels and a space full of small round tables and lots of chairs. The decor was modern and welcoming, such a contrast to the Marconi shop. She wanted to tell Lino how much she liked this place, but instead, she looked about the room, hoping to meet her dad.

"Hey, Lino," a girl behind the counter said. "Who's your friend?"

"Lunetta, this is Kate. Kate this is Lunetta, my cousin. And that funny looking guy down there on the end, that's Peter. Another cousin. Both awesome." They beamed at the compliment. "What's the flavor of the day today?"

"Coconut and caramel." Lunetta walked toward him with two bagels in hand. He took them and led Kate to an empty table. After taking a seat, he laid one bagel in front of him and another in front of her. "Let's see if this one's any good."

Kate nibbled at it. Her stomach churned.

"You have to take a bigger bite, or you won't get the full effect." He took a big bite of the chewy bagel.

Kate looked around again.

"You looking for someone?" Lino asked after swallowing.

"Sorry. I'm a little distracted." She swung her arms out to the side and then smacked her hands on her legs.

"Your family?" It was about her family, but little did he know what was going on in her mind.

She nodded. "Is your boss going to show up?"

"He doesn't mind us eating a bagel or two during the day. Trust me." He thought she wasn't eating because she didn't want to steal. One point for Lino.

"Oh, good," she responded. "I like things to be on the up and up. I wouldn't want to get you in trouble."

"My boss is great. Laid back for the most part. I live with one of his brothers, Marcel. They're both great." The front bell rang, indicating there was a new customer. "Speak of the devil." Lino stood up and met the man. Her father. Today he wore a red button-down, sleeves pushed up to his elbows, tan pants with a dark leather belt, with pointy, shiny dress shoes. He wore three necklaces. Two like a surfer might wear made out of tiny brown shells, one slightly longer than the other, and a thin gold chain that was being pulled to a V shape by something hidden beneath his shirt. She wondered what dangled there. He was handsome, and his smile was warm, soothing. He seemed to be a cool guy, considering his choice of clothing. She stood too and tapped her foot against the floor while twisting her hands in anticipation. They moved toward her. She thought her head might explode with the pressure building up in it. Everything seemed quiet and yet loud at the same time.

"Kate," Lino said, "This is Vincenzo, my boss."

16

Vincenzo's eyes sparkled with delight as he held out his hand for her to shake, a stark contrast to the darkness outside. The storm was gathering for sure. When their eyes met, he squinted slightly and cocked his head slightly to the side. "Have we met before?"

"No," she croaked and then cleared her throat. "Sorry."

"Well, you saw her from a distance the other night at Rinaldo's," Lino said.

"Ah, got it. You're visiting? And where are you from?"

"Texas."

"Huh," he said, his chin raised slightly. It gave him the appearance of an important person looking down on her. But, behind it all, she could see nervous energy working in him. "Well, it was nice to meet you, but I have to go. Enjoy your tour."

As he walked away, she thought she heard him sigh loudly. A huge thunderstorm hit outside at almost the same moment, and the heavens sent huge drops of rain down on the streets. It didn't take long for puddles of water to form as unprepared pedestrians entered the shop. Lino watched, and his agitation grew as he did. He looked at Kate and grimaced.

"Don't worry about me, Lino," she said absentmindedly. She had talked to her dad. Her birth dad. "I don't mind if you go help out. I know you have to work in a few, anyway."

He grabbed her hands and squeezed them. She barely felt the pressure. She stared down the hallway Vincenzo had gone down. "Thank you. I'll only be gone a few seconds. Just long enough to get that water up and put some caution cones down. I'd hate to see someone slip and fall."

Like a magnet being pulled to its opposite, Kate's eyes stuck to the hallway Vinny had gone down. Vinny had obviously recognized something in her. Something that threw him off. Did she dare tell him she was his daughter? She had to be. Nothing else would explain the locket and the painting. He was nice, but connected to Andre and the other Marconis. He could be a gangster. A rare mix of fear and hope filled her.

She licked her lips. There was the chance that he could have ordered her killed. It was a Marconi that had signed that note to Cremashci, the note she believed was given to him as a permission slip to adopt her out. What did that tell her about Vincenzo? He could have been the one who wanted to hurt her. He could have been the one who killed her mom. He had told Lino that the girl in the oil painting caused him pain, but it didn't feel right to think that he'd hurt her. Maybe the pain came from her mom's death. Her limbs tingled, and her breath seemed to be bottled up in her chest. She had to risk it. She had to. She'd come this far. As she passed the sales counter, a strong whiff of garlic and onion filled her nose. Her stomach churned. She pushed on. If she made a fool of herself, so be it.

His door was open, and he stood staring at the painting on his wall. She took a quick glance and then moved inside. He stood up with a jerk and faced her, his hand behind his back. Kate opened her mouth, but nothing came out.

"Is there something you need, Kate?"

She moved her tongue around her mouth to produce much needed moisture. She took in a shaky breath. His nose flared, and he raised his eyebrows. "Well?"

Her nerves ran away with her. What proof did she really have that he was her father? She had undeniable proof that the woman in the picture was her mom, but maybe her dad was someone else entirely. She needed more information.

She licked her lips. "Your wife?"

He gave no indication.

"She's lovely."

"She was lovely."

"Oh, I'm sorry, I didn't know." So her mom was dead.

"Some things are better kept in memory."

"When did she die?"

"I didn't say she was dead." He flicked his eyes from the painting to her.

She noticed there was a date on the title plate. Fifteen years previous.

"Did she have children?" Her heart raced like never before and crickets filled her belly. She had to know one way or the other. She had to.

"No." His voice turned cold, hard in an instant, and he turned from her. His words echoed through her as false. He was lying to her. He knew something. She threw caution to the wind. This was it. Now or never. "Vincenzo. I am Constanzie, Carmela's daughter—and I believe yours, too."

His face paled. "No. I have no daughters."

"But you do, and having a painting made that removes me from the picture won't erase that fact." She took the locket off, and his eyes showed a spark of recognition that was gone in an instant.

He huffed now and spit his words at Kate. "I do not have a daughter and never will."

"I believe you gave me up to keep me safe. From what, I have no idea." She moved toward him.

He jerked toward her, and she pulled back. "I don't know what you're talking about." Red splotches crept up his neck.

"It's okay. I understand. I'm not mad. You saved me." She licked her lips with cautious hope as an excited flutter found root in her belly. "Look at this picture." She clicked the locket open.

"I'm going to say this one last time. You are not my child. I have no children, and I want you to leave and never come back. If you show up here again, you won't like the consequences." His lips pinched together in disgust, and his hands clasped the top of his desk, his knuckles white.

She backed up into the door, closing the locket and shoving it into her pocket. She felt behind her for the knob. Heat rushed across her cheeks. She twisted the knob, yanked it forward, blinking fast to clear her burning eyes. She wanted to crumple onto the floor, but she knew it was not an option. He turned from her, exposing a gun shoved in his waistband. She ran to the seating area and grabbed her purse before running past Lino and out into the humid air.

She ran blindly, not caring who saw. She'd been rejected by her father. Somewhere in the back of her mind she could hear Lino calling her name. Out of the corner of her eye, she saw a cab drop off a fare, and she ran across the street to get to it before it could drive away. She had to slap her hand on a window to get him to stop as he pulled out into the street. He did stop and waited for her to climb in. She gave him the address of the resort, and he took off. Lino stood across the street, hands out, palms up in question. She wanted to feel bad about leaving him, but couldn't find room for anything but her own hurt and disgust.

She needed to distract herself from her pity party. She grabbed her phone. No texts from anyone. Not Ellie. Not Colby. Not Jace. None. She closed her eyes. She'd been so stupid to listen to Ellie. She never should have let the likes of Jace McCollum into her life. He had targeted her, and she'd fallen right into his trap. She was such a stupid girl. What else could go wrong? First Jace, then Andre, and now Vincenzo.

Once back at the hotel, she used her keycard to go in a back door. She hurried into the elevator. As the doors shut, she found herself alone and looking at her phone. As she stared at the screen, a text popped up from Ellie. *Word is out that Jace is on the beach somewhere. We've been scouring it for hours and nothing. Going to keep looking. I hope everything is going well with your search. Let me know what's happening.*

She grabbed her hair near her forehead and screamed out. Was there no one she could count on? Finding no one in the hotel suite, she leaned against the wall, slouched down it, and bawled.

At some point, she got her wits about her and texted Ellie.

Any luck? she typed, blinking the tears from her eyes.

None. If he's here, he's well hidden. What about you?

Long story. Fresh tears welled up in Kate's eyes as she typed. *Tell you when I see you next, which will be?*

Not sure. Come join us on the beach. We're only about a half a mile from the hotel. Head North. We'll find each other.

I need a nap first. I'll call you when I leave.

She slid into a hot bath, hoping it would soothe her. What she really needed was her piano. But she wasn't about to go downstairs and risk being heard by anyone. Besides, her memories of Jace were tied up with that blasted piano. She lay back and let the jets pound her body. She was about to get out when the jets stopped of their own accord. A light knock came from the other room. She grabbed a plush white robe to investigate. The last thing she wanted was to have housekeeping come in while she was naked in the tub. When she opened the door, Jace fell in. He'd been sitting on the floor, leaning against the door. "Whoa!" he hollered, unnaturally loud, as he looked up at Kate. "It's about time." He grinned, a definite slur in his voice. "I've been knocking and knocking and knocking." His head lolled slightly side to side as he talked.

"What do you want, Jace?" He'd been drinking for sure.

He rolled over on his hands and knees and stood. "Are you mad at me?" He scratched his chin.

She took a deep breath. She was being ridiculous. Sure he hadn't called, but he was here, now. And it hadn't even been a full day. Maybe he'd been really busy earlier and couldn't text or call. "I'm not mad.

Come on in." She motioned for him to enter. He used the wall to stand and then weaved as he entered. She walked over to the big leather couch and took a seat. He sat right next to her. Almost on top of her. She scooted slightly to the side. "What've you been doing today?"

"I slept in and then got a call from my dad. I went to see my therapist so that it wouldn't ruin my whole day."

"Talking to your dad ruined your whole day?"

"I'm never good enough. I'll never be the son he wanted. I embarrass him on TV."

Kate squished her eyebrows together. "Was your dad telling you this?" She was so used to her parents continually encouraging her. She couldn't imagine a parent tearing their child down.

Jace nodded and moaned.

"He must be upset about something else. He didn't mean it." He couldn't have. This was the first time she realized just how broken Jace really was.

"He's said it enough. He means it. He's right. I am good for nothing."

"Don't you dare say that. I was sad last night, and you made me feel better." She gave him her best smile even though she didn't feel like smiling. "And if it makes you feel any better, I've never fit in with my family either."

"Are you going to make me feel better today?" He was going for silken, molten, but the slurring was preventing it. He hooked a finger over the front of Kate's robe and tugged downward.

Kate scrambled to pull it back up. She held it tucked under her chin. "What are you doing?"

"You said I made you feel good last night. It's your turn to make me feel good." He moved to kiss her.

She leaned back. "Uh, no."

"What do you mean, no?"

"You're drunk, Jace. You need to sleep it off."

"No. All I want is you. I came to see you. I waited and waited." His words slurred and stumbled, his eyes half drawn.

"You should have called me first."

"My phone broke." He puffed out his lips.

"What?"

"Little pieces." He made a motion with his hands like an explosion.

"Did you throw it after talking to your dad?" He hadn't called her because he couldn't.

He nodded. "He's mean. I hate him."

"You don't hate him. He has to have some good in him if he had you." She thought of Lino and what he'd said about family.

"No. No. He's right. I'm bad. I'm on a bad show, and I do bad stuff." He frowned.

Kate stood and retrieved a fresh blanket from the closet. "Lay down. You need rest." As he lay down, she covered him with the blanket. She patted his shoulder. "Sleep now. We'll talk when you wake up." She changed into some clothes and sat next to his head and played with his hair until his breaths evened out. She scooted over and lay with her head next to his and slept too.

When she woke, her head was in Jace's lap and he was asleep sitting up, his mouth slightly ajar and resting back on the couch. She smiled. He was a good kid. Hopefully, he'd feel better when he woke. Someone cleared their throat, and Kate's head whipped to the other side of the room. All four of the Lamberts were standing opposite them, staring.

17

Kate whipped her legs around and set her feet on the floor. The scowls on the family's faces said it all.

"How long have you been there, staring?"

"We just came in," Colby said. "What's going on?"

"Look guys," she whispered. "It's not what it looks like." She glanced at Jace.

They stood, and Ellie's mom pointed to their master suite. Kate thought her room had been nice, but this room was twice the size of hers and had a sofa and two chairs tucked at one end. Kate sat in the first chair she saw, and Mr. Lambert shut the bedroom door. They stared, waiting patiently for her to explain.

"Look. I was taking a bath, and I heard a knock on the door. It was Jace. He was drunk and needed to sleep it off, so I let him use the couch. I guess I fell asleep, too."

"In his lap?" Ellie said in a low growling voice.

"No. He was lying completely down when I fell asleep, he must've woken and shifted." Kate squirmed in her seat.

"And how exactly did he know to come to your room?" Mrs. Lambert raised an eyebrow.

"I met him last night on the beach, and he walked me back up here." Kate blurted it out without thinking her answer through. She could have eased the blow that she not only knew where Jace was last night but that she'd also spent several hours with him.

Ellie's eyes were the size of apricots. "You met him on the beach?" She clenched her fists.

"And you didn't think this might have been something we'd want to know about, considering we'd been looking for him all day today?" her mom asked, her smile grim.

"I told Ellie I had news last night. I was going to tell her this morning, but you got in so late, and I was asleep when you got here, and then he caught me off guard."

Ellie waved her phone. "All you had to do was text, 'Jace is here.'"

"Not cool, Katie-kins. Not cool." Colby shook his head. Kate knew Colby wanted his sister to be happy, and she had endangered that.

A sour mix of anger and embarrassment swept through her. The back of her neck heated, and she swallowed hard. "Look, I'm sorry. I really am. I didn't intend on keeping it from you. I didn't have my phone on the beach, and today, I've got a lot going on." Her hands flew about in an awkward dance.

"You had all day to tell us." Ellie's eyes were on fire. She would not forgive Kate any time soon.

"It might interest you to know that my day was quite awful, too. Jace wasn't the only thing I had on my mind."

"Nothing could be more important than this. Nothing," Ellie said, revenge playing on her face.

Like a balloon that suddenly lost all its helium, Kate deflated. She grimaced. A sharp tone entered her voice. "You're right, Ellie. Nothing is more important. Nothing like you abandoning me today when you said you'd be there." Kate stood.

"Did you think you could keep him from us?" Ellie nearly screamed.

Kate shook her head. She had to get out of there and fast before she said something she didn't mean. There was a knock on the door. Everyone froze but Kate. "Good grief. He's only a person." Kate yanked the door open.

Jace stood there smiling, scratching his head. "I wondered where you went." No longer drunk, he appeared to be fighting a hangover. "I wanted to apologize. . . " He noticed they had an audience and stopped mid-sentence. "Oh, hi." They scrambled to their feet and practically pushed Kate out of the way to get to him. Their gushing made her sick, so she hurried to her room to change and freshen up.

When she came out, everyone was drinking smoothies, besides Jace who had black coffee, laughing and talking. Jace had his arm around Ellie. A zing of hurt whipped through Kate. Ellie's attention fell on her, and she grinned a wicked grin. She was baiting her.

"Kate, you're finally back." Jace turned to Ellie. "I told you it wouldn't take her longer than half an hour."

"Yep. You were right," Ellie said, and put a kiss on his lips. He didn't hold back. He leaned in and gave her all he had. Kate thought on last night and how his lips had been all over hers. Jealousy and resentment slammed into her. Her kisses had meant nothing to Jace, and her friendship meant nothing to Ellie. As she looked on, emptiness replaced the jealousy, and apathy replaced the resentment.

"I've got to go." Kate's words came out soft and almost inaudible.

Not one person acknowledged her.

She walked the boardwalk, going over everything that had happened. What a mess. Her life had to be the biggest mess in the world. Jace had been such a terrible decision. She wished she could talk to someone about it. The painted image of her birth mother washed over her. She didn't need Ellie, Colby, or even Jace. And she didn't need her adoptive parents either. Lino was right. She couldn't trust anyone but the family she chose. And she was choosing her birth mother. Her birth mom was the only one she had left to trust. She had to be alive—hadn't Vinny intimated that? And she thought she knew the way in, through Lino and his keycard to the bagel shop.

***

She should have gotten Lino's number from Ellie. But her best friend had betrayed her, and now that was impossible. Lino might not even want to talk to her after she burst out of the bagel shop. Vinny could have told him any number of terrible things about her. Still, she wanted to talk to him. He had the connections she needed to find her mom. He didn't need to know what she was up to. She'd be gone in a week anyway. It's not like they could have a lasting relationship when he lived here. Still, he seemed the most real thing in her life. Only, he was at the bagel shop. The shop where her father rejected her. She couldn't go storming in there to ask for Lino. Her own father had threatened her to stay away. But it was the only place she knew to find him. There was also Rinaldo Marconi's house, but who knew when Lino might end up there. It did give her a measure of relief that she wasn't a Marconi. She desperately hoped the Bellinis were not mixed up in the garbage she believed the Marconis were.

She waited outside the bagelry and realized it would be closing soon. Vincenzo came out of the building and headed for a car parked on the street. Without stopping to think, she ran toward the car. He could lead her to her birth mother. Immediately when the beep sounded, telling her the car was unlocked, she climbed inside the passenger side as he climbed in the driver's side. He jerked to look at her and, to her shock and horror, in a flash, he held a knife to her neck. "What are you doing here? I told you to disappear." His voice was a low rumble through the vanilla scented car.

She didn't speak, afraid the knife would slice her if she did.

He pulled back, the knife retreating.

"You can deny it all you want. But I know you're my dad." She didn't look at him until she'd finished speaking.

"You don't know what you're saying." He looked out all the windows like an FBI agent might when looking to see if he's being watched.

"I do. And I know that painting in your office is of my birth mother." She would not back down until he admitted it.

"That painting? Beautiful isn't it? It's a nice little moment from our time together. A memento that reminds me to never again be duped by anyone, including a pretty face. "

"What are you talking about?"

"Your mother, that witch. She strung me along, taking all my money and then she held the one thing over me she knew would hurt. Family. I wanted a family. A son. Someone to carry on my name, but I knew she was a whore when she came telling me she was pregnant and that it had to be mine. It couldn't have been mine. I can't have kids. She wanted to hem me in. Trap me. With you. I told her to get rid of the bastard child, that it wasn't mine. She came groveling back to me sometime later, begging me to take her back. She told me she had taken care of you. But now here you are, sitting beside me, sharing many of her features. And you've bought the coffee too, telling me I'm your dad. I'm not. You were supposed to have been taken care of. She must've lost her nerve. Lousy, lying witch." He spit the words, his face a mask of rage. "Now you know all about me and about your lying, conniving mother. Now get out. I never want to see you again." He turned and looked out the driver side window.

Kate couldn't move. She was frozen. Every muscle in her body had locked up. But her tear ducts hadn't gotten the memo. Tears poured in rivers down her cheeks. She didn't make a sound. The man next her, not her father after all, didn't make a sound either. Like they were lost in time, nothing seemed to move or change. The tears dripped off her chin and onto her lap.

"I said, get out of here." Was there a hitch in his voice? First she blinked. Then she turned her head to the man who had dashed her every hope. Her mother gave her away to be with this man? Her mother was a con artist wanting him for his money. It couldn't be true. She had to see for herself. "Do you know where I would find this witch mother of mine?" She drew in a quick breath as if she'd been sobbing for hours.

"Probably dead on the street somewhere like most whores end up, and that would be a better end to her than she deserves. Go home and love whoever it is she suckered in to taking you and be grateful they did.

Forget about her and whoever she used to spawn you." He didn't turn to her but she could feel the ache in his voice. Her birth mother must have really betrayed him to get him to say the things he was saying. She felt a little ping of sadness for this man. And it was her birth mother who had broken him. She pulled on the door handle, ready to get out.

"You won't see me again."

He was unnaturally still, and Kate thought about the knife he'd held to her neck. His shoulder twitched, and that was enough to push her out of the car.

She walked past the bagel shop and toward the beach, walking as if on autopilot. Someone honked at her. She ignored it and kept walking. Car after car passed her. It was a ways to the beach. She walked without seeing what was right in front of her. She walked only seeing the end goal—the ocean. She stopped at a light, a group of people halting her progress. A hand grabbed hers. She jerked it away. "Kate. It's me. Lino."

She turned to him. For some reason, the sight of him sent pure relief through her, and she grabbed and hugged him. His chin rested on her head. "It's going to be okay. When I saw you start down this street, I was dying to catch up with you, but I had to finish closing the store. I had things I needed to do first. As soon as I was done, I came for you." The people around them walked across the street, leaving them alone on the corner.

"Why? Why would you come for me?" She was useless. Nobody cared about her.

"It was something about the way you looked. So totally dejected and alone. I had this feeling you needed me."

What he said had the ring of truth, and guilt swept over her. He was the only one who was there for her right then. And she had planned on using him in a very bad way. Had his boss not revealed the truth, she would have gone through with it.

"Tell me what happened." He led her down the road to a bench, where they sat.

"I found my dad, or at least the man I thought was my dad."

"That's great news. Why are you so sad?" He put a hand on her leg and turned his body to face her.

"He wasn't really my dad, and he both hated and loved my mom."

"That sounds about right for married couples." He squeezed her leg, a comforting gesture.

Kate told Lino everything she had learned from her dad, though she left out his identity. "And he wasn't even my dad after all."

"I'm sorry. That's awful."

"A part of me wants to locate my mom, but the other part wants to stay as far away from her as I can." If she had such a reception from her mom, she'd be devastated.

"It's not a decision you have to make now. Step back and take some time to figure out what you really want."

"Thanks for being there for me."

He pulled her into a hug, and they walked the rest of the way to the beach.

18

She woke feeling chilled, the sand feeling a bit wet underneath her. Her head lay on Lino's chest. She and Lino had talked and talked until they'd fallen asleep. She looked at his face, free from worry and every care. There was no sun, but the sky was growing brighter. Dawn approached. She smiled up at the fading moon; fate had smiled on her when it brought Lino into her life. He was the kind of guy she could see being friends with for the rest of her life.

She sat up, hoping not to disturb him, but his eyes popped open. He spoke through a stretch. "What time is it?"

She pulled out her phone. "Five." She had a few texts from Jace and Colby. She decided not to open them. She focused on Lino, who sat now, arms wrapped around his knees.

"Thanks for last night." She leaned into him.

"No problem. I can't believe we fell asleep." He leaned into her.

"No kidding." She shivered.

"You're cold." He pulled her close, his heat filling her.

"A little. You tired?"

"A little." He grinned. "But it was worth it."

She drew her legs up close. "Yeah. Definitely. Oh, look. The sun is coming up."

"I'm starving. Let's go get something to eat."

"Sounds good, but no bagels." She couldn't stomach the idea of running into Vincenzo again. Besides, she'd promised him she'd disappear.

"Tired of them already?"

"No. Just up for something different. Something greasy with bacon. Yes. Definitely bacon."

"I know the perfect place." He stood and helped her up.

After a short walk, they ended up at a diner that fit the bill. She ordered a big plate with bacon, eggs, hash browns, and waffles. Lino did, too. She smothered the waffles with raspberry syrup and butter. They were early enough to miss the rush of people that Lino promised filled the diner during peak eating times. "I hate to say it, but I've got to go soon. It'll take me a good twenty minutes to get back to work."

"No. It can't be six already." She looked at her phone. 6:01. She groaned.

"You should probably catch up with Ellie. I'm sure her family is worried about you. I'm sure she's worried about you."

Six texts waited for her to open, and she'd missed eight calls. None from Ellie, though. "I'm not so sure about that."

"I don't know what you fought about, but whatever it was, it couldn't be big enough to end a life-long friendship."

"You might have a different opinion if you knew exactly what happened."

"As much as I'd love to know all the gory details, I've got to go." He stood up, leaving enough money on the table to cover everything.

"I'll call you a cab. I owe you that much." She pulled up the cab company's number and ordered a cab for him. "Besides, I want more time with you."

"I have Ellie's number, but not yours, and I have a funny feeling that calling her won't get me you."

"You've got that right." She took his phone and put her number in it. He immediately called her. She captured the number and put his name in her phone, snapping a quick picture of them to accompany it.

Cindy M. Hogan

"Now we have a connection that can't ever be severed." He bounced his phone out in front of him.

"Except by deleting it."

"Which you would never do to my sacred number."

"Right again."

The cab pulled up in front of the cafe. "Make up with Ellie and think about what you're going to do about your mom. If you want to go tonight, I'm free after three."

"Thanks again." Kate stood and hugged him. He made her feel safe, secure.

She gave the cabbie some money and waved as the cab drove away.

She sat on a bench on the boardwalk for a good twenty minutes before convincing herself she should look at the texts.

The first was from Colby. *Where are you, Katie-kins?*

Kate opened the next. *This is Jace. New phone. I talked to my producer, and she thought it would be awesome to give you a walk-on part on the show tomorrow. We could play one of those duets together.*

The next was again from Colby: *We're going to a taping tomorrow at ten. If you don't show, I'm going to the police.*

Jace: *Ellie told me you still haven't showed up. You better not be alone. And if you are with someone, then I'm super confused. You wouldn't stay with me, but you will with some stranger?*

Jace: *Okay. It's a free world, you can stay with whoever you want to, but I thought we had something. I can only assume that something happened to you. You seemed like the very organized type and all.*

Colby: *You're still not here. I take it back. I'm calling the police now.*

Kate sighed. Colby had sent that text twenty minutes ago. She texted him. *Don't call the police. I'm fine. Needed space.*

Colby replied, *Sorry about last night.*

This is one of the reasons she adored Colby. He didn't couch his apologies with excuses.

I get it.

159

Kate Unmasked

And even if Ellie won't admit it, she is distraught over your disappearance.

Did she say that?

There was a pause

No, but I can tell.

Kate rolled her eyes. *I'll come back when she's ready to apologize.*

Don't be so stubborn. And she wasn't totally at fault.

You did not just say that.

No, I texted it.

Before she could respond, she got another text from Jace.

Where are you? Get over here. You're making me look bad.

Kate thought about Ellie. She'd freak if Kate was a guest on the show and she didn't know. At the moment Kate didn't care. She would go on the show just to make Ellie mad. She deserved it. She hadn't even worried about her not showing up last night. She probably went to bed early and didn't have a second thought about her not being there.

Address?

The hotel. We're shooting live. Hurry.

On my way.

***

Kate stared at the person in the freestanding mirror in the large changing room. How had the makeup artist created the person in front of her? Kate knew a lot of the things that happened on reality TV were fake, but not as much as this. Her whole scene was scripted, and she was working like the devil to learn her lines. She also didn't realize she'd make so much money for being on the show. She was being paid as much as her friends working fast food for probably an entire year. She looked at her phone. No texts from Ellie. Well, she wasn't going to be the first to apologize. Kate blew out a puff of air that made her bangs fly up. It was Ellie's fault that she didn't know Kate was going to be on the show. If she would've cared one bit about what had happened to Kate yesterday and the day before, then she'd know, but she hadn't. If Ellie was going to be a bad friend, so was Kate. Kate's chin quivered as she thought about just how bad a friend she was about to be to Ellie.

***

Kate played her part well, despite raging nerves. She quickly discovered that while it was scripted, Jace hadn't received the script or hadn't bothered to learn it. In truth, Kate felt like the unscripted version was better, more natural. She even got the chance to reject a kiss from Jace. It gave her great satisfaction. It was like slapping him, without actually slapping him. He was waiting for her in her dressing room when she arrived. "You're a natural."

"Thanks." She wiped at her face with makeup remover.

"Of course it would have been more natural for you to kiss me." He grinned. .mischievously.

"You went off script." She threw the towelette away and began putting makeup on how she liked to wear it.

"You know what we did was better." He stood next to the makeup table.

She nodded.

"Except the kiss, that is." He took the blush brush from her hand.

"I value kisses differently than you." Memories of him kissing her senseless filled her mind. He *was* an amazing kisser.

He jerked back. "What's that supposed to mean?"

"I don't kiss just anyone." She reached into her make up bag for mascara.

He stepped back. "And I do?"

"I watch the show, remember?"

"Okay, so I'm liberal with my kisses on the show, but I thought you understood that the show wasn't me" He moved his hands back and forth between them. "It doesn't make our kisses any less meaningful."

"It does when you kiss my best friend." She worked hard getting the mascara on her lashes without letting her complete hurt show.

"Hey, she kissed me." He moved next to her again.

"She pecked you, and you devoured her." She stood up, fury filling her for being such an idiot and falling for his charm.

"Well, I had to leave her with a real kiss, right? If she was going to tell people we kissed, I wanted her to give me a glowing review."

"A glowing review? Please. You weren't being filmed. You need to learn to separate real life from what isn't."

"Whoa! Are you throwing what I told you in my face now? I confided in you the other night. Not cool." True hurt played across his face. "I thought we connected, that you really liked me, but you're just like your best friend's family and everyone else who wants to use me."

She reached out to him, but he retreated, shaking his head. "Don't touch me. I hope you enjoyed your fifteen minutes of fame at my expense."

"I'm not like them."

"You proved that wrong today." He turned and hurried out.

She growled and chased after him, but he was nowhere to be found.

"I mess everything up," she murmured, returning to her changing room. She put the expensive clothes back on the rack and looked at herself in the mirror. Her motives for being on the show were anything but altruistic. She owed Jace a huge apology. She called him. No answer. She left a voice message saying she was in the wrong and wanted to make it up to him. She also left him a text message. *Call me. I'm sorry.*

She took the bag of makeup and the check for being on the show and headed outside. Ellie was standing with a crowd of people waiting for the cast to appear. Kate guessed it was like getting backstage passes to a rock concert. Kate spied the rest of the family mingling about. They'd seen her perform. They wouldn't have to wait for the show to air. She had no time to give excuses for her behavior. She was sure Ellie was out of her mind with jealousy. Kate wouldn't face her now. She couldn't. Kate found a hotel employee and asked for a back way out.

She hurried up to the room and changed before writing a note to the family. She would take her cue from Colby. Short, sweet and to the point.

I'm sorry for not texting you the second I met Jace. I didn't mean to keep it from you. It wasn't my intention to hurt anyone. Please forgive me. I'm safe. Staying away to give you time and space to forgive me.

-Kate

P.S. I love you all more than you know.

19

Kate headed for an Internet cafe to do some research on her mom. She liked to have the full screen when searching for things instead of her phone. There was nothing. Nada. No matter what she tried, she got nothing. She needed Ellie's help. She had about half an hour more time on the net so she decided to look up the Marconis. She wanted to look up that link to a story about them and the mob. She wanted some proof of who she thought they were. When she'd first scrolled through the results, she'd skimmed over a lot of them because they seemed not to apply, but after what she'd seen in the alley behind the bagel shop, the mafia connection had new meaning. Mixed in with the Nobel Prize Marconi articles, were articles about the Marconi crime family.

She skimmed through the articles, reading about how the FBI had botched a crackdown on the family. She jotted down information in her journal. The family claimed innocence, of course, but the evidence, had it been collected properly, showed their hand in all types of corruption and wrongful deaths. The newest article indicated the family's move to white collar crime within the stock exchange. This however, was not backed up with the proof they needed.

Her heart sank when she found the Bellini family mentioned in two of the articles. The connection was not undeniable, but it was apparent. She printed out those articles and taped them into her journal. She would have to ask Lino about them. She dug into more articles about crime families and happened upon a series of videos about the mafia. She paid for the first one and watched it. She took a ton of notes. She immediately paid for the next and watched it. The documentaries were mesmerizing. By the end of the sixth half hour program, her mind swam. She had the distinct impression that if her birth parents hadn't given her up, she would be neck deep in the family business.

She thought of Lino and what he'd told her about Vincenzo saving him. The reality was that he had been recruited. He started at the bottom as a gopher. He did all the grunt work, most likely collecting sports bets, bribes, and the like. He then moved into being what they called an earner, someone who found various non-law-abiding ways to make the family money. Only because he wasn't good at it, was he put on a different path. A path that would make him into an earner with white collar crime and the stock market. He'd been with the Bellinis for eight years. He had to know what was going on. He had to.

She wanted to believe that her mother hadn't given her up to keep her out of danger, but instead to save her from a life of crime. But after watching those shows, she figured that was a pipe dream. She paid particular attention to the reasons the mafia turned on their own, and it didn't take much. There were three major things that would get you killed by your own family if you were part of the mafia: sleeping with the mob boss's wife or daughter, being an informant, or disobeying the boss. If her dad had slept with Rinaldo Marconi's wife, he'd be dead. If he'd disobeyed the boss, he'd be dead. Only one thing stood out as a possibility. Her mom must've been an informant.

Was her mom killed for snitching? She couldn't make herself believe that. Her mind wandered. Perhaps her mom was working for someone. Yes. This made more sense to her for some reason. Maybe she was like the informants on the shows she'd watched. Maybe her mom was working for the FBI and had embedded herself in there to take the family down. Maybe the family found out. Maybe she was dead. But if she was an agent, she could be alive. She latched on to the possibility.

She wanted it to be true. She wanted her birth parents to be good people trying to either make things right or to escape the life.

Her drive to find her mom sky rocketed now. If her mom was in the FBI, then Carmela was most definitely not her name. She grabbed the journal and on the page dedicated to Carmela, she wrote, *How do you find someone who used a fake name? Father?* Could it have been a fluke, and Vinny was her father? Could his little swimmers have been valid one time? *Boyfriend? True boyfriend in real life? How did she get pregnant?* Her birth mom could actually be a successful person contributing to society and not a hoodlum. While all the evidence before her led her to believe her mother was no angel, she clung to the idea and hoped for it.

Her phone vibrated. A text from Ellie: *I'm sorry. I was jealous.* Kate felt more relief than satisfaction. She knew she still couldn't count on Ellie to be fully present for Kate's quest, but she'd at least have some help. And she wanted desperately to have her best friend back. She no longer cared whose fault it was.

She texted back, *I'm sorry. I knew how important it was to you, and I didn't pull through for you. Please forgive me.*

Instead of waiting for a reply, Kate called Ellie. "Kate?" Ellie asked.

"Ellie, oh my gosh, I have so much to tell you—"

"Have you seen the news?"

"What news?"

"Jace. His body washed up on the shore half an hour ago. They're saying it was suicide."

Kate didn't respond, she couldn't. A heavy weight sank in her gut. She couldn't seem to get any air and when it finally did come, she gasped, sucking in more air than she needed, and she coughed and sputtered. Jace's hurt face filled the screen of her mind, their conversation replaying in her mind. She should have searched harder for him. He must've left her and gone straight to carry out the act. "Kate?"

"No. This isn't happening."

"Please come back."

"I am."

Cindy M. Hogan

***

Ellie was waiting for Kate in the lobby. She wore big sunglasses and a hat like someone going incognito. She waved Kate to the side and put a big floppy hat and sunglasses on her. "Don't say a word," she whispered into Kate's ear. "We're going straight up." Ellie signaled the concierge, and he called the elevator car. He nodded at Ellie. "Walk slowly and carefully. Don't bring attention to yourself."

Kate said nothing, but followed her instructions. As they reached the elevator, the doors opened. They stepped in. Ellie pushed the close door button and the elevator operator stepped in front of the open doors. A casual, but effective movement. The two girls stared out at the frenzied crowd of media when someone yelled. "It's her. She's in the elevator." Lights, cameras, and bodies pushed forward as the scene disappeared with the closing of the doors. Kate didn't say a word until they were safely in the suite.

"Is the paparazzi after you?" Kate asked.

"No." She took her glasses and ridiculously large hat off, setting them on the table. "They're after you."

"Me? Why me?"

"You were the last person to have contact with Jace. They want a statement. Don't worry, Sally's on it. She's on her way. On a plane, I mean. We need to stay inside until she arrives." Ellie must have noticed the concerned look on Kate's face, so she amended her statement. "It'll be fun. We'll order room service, and we have the staff at our beck and call." The remaining three in Ellie's family stood just inside the kitchen staring at her.

"Any way we could talk in the living room?" Kate asked the whole Lambert family.

Only minutes later, the whole family was seated in the room, looking expectantly at Kate. She spent the next hour filling them in on what had happened the last two days. She started with Jace. It couldn't wait. She cried as she talked. Ellie had her arm around Kate, and everyone got up and hugged her. "Kate, you were not responsible. Put

167

that out of your mind." Ellie's dad was always so practical in his advice.

"That's right, sweetie." Mrs. Lambert said. "You had a lovely time with him and gave him a lovely time. Focus on that."

Kate sniffed and recognized that she needed to tell them about the Marconis and Bellinis and their connection with the mafia as well as her conclusions about her mom and dad. When she was done, the room erupted in conversation.

"So you think your mom is an undercover agent?" Mrs. Lambert said.

Kate nodded. "I'm hoping anyway—the alternative is not a good one."

"And Vinny might be your dad after all?" Ellie said.

Kate shrugged. "I have no idea. Maybe."

"If this has to do with the mafia, Kate," Ellie's dad said, "then maybe you should let sleeping dogs lie."

"I can't. I have to know."

"But you could be putting a lot of people in danger by pursuing this." Colby gave her a concerned look.

"If you were me, would you give up?"

Colby looked her dead on. "I'm not you."

"Please, help me. This is my only chance to find my birth parents. My last chance. Let's face it. When I get back home next week, my parents won't let me out of their sight, and they most definitely won't let me come back here."

Mr. Lambert tipped his head to the side, obviously considering what she'd said. "I'll tell you what, I'll see what I can find out from the FBI—if I can get anyone to talk to me. This whole thing seems a bit of a stretch, but I'll do my best."

"I'll take it."

"We should go see the priest again." Ellie bent over in her chair, her elbows on her knees. "He's faking it, after all. We can get more information."

Kate hadn't thought of that. "What more could he tell us?"

"Why your mom disappeared."

"You think?" Kate thought for a minute. "No. We'd never get him alone. On top of that, the receptionist is a Marconi. Aren't they the ones keeping Cremashci there?"

"Actually," Ellie broke in. "I think the mafia bosses were getting too close to what he was really doing and he's faking Alzheimers to avoid them killing him. If that receptionist saw us again, then something really bad might happen."

"You have a point there."

"I could go," Colby said.

Mrs. Lambert broke in. "I think it would be more believable that an older person would go and see him. An older devotee."

"Yes. We'll go together," Mr. Lambert said.

"No. I don't want to get you two involved. I'm okay with the FBI thing because I think you two are more believable than a seventeen-year-old girl, but no one is going to see that priest. He was way too freaked out."

"If we hope to get any information from the FBI, I think we better get going," Mr. Lambert said. "I want you kids to stay here. This is the mafia we're talking about. Let's allow the FBI to take the lead. Don't go anywhere. You hear me?"

They all nodded, but Kate's nod was not sincere.

After the door shut behind them, Kate noticed Ellie had been biting her lip, her tell-tale sign that she was thinking hard. "What are you thinking about, Ellie?"

"Nothing. I got nothing."

"I might have a way to uncover information about my birth mom. I'm not excited or comfortable with it, though."

"What is it? Maybe we can make you excited about it." Colby flashed his dashing smile.

"Vincenzo Bellini, the one who might be my father—he claims he keeps that painting of my mom in his office to remind him to stay away from a pretty face, but I think he keeps it because he still loves my mother. And Lino said he doesn't like people in his office when he's not there." She laid it all out for them slowly, though she already had the plan all figured out. She wanted to give them a chance to catch up. "I bet he has information on my mom in there. It's only a hunch, but I'd bet just about anything that I'm right."

"And you're going to use Lino to get into the office," Ellie said, smirking.

Kate did have an in with Lino, a connection she had been willing to exploit earlier, but now her conscience poked at her. Did she really want to use him? He was such a nice guy; it seemed the wrong thing to do. Maybe she could simply ask him to help her. He obviously cared about her. Maybe if she laid everything on the line with him, he'd be more than happy to help her out. Then again, the way he talked about the Bellinis and family made her think she couldn't count on that happening. And from the movies she'd seen about the mafia and how they treated traitors, she couldn't stand to think of putting him in that much danger. No. She'd get the keycard from him this afternoon after he got off work, and she'd sneak in sometime after they closed for the night and before the early shift came in. She'd find a way to give it back to him before his next shift. He wouldn't even know she'd used the card.

"I can get his keycard and sneak into Vinny's office. Hopefully, I'll find what I need in there."

"Get in and get right back out," Colby said.

"I will," Kate said. She definitely wouldn't be hanging out in there longer than she needed to.

"I mean it. In fact, I'm going with you," Colby added, a resolute look on his face.

"Me, too," Ellie said, putting her arm through Kate's as if that made her declaration stronger.

Kate shook her head. "No. Too many cooks in the kitchen. I've been there, I know the layout of the place, you don't."

"I don't like it." Ellie scratched her neck.

"We don't have to go in with you," Colby said. "We'll be your lookouts."

That plan did have merit. "All right. Let's do it." Kate sat back in her chair and sighed, the thought of finding her birth mom filling her with sweet anticipation.

20

With the help of key hotel staff members and a delivery boy, the three conspirators snuck out of the hotel. It was quite amazing what the Lambert's good money could buy in the service sector. The manager dropped them off five blocks from the hotel, and a cab carried them away. Kate, Colby, and Ellie were going to the beach and shopping near Bellini's Bagels to wait for Lino to finish his shift. Ellie tried on a bunch of different clothes and bought several things. Kate tried a few things on, but she couldn't spend any money; she needed what little she had left to get her around town.

Lino was about to be off work. She said good-bye to Ellie and Colby, hailed a cab, and texted Lino on the drive toward Bellini Bagels. *I'm heading your way. I hope you meant it when you said you wanted to hang out.*

He didn't answer right away, and doubts entered her mind. Maybe Lino didn't feel about her what she thought. Maybe he seemed like a nice guy and really wasn't. She didn't stop the cabbie from continuing to drive her to Bellini's. She had to hold on to hope.

At exactly 6:31 that evening, he texted her. She should have known that he wouldn't text on the job. He would have to be on break or off in order to answer her. He was a boy scout, and she couldn't deny that she found that very attractive. It wouldn't be easy to get that keycard. It occurred to her that she couldn't let him go home. What if he left his keycard there? For her plan to work, Lino had to have his keycard on him, otherwise she wouldn't be able to take it.

I did mean it, but I really should shower and change. She'd seen that coming.

Didn't I see a shower inside the shop? You could shower and put the clothes you were wearing this morning back on. She added a smiley face.

If it gives me more time with you, then I guess I'm game, but no funny comments about my wrinkly clothes.

My lips are sealed. As she typed it, his lips popped into her mind. She didn't want to feel anything for this boy. She only wanted friendship, and she wasn't sure even that would be a possibility after tonight. She sighed and closed her eyes. This had to be done.

I'll be waiting next door in a cab, she sent.

You could come in and have a bagel.

No thanks. Just ate.

I'll hurry.

No rush. In truth, she wanted him to be super fast. The ache in her chest continued to grow the longer she had to wait.

She texted Ellie and Colby with an update. As soon as Lino came out, he rushed to the car. It had only been fifteen minutes, and Lino looked like he'd taken his time getting ready. She opened the cab door and got out. A smile stretched over his face, making him more attractive still. He had his duffle over his right shoulder. He hugged her. They climbed back in together. The cab smelled like fake lemons, almost like the scent of Pledge. The cabbie wore a headscarf and had a little gray, fraying mustache.

Lino had the driver take them to a carnival nearby. The smell of cotton candy, sweat, and hot dogs with relish filled the air. They stopped by a clown who was blowing up balloons and creating various things out of them. He made Kate a heart with a small monkey hanging in the middle of it on a swing.

"I've never seen anything like it. It's so elaborate."

"Me, neither. Awesome." She loved it when he said awesome, his accent was super cute. At this point, she only needed to wait until it was dark outside. She'd concentrate on moving slowly through the carnival to drag out the experience as long as she could. They rode a few rides and slid down the huge slides. Fun, but she was ready to relax a bit.

"I think we need to do some serious people-watching." Kate led Lino to a bench, and they watched and talked about the people they saw. The laughing was the best. When the sun moved from behind the tree and started to cook them, they got up and got a snow cone. She hadn't had the chance to fish for his keycard yet, but had seen it in his wallet when he'd paid for the boat ride they were about to take.

They played a few more games, and he won a few prizes. Kate won a real fish and gave it to a little boy, who oohed and ahhed over it.

The park lights lit up once twilight set in. The smells of popcorn and fried sugar floated on the air. It wasn't cold, but chilly. She shivered. He gave her his hoodie out of his duffle, and she happily put it on. It was time for her to make her move. It was already eight thirty. They stopped to play a car game, where the prizes were super fun and big. With purpose, she crashed her car, which ended her game. Lino was determined to win her the big prize, though, and she knew it was time to ask for what she needed. "I hate to ask, but I'm thirsty. Could I get a drink?" She felt like an idiot asking for money, but was certain it was the only way to get that card. He was nearing the end of the course and would most likely win if he kept going.

"Sure. Grab my wallet from my back pocket."

"You're so close. I've got a feeling I'm going home with that awesome bear tonight."

"Yes. Yes you are." He kept his eyes steady on his car.

She had to concentrate on not trembling when taking his wallet. "Thanks. I'll be right back." As she paid for the drinks, she slipped the keycard out and put it in her pocket. It was time to break away. She texted Ellie that she needed her to give her an excuse to leave in about twenty minutes, that she had the card. She put the sound on her phone. When she got back to the spot she'd left Lino, he was standing there with the big bear she'd pretended to want. Her heart tripped, and she had to work hard not to stop walking toward him. Could he be a better guy?

She forced herself to smile and pick up the pace to get to him. "I can't believe you actually won it! You're too good to me." She handed him his drink, and he handed her the big bear which she almost couldn't hold while holding her drink. She laughed and carried the bear to a table and set it down.

"Do you even have space in your room for that thing?" he asked.

"I guess I'm going to have to find room."

He had a self-satisfied look on his face. "Let's get some pictures with it." They set it in different places and took funny and ridiculous pictures. "Find some cute kid to give it to before you get on the plane."

"Thank you. I sure wish I could take it back to Texas with me." She said it with a sincerity she had to dig deep for, not because she wasn't thankful, but because her guilt was making her feel disingenuous.

"I love seeing you smile." His eyes sparkled and fell to her lips. She panicked and took a sip of her drink through her straw. He pulled back and drank from his. "What is this?"

"A rodeo."

"And what might be in a rodeo?"

"Coke, Dr. Pepper, Pepsi, and Mountain Dew. The combination will make you spin for a while and then leave you on your butt. Do you like it?"

"Now that I know what's in it, it makes me wonder why I liked it."

"Never met a guy who didn't like a rodeo." He drank more and so did she. "You ever been to a real rodeo?"

"Yeah. You?" They sat down on a nearby bench under a lamp that lit the area now that it was dark.

"Four or five. They're pretty interesting."

"I've never really understood why someone would want to be in a rodeo or watch one for that matter."

"That's because you're a city-slicker. Once you go to one and get it all explained to you, you gain a new appreciation for it."

He pressed his lips together and nodded. "Sounds like someone's going to be taking me to the next rodeo."

"It's a plan." That would have been fun to do. Too bad she'd be in Texas, and he'd be in New Jersey when the next one rolled around.

He took her hand. A fuzzy zing sailed through her, and her breath caught. "I've had a lot of fun today. I really love hanging out with you."

"I love hanging out with you, too," she blurted without thinking it through. His thumb moved over her hand, and an aura of seriousness settled over them. Her heart raced as his head moved closer to hers. He moved so slowly, she held her breath. "I'd like to kiss you," he whispered into her ear, "but this hardly seems the right place."

She was surprised at the want she felt. She wanted to kiss him. But he was supposed to stay in the friend zone. This was not acceptable.

"If we were in the right place, would you like to kiss me?" His nose brushed hers, and she closed her eyes. At the moment, the answer was yes, but if he kissed her any time soon, things would get way too hard for them. Her eyes popped open as he rested his cheek on hers.

"Right place. Right time. I'm in." She would have to make sure there was no right time or place.

He pulled back. "We're going to have to make that happen." Her phone rang. She reached for it and stood up to take the call.

"Oh, okay. Sure. I'll be right there." She gave Lino a sad look and hung up. "Looks like I've got to go." She called a cab before he could protest.

"Good thing I showered at the shop. But even doing that didn't give me enough time with you."

"Sorry. I know."

"I work the early shift tomorrow, anyway. An early night will be good for me even though I don't want it to be."

"Do you always find the silver lining of everything?" Most of Kate wanted to step back and tell him everything and enlist him to help her. She couldn't imagine him refusing, but the videos and his own words about the importance of family sticking together made her hold back.

"If you lived my life, you'd learn to, that's for sure. Are you still fighting with Ellie?"

She shook her head. "No. Thank heaven."

The cab pulled up. "We'll take you home first," Kate said.

"No. You go. I'll catch the train. That bear's gonna take up the whole back seat."

"Thanks again," she said. He opened the door for her, and she climbed in. He brought the bear to the other side and shoved it in. It took up a good two-thirds of the back seat.

She waved as they drove away, a sick feeling invading her. When she picked both Colby and Ellie up near the boardwalk, they gave the bear to a little girl sitting with her dad on a bench. The two teen Lamberts carried a bunch of bags, which the driver put in the trunk. Ellie pulled out a receipt and wrote some instructions on it. When the driver got back in the car, she handed him a fifty dollar bill and the note. "Take our bags to the front desk of the Seaside Hotel with this note. Say nothing. If you follow the instructions exactly, you will have another fifty waiting for you.

He nodded. "You got it. Where to now?"

Ellie pretended to look at some note in her hand and told him the address. It was two blocks south of the bagel shop. They pulled out into traffic.

Ellie stood watch across the street from the front of the store, and Colby stood outside the alley, the only passage leading to the back door. Kate hugged Colby to help calm her nerves before walking down it. She'd seen the store was dark and empty as they passed the front windows. Only one sparse light illuminated the area near the cash register. She pulled Lino's hoodie over her head and tightened the drawstrings slightly before swiping the card and pulling on the handle. The door opened without a problem, and she rushed inside. She popped on the flashlight and hurried to the office, praying it was open. The door was shut and a moment of fear raced through her. If that door was locked, all the sneaking around had been for nothing. The knob turned when she tried it, and she sighed in relief. It didn't seem like Vinny cared that people went in his office. It'd been wide open the other day, and he kept it unlocked.

She thought about flipping the light on, but it scared her too much. With the hoodie still in place, she opened the file cabinets and pulled each file out, taking a quick glance at the contents. Nothing. All the files were personnel or financial records. She turned to the desk and pulled out the drawers. Her jaw dropped when she opened the bottom folder. Her mom's face looked out at her. A big red x crossed over her face and the word *snitch* was written in cursive just under her chin. A smaller picture fell from the file onto the floor. Her fingers scrambled for purchase. When she finally retrieved it, she took a quick breath in. It was her as a child, maybe two or three years old. A red x crossed her face. She looked up at the man holding the child's hand. Vinny.

21

Her hands shook, and the file and all its contents fell to the desk. All the evidence was falling together nicely to fit her hypothesis. Her birth mom had to have worked for the FBI, and she'd been discovered. It made it all easier to deal with. Had her birth mom escaped? She sat hard in the soft office chair, the leather squeaking as she did. So Vinny was her father after all. Why had he lied? Losing all sense of time, she sat motionless in the chair. Male voices startled her back into reality. She stood and peeked out the office door. Men stood at the back entrance, using a keycard to go through one of the doors that she'd never seen behind. The tall men looked serious, mean. They all went into the room and as far as she could tell, the door shut behind them. She looked at her phone. No warning from her lookouts.

Then a text came through, from Ellie. *Mom and dad texted us, said they're leaving the FBI field office now. We're going to run back to the house and pretend you're sleeping so we don't get busted, then we'll sneak back out. Don't let anything happen while we're gone.*

Kate shook her head. She wasn't sure if she should be grateful or mad. Kate rubbed at her chin and sighed. She was alone on this one, and this one might find her caught red handed. She grabbed up the entire folder and stuffed it under Lino's hoodie. She went straight for the front door. There wasn't a key swipe dock. She looked around and found nothing. The door had several keyed locks, and she could see where they crossed the divide and held the door in place. The front door was a no go. She also noticed the alarm running to it. She felt the folder shifting under the hoodie, about to fall out. She shoved it into her waistband to help secure it.

She had to use the back door unless she found a window she could open. Then again, they were probably alarmed, too. She had no way of knowing if anyone else was coming tonight. The door was solid, with only a tiny peephole. At least she'd be able to tell if someone was right outside the door. She sidestepped back to the hallway, pulled the hoodie's drawstring tight and then started creeping down the hall without using the flashlight. Once she hit the section with all the equipment, she dropped into a back corner and took a bunch of long, deep breaths to recover from holding her breath as she slinked from the front of the store to her new position.

Kate remained for a few minutes longer, gathering courage. She stood and made her way to the hallway entrance. She pushed her back up against the wall and started taking more shallow breaths. She entered the hallway. Only twenty feet and she was home free. The door to the alley opened, an arm pushing it inward. She darted back, her heart thundering against her ribs. She glanced to the far corner and wondered if she could get there without making a sound. There was a window with a latch. She could probably fit through it, but it was most likely wired.

She heard male voices, but they didn't seem to be coming nearer. Just in case, she inched her way along the wall, trying hard not to breathe. She heard one door shut and then another. Was she alone again? Were more people coming? She knew she had to act fast. She scurried with silent feet to the hall. It was empty. She moved quickly to the door leading out and peeked out the peephole. She couldn't see anyone, and the peephole seemed to give her a pie slice view of the alley. Thinking she'd verified no one was out there, she opened the door.

Two large goons stood to the side of the door, talking to each other. She popped her head back in, but it was too late, the goon facing her had seen her and she'd seen him. She pushed on the door and it clicked shut. She could only hope they didn't have a keycard. She dashed to the only room she'd seen a possible escape—the bakery portion of the business. She pushed a cart up to the window and climbed on top, the folder pushing into her ribs as she bent. Someone banged on the door. So they didn't have a key. That would give her a few precious seconds. Alarm or not, she had to get out that window or she was dead. That mafia documentary told her that much. Her hand slipped on the window lever, and it wouldn't budge. She used her elbow to slam down on it, and it started to give as someone down the hall shouted, "What's going on?" Someone from the secret room must've come out into the hall. She slammed harder with her elbow. She would have a terrible bruise.

The window fell open, and she pulled herself almost all the way through. She heard something hit the floor inside and she paused. A hand grabbed her foot. She kicked. Inside, people were yelling, but she couldn't make anything out over the blood rushing through her ears. She kicked again and made contact with something hard. She fell out the window, one hand barely keeping hold of the window casing. She cried out as her body weight jerked her to a very temporary stop before she continued to the ground. She had sense enough to roll once her feet hit, but the balls of her feet still stung and her shoulder throbbed.

Pushing all discomfort to the back of her mind, she popped to her feet and started to run. A bullet zinged off the cement beside her. She ran for her life, bullets spraying all around her. She turned a corner but knew being out of sight wouldn't stop them. A taxi sat on the street in front of a small motel. She climbed in.

"I'm taken. Sorry."

"I'll pay you double the fare with a tip if you drive now." She pulled her hood tighter around her face to keep her identity secret, but there was no hiding the fact that she was a girl from the cabbie.

His eyes popped wide. "I don't want any trouble."

She peeked out the back of the cab and saw one of the two men from outside the back door of the bagelry whiz around the corner.

"Triple," she yelled. "But don't drive away fast."

"For that, you got it." He pulled away from the curb and drove off as if he was carrying a normal fare. Kate lay on the floorboards out of sight, her breaths coming out in ragged, breathy pushes and pulls. Her arm throbbed with pain, but she clenched her jaw to keep in any possible screams.

"We have driven two blocks. No one is following us. They went into the hotel after we drove away. They will soon know you commandeered someone else's cab. I suggest you tell me where to go before I am ordered to return you. Those were Bellini men, weren't they?"

"Just take me to the boardwalk, please." She spoke through those clenched teeth.

"I'm sorry. I'll have to tell them I took you here if I'm asked, which I will be. Those Bellini men get what they want when they want it. Be careful." He drove quickly to the destination.

She gave him the cash, glad to find she had enough, and then rubbed her shoulder. The pain was increasing. Her arm didn't seem to work right. "Triple the fare. Thank you."

The sheer agony in her shoulder would not be ignored any longer. She supposed adrenaline had kept her from feeling the pain of it earlier. She headed the opposite direction she planned on going. If she had been able to buy the driver, Bellini's men, with their mob money, would own him. She had to give them a false trail. As soon as he was out of sight, she ran back the other direction. That's when she remembered she couldn't simply walk back into her hotel. She ducked behind some garbage cans and texted Ellie, *911.* She gritted her teeth to stop the uncontrollable desire to scream.

No response. She texted Colby. Still no response. Where were they? She couldn't rely on anyone. She called the hotel and asked for the doorman. He was no longer on duty. "This is Ellie Lambert from Suite 804. I need safe passage into the hotel. I don't want to be seen by the paparazzi."

The man said, "One moment please."

Cindy M. Hogan

With the adrenaline leaving her and sweat dripping down her forehead, she started to chill. She pulled her legs up tight against her and rocked to distract herself from the pain. She was very aware of the folder under her hoodie.

"Ms. Lambert. We have a car to pick you up and to bring you to the laundry. Where can they find you?"

She stood up and found a street sign. She gave him the coordinates. "They will be there in five minutes in a white laundry van. There will be no markings on it."

"Thank you," she said. She put her hand on her forehead and sighed. Her t-shirt clung to her skin under the hoodie, and she adjusted the folder. She hugged herself, tucking her head low to avoid the wind. She bit on the sleeve of Lino's hoodie. It seemed to help with the ever-growing pain. Pounding feet headed her way. She jerked to attention. The two hulking men from the bagel shop thudded their way down the boardwalk. She slunk down and around the corner to avoid them, but they spotted her. They were faster than they should have been.

A big white van pulled down the street, and she took off toward it, glad she still had the hoodie on and couldn't be recognized. The man driving the truck saw her running toward him and in the sparse light she could just make out his frantic effort to lean over and open the van door for her. As she slipped behind the door, a shot pinged off the edge of it. The driver swore and started to drive. "Wait!" she yelled, grabbing on to the seat and planting her feet on the foot ledge. He swung around, the door swinging wide before hitting into her backside and bouncing back out, leaving her completely exposed to the Bellini men. Shots zinged all around her. She screamed and the van completed its turn before the driver floored it, racing down the street. Kate held on for dear life until he turned right. It gave her the momentum she needed to pull herself in and shut the door. She buckled up and sighed.

"Who in the hell were they?" The man driving the van asked.

"Paparazzi?"

"I hate to break it to you, but the paparazzi usually don't shoot at

183

you with bullets, only cameras."

"Thank you for coming for me. If you hadn't, I most likely would have been dead." She moaned, her arm aching worse than any injury she'd ever experienced.

"Ya think?" He swallowed hard. "I don't make enough for this. You need a body guard."

"You might be right," she mumbled before lifting her head. "And you might want to lay low for a while."

"Great. Just great. The hotel better provide security for me. I didn't sign up for this."

"I'm sorry. Neither did I." She could feel the folder under the hoodie and as desperately as she wanted to remove the hoodie, she didn't. She didn't really want the guy to know what she looked like. He pulled into the laundry area of the hotel, and Kate climbed out. "If the hotel won't take care of you, let me know and I will." She hoped the Lamberts would be able to do something for him, anyway.

He nodded and swore over and over. She took the laundry elevator up to her floor and was pleased to find the hall empty. Once inside the suite, she called out for the Lamberts as she pulled the folder out from under the hoodie and put it on the table. She called out again. When no answer came, she undressed right there before grabbing a robe from her room and putting it on. She couldn't get her arm inside the robe. She needed a doctor. She rubbed her shoulder, but it seemed to make it hurt worse, so she dialed for a massage. She texted Ellie. *Where are you?*

A message came in from Ellie a moment later. *I'm sooo glad you're safe. My mom insisted we go over to Sassy's night club. We couldn't get out of it. The cast from Never Give Up is there. Here for the funeral. Did you get what you needed?*

Kate shook her head, then texted back. *Can you come back? I need you.*

I'll ask.

Kate had started whimpering from the pain in her shoulder.

Ellie texted, *My mom said I should have woken you up and brought you. I don't want to get you in trouble. What's wrong?*

If Kate told her the truth, she'd come, but at what expense? Ellie'd lied to her parents and covered for Kate. She'd get them in a lot of trouble. She owed this family so much; she didn't want to cause any more problems. *I guess it can wait until you get back.*

I'd tell you to call me, but I wouldn't be able to hear what you said. What did you find out? I'm dying here.

Kate replied, *He's my dad. She's my mom. No doubt. She was an agent. Well, maybe. Found her picture with snitch written across it. Did your parents find anything out?*

They filled out a report. The office said it could take up to two weeks for answers.

Great. So nice of the FBI to be so punctual. I'll see you later. Wake me this time no matter how early it is.

There was a knock at the door. It was the masseuse. He confirmed that the shoulder was out of its socket, but massaged the rest of her body. Kate called the concierge to locate a doctor who would make a house call. When he arrived, it only took a minute to put the shoulder back into place, but the bill was five hundred dollars. Truth was she would have spent three times that to fix the problem, but she was down to one hundred dollars. Her life savings gone, searching for her parents and what had it gotten her? At least she had the money from the show. She gave the doctor the money. He instructed her to ice for twenty minutes and heat for ten for the next several hours.

She sat at the table to do the icing. Her hands shook as much from the cold as the fear that coursed through her. She looked at the picture of her mom, her face X'ed out and then looked for the photo of herself. It was gone. That must've been the object that fell when she climbed out of the window.

She reached for Lino's keycard. It wasn't in her right pocket or her left. She thought back, patting herself down, trying to locate it. Then she remembered. She'd had it in her hand when she'd seen those goons outside. Had she dropped it? No. This couldn't be happening. In about an hour, Lino would be heading for work, puzzled by the fact that he didn't have his keycard. He'd think he left it in the shower at work or something. Maybe she'd dropped it just inside the back door. Maybe he'd borrow a keycard from someone, and he'd find his when he came into work. Then again, maybe the Bellinis had found it and thought he was the one used to sneak into the store. She looked at the discarded hoodie. Would they have seen Lino in that hoodie? Did they already think she was Lino? No. They couldn't. He was much taller than she was, and they never called out his name. Surely they wouldn't have made that mistake.

22

After grabbing a drink, she sat back down at the table and opened the folder she'd taken. She moved the picture of her mom to the side to reveal the papers beneath, being careful not to move her arm too much. A few handwritten notes were included, but that was all. The first one looked like a page ripped out of a journal. The date at the top was fifteen years previous.

Only two more weeks, and we'll be free. I wish I could tell him. I'm sure he wants something better just like me. He has to. Who would choose to be ruled by an iron fist? He might be mad when he finds out, but that will quickly fade when he discovers we will be finally free.

Kate's birth mother must have been deep undercover to have lived with Vinny long enough to have had a baby with him. The next paper looked like the first, only with a date a week and a half later.

It's only a few days before the trial, and I'm scared. I keep thinking I'm being watched or that they know. But they can't. I'm being protected, and I have to believe God is protecting me, too. These people. . . I can't wait to free us.

The other pieces of paper included a ballet ticket, an opera ticket, a subway ticket, and a receipt from what must've been an expensive restaurant. The bill was two hundred dollars for two people. And last were two locks of hair, one darker and coarser and the other fine and lighter, but still dark brown. Each had a small piece of twine tied into a knot around them. Her birth mother's hair? Her hair? She thought about the FBI's response and the idea that it would be at least two weeks for any answers. It wasn't fast enough.

Her finger traced the outline of her mother's face, and she stared into her eyes. "You are my mother, aren't you?" Tears rolled down her cheeks. She stood up, her shoulder aching. She got some fresh ice from the freezer. She looked at the clock. It was already two in the morning. Lino would be heading to work soon. To her surprise, he texted her.

Hey. You up?

She started to text him back but stopped. Should he know she was still awake? Would he suspect her of using his keycard?

A few minutes later, another text came through. *I didn't think you would be, but I can't find my keycard. I was hoping you could check the hoodie pocket and see if it somehow got stuck in there or something. Vinny is going to kill me if I don't find it. Anyway, when you get up, if you could check, I'd appreciate it.*

She let out a hard breath, glad she hadn't texted him back. She'd wait for a respectable time tomorrow and text him.

Ellie didn't text back.

About twenty minutes later she got a text from Lino again.

Looks like someone broke into the bagelry. This is going to be a long night.

Kate's heart sank. A terrible thought occurred to her. What if the shop could tell which card opened the door? It most likely could. She'd wanted to get in and out without anyone knowing, but that's not what happened. Now Lino was going to get into trouble—because of her. She hit her fist on the table, her eyes lingering on the hoodie. They could think it was him simply because she had worn his hoodie.

Dread hit into her like a locomotive. She moaned, thinking about the videos and what the mafia did to those who crossed them. They killed first and then asked questions. And Lino, innocent, kind Lino walked into work without any idea that he was in danger. She looked at the hoodie and then at the picture she'd added to her phone of the two of them at the carnival. She'd put him in some serious danger and that wasn't right. It was two forty-five.

She needed an excuse for showing up at the bagel shop. It would mean putting herself in danger too, but she wouldn't be able to live with herself if she didn't fess up and he got killed or something. She had to go try to save him. She had to. She slipped the hoodie back on and left a note for the Lamberts.

They caught me, but I got away. I found this folder. Now I have to go try to save Lino.

-Kate

23

Kate called a cab. She didn't care if the paparazzi recognized her. Maybe a few of them would follow her and get the confrontation on film so her family would know what happened to her. So her birth mom could be proud of her for acting with honor as she died. She wasn't giving up, but the graphic videos of mafia hits played through her mind. She had decided on a story and would stick to it. That was all she could do. She left the folder and her journal for the Lamberts.

No one followed her. In fact it was like no one even noticed her. While in the car, the radio show host was talking about Jace's death. Her heart swelled with grief. It would probably be her in a few hours. Jace's funeral was tomorrow, and she would miss it. She wished she'd had a chance to say goodbye, to tell him face to face that she was sorry, that she did care about him and she was sorry she misjudged him. The cab pulled in front of the shop and dropped her off. Tough looking guys stood out front, but not the ones who had followed her. They stared at her as she walked around to the back alley. The two guys who had chased her stood by the back door with three others, all smoking and talking in low voices. Most likely Lino's cousins. They didn't notice her until she was only fifteen feet from them.

"Looking for me?" she asked. The men stared in complete astonishment. "I've come to turn myself in." She saw the door with the store name on it. What would she be up against behind that door?

The two men from the docks took four steps, grabbed hold of her, and yanked her inside. The heavy door slammed shut behind them. She cried out in pain, her shoulder not wanting to be yanked at all. "Be careful! My shoulder!"

They only took about five steps and stopped before knocking lightly on the door. Two short, quick raps and three loud ones. The door swung open, smoke swirled out of the room, and Kate coughed. "Look what the cat dragged in," one of the two said as they threw her into the room past the man holding the door open. She stumbled and fell onto her hands and knees. Her shoulder gave her another jolt of pain. She pulled herself back up to standing. She was surrounded by gaming tables like could be found in a casino. Three feet away, Lino sat in a chair facing three men, one of whom was Vinny. She didn't know who the others were. In the background, she could hear the whip of large mixing bowls churning dough. The sharp smell of yeast tickled her nose.

The man who'd held the door open pulled a chair over and set it about a foot from Lino's, facing the same three men. He pulled Kate by the upper arm, luckily not the injured one, and sat her down hard on the chair. She turned to Lino. "I'm sorry Lino, I didn't know. I didn't mean to—"

The guy slapped her across the face. "Don't speak unless spoken to." Her cheek stung, and her jaw throbbed. That's when she noticed Lino's eye was swollen and his cheek cut. He did not look her way. Her eyebrows scrunched together.

This was it. She was going to die alone. No one would stand for her. No one would come to help her. Her parents wouldn't even be sad that she'd died. Her birth mom would never know she'd sought her. Vinny would be happy that she was punished for not listening to him. Jace was already dead. Ellie's family would have one less thing to worry about, and they'd be able to put all their efforts into making it onto a TV show. Her family had enough brothers and sisters that she wouldn't be missed by them. She had no one to turn to but herself, and all she had going for her was her desire to see the right thing happen.

One of the three seated men spoke. He had longish, bright white, wavy hair. His dark skin and eyes contrasted sharply with his white button-up shirt and double breasted blue jacket. His jeans tapered slightly near his dark brown leather loafers. "Did you break into this establishment tonight?"

"I did." She looked them straight on so that they would know she was telling the truth.

"How did you do it?"

She looked at Lino and sighed. "I stole Lino's keycard while we were at the carnival." Another slap came at her. Her teeth vibrated with the hit.

They looked at Lino, and one of the guards kicked his foot. Lino flinched.

"Are you telling me he didn't know you took his wallet and stole the card?" The three men laughed, even Vincenzo. Kate wasn't sure what to make of that. Why were they laughing?

"I told him I was thirsty while he was busy so that he wouldn't know I took it."

"So you wanted to steal from us?"

She shook her head. "No. No. I—I—" Her head swam. She didn't know what to say, what excuse to give.

"Where's your family?"

"Nowhere."

"You have no family?"

"I do, but I don't know who they are." Had Vinny not told them anything?

The man with white hair laughed again. "You're lost?"

"Yes," she said.

"Galtem, show her where she is."

Another slap came. Her head ached. She didn't know what they wanted to hear, but she remembered Lino's story and thought she'd mimic it.

"I think my parents are dead. I needed a place to stay."

"So why did you run?"

"I found a spot to sleep, but before I could get comfortable, I heard voices. I was so scared I'd be caught and get into trouble that I tried to leave. That's when I ran into them." She indicated the two big goons. "I freaked and went for the window. It was stupid. I should have stayed and fessed up."

"You put us in a very awkward position. You see, we don't put up with people stealing from our family. And we don't put up with family members who enable thieves."

The man next to Lino punched him in the jaw. His head flew to the side, then swung down to his chest. A groan escaped his lips. Blood trickled down his chin.

"Please don't hurt him. He didn't know." Her lip quivered uncontrollably. "Hit me. Kill me if you have to, just leave him alone. He had nothing to do with it."

Vincenzo spoke up now, "But he did. He let a girl hypnotize him. He let a girl make him stupid." His eyes said what his mouth wouldn't. *I told you to never come back. You are just like your mother.*

"I didn't take anything."

"You took the keycard. You took his honor. You spent several hours in our shop sleeping. You caused us to fire many bullets at you. Bullets cost money, you know. And the manpower. All that manpower. And now, we had to stop our game and deal with this. We had to send our friends home without a good evening together."

Kate looked around, an illegal betting playground. The mafia was famous for places like this.

"How do you propose paying the family back for all of that?"

"I can get you the money with interest."

The man talking laughed. "Of course there'd be interest. But how do you propose to do that?"

"I was on a TV show, and they paid me a lot of money."

He nodded. "That's a good start, but it won't cover the damage you've done to our reputation. It takes a lot to cover that. You two agree?" He looked at the man on his left, who was youngish, in his thirties maybe, with a stylish button-down opened to the third button, several thin, gold chains hanging around his neck, and then at Vincenzo.

They both nodded.

"I think maybe, just maybe your life and Lino's life might pay that debt." Immediately, the large man next to Kate put a knife up to her throat and the man next to Lino did the same. Kate screamed.

Her dad put his hand on the white-haired man's arm. "She does have skills. She could possibly be a good earner."

"She's a girl. We don't use girls to earn." That was true. In the videos she'd watched, they'd barely even mentioned women. There was one she'd seen at a club who informed on someone, but that was it.

"Maybe there's a first for everything. Look at her. She has a pretty face. A good body. She could be a club girl and earn her way through information. She tricked Lino."

Kate held back a sob. Her life was over, one way or another.

The man nodded. "I'm starting to see that." The way he looked at her made her flinch.

"And Lino. He's loyal. My best worker. He's smart, and he'll be a good earner after college. He won't make the same mistake again. Will you, Lino?"

"No. Never," he mumbled.

"We brought you into this family, no questions asked, and you let us down like this?" The man with the three gold chains said. "I don't know."

"I won't make the same mistake. I won't." He spoke with a clear voice this time.

The main guy sighed. "With the right clothes and makeup," he nodded, "I think you're right, Vinny. She could get anything out of anyone. We could train her to do other stuff, too. What do you think?" He looked to the other two men and then Kate.

Kate didn't speak and the big guy slugged her in the gut. A gasp

7

sprang from her mouth, and she couldn't breathe. "Did you understand the terms of keeping your life, girl?"

"I-I- think so," she sputtered.

"You will work for the family, night and day, non-stop until you pay us back."

"How long?" She scrounged for air.

"Well, we'll be taking care of you and training you as we go, which puts you further in debt. It's your life in death or your life in living. Which will it be?"

Kate stared at her dad. How could he be doing this? She turned to Lino. She really had no choice. She had to do this for Lino. "I'll do it."

"Do what?"

"I'll work for you."

White-haired guy nodded, and the big guy moved the knife away. "Take her to my car."

Vinny put his hand on the main guy's arm again. "I was hoping to put her to use in the store first. Lunetta could train her part time, and I'll train her also. I'm short a worker since Gino was taken. She's obviously as green as a meadow. I'll toughen her up for you."

Gino. That was the guy Andre Marconi had mentioned needed to be taken care of. They'd killed him.

He nodded. "I like it. She's yours for now."

The three men stood, and two left with most of the guards either in front of them or behind them. Only four remained, and Vinny instructed them to take Lino to the showers to get him cleaned up so he could get to work. Two guards carried his weakened body out.

He dismissed the other two men then turned to Kate. "I told you to stay away. You just couldn't stay away, could you?" He ran his hands through his thick gray hair. He sighed a deep sigh. "You have no idea what you've done."

Her stomach knotted, and she decided not to say anything. She knew he'd saved her. He had been sneaky about it, but he'd done it. She knew it, but he didn't know she knew. She tucked that fact away to a far

195

corner of her mind.

"Can I go home?" She clutched at her aching stomach.

"You are home. You will serve the Bellini family day in and day out from now on."

"What does that mean?"

"It means that you have lost every ounce of freedom you ever had. The family will check on your progress, and you must not fail to show said progress."

"But I'm here with friends. They'll worry about me."

"Yes, they will. They'll probably even put missing signs with your picture up. They'll probably go to the news, to the papers, but none of it will change the fact that you are dead to them. You must understand that. Your life before tonight is gone. You can never return."

"That doesn't make any sense. Someone will find me. All I have to do is go tell a cop what happened."

"We own the cops. You do that and one of two things will happen. You will either be killed, or Salvatorio Bellini will find your family and kill them."

"Salvatorio?"

"The head of our family. The boss. He had the white hair."

Her jaw dropped. He paced. "This is no joke. Consider yourself a life-long slave. You might have fared better with a death sentence." He shook his head. "Come with me. And behave. I can have you killed as easily as he could."

She followed him to another room that she hadn't been in. It was a bunk room across the hall from the gaming room. "This is where you'll sleep. I'll bring you some clothes later. Tomorrow morning you start your training."

24

Finding herself alone, she immediately searched for her phone, but it was gone. When had they taken it? She had no clue. She thought she'd never be able to fall asleep, but the truth was, she was totally exhausted, both emotionally and physically. She'd been scared spitless more in the past day than in her whole life combined. It only took about five minutes for her to be out.

She woke to a knock on the door and the door opening. Vinny stood there with a bag of clothes and supplies. "I'll take you to the showers so you can get ready for the day."

She followed him out, rubbing sleep from her eyes and feeling the ache of a bruised face and gut. They passed the workers, and he indicated she should go into the room to the left. He held the bag out for her to take. She did. The hot water pounded her back and shoulders. Her shoulder ached. Missing the ice and heat had really slowed its healing. She had to get out of there, and she'd have to take Lino with her. If she left on her own, they'd punish him and maybe her dad, too. Did she care about Vinny enough to worry about that? Lino's bruised and bloody face came to mind. Had she even helped him? Well, he wasn't executed last night. That was something.

She dressed in the fine clothes Vinny had brought her, which was weird considering she'd be working in a bagel shop. She thought of all the Bellinis and Marconis she'd seen—they always dressed up, no t-shirts, ever. So, perhaps it wasn't so weird. The pants were a little long, but the wedges he'd brought her lifted them from the ground. She was going to have some achy calves at the end of the day. She fixed her hair into a fashionable low ponytail and used the makeup he'd provided to try to hide her bruised and puffy face. What were her parents going to think when she didn't return with the Lamberts? They would find out she didn't go to Mexico. What would the Lamberts tell them? The faces of her wild and crazy brothers and predictable sisters flashed through her mind. She locked them up in a distant corner of her mind. She couldn't think about them. Not now, maybe not ever. It hurt too much. She grabbed up her ruined clothes and put them into one of the three bags that had held her new clothes and supplies.

When she tried to open the door, she found it locked. She knocked with a light hand. Immediately the door opened. Vinny stood there. "You ready?"

"Yeah." She held up the bags. "Where do you want me to put these?"

"You can put them back in your room."

That was her room as in permanent room? No way. Had they put Lino in a room like that, too? She looked around for him.

"Looking for Lino?" Vinny started back to her room.

How had he known? "I'm worried about him." She followed Vincenzo.

He shook his head and sighed, turning his head toward her for a tiny moment. "You can give it a rest. The deception is over. There's nothing more you can gain by pretending to be interested in him."

She stopped. He didn't. She scowled, placing her hands on her hips. She could tell he was talking but she couldn't hear what he was saying. He turned in an abrupt movement. She continued to scowl, and now his face soured. "What are you doing?"

She charged forward then, "Look. I do care about Lino. I meant to borrow the card and return it to him before he came back to work."

He raised his eyebrows. "Please!"

"It's true." She lowered her voice as they passed the people working. "I only wanted to find information about my birth mom and then get the heck out." She wanted to shout in his face that she had had to do it because he had lied to her, but she would save that card for another day. "I was going to sneak back out as Lino arrived at two thirty to give him his key. You have no idea how terrible it is to live like I do." She cringed at the thought of her parents' deception.

She watched his face carefully to see if any hint of remorse crossed it, but he turned away before she could get a good read. She was only feet from him now, and he opened the door to what she now realized was her cell. "It's about to get a lot worse."

She walked into her cell and put her bags on her bed. "You're going to learn how to run the front of the shop today." Vinny's voice was flat. "Don't get too comfortable. We're going to have to transition you into an earner as quickly as possible. Otherwise, he will use you for things you thought only happened in the movies."

She wondered who *he* was. She glanced over at the clock. It was one o'clock already. "You let me sleep in?" A twinge of hope glided through her. He was showing her tiny kindnesses. Maybe he wasn't lost after all. She followed him toward the front of the store.

"I figured you'd be worthless without it. Lunetta will be showing you the ropes. I want you to shadow her for the first hour. Don't touch anything or speak to anyone. Watch and learn. Second hour, you can start filling orders. Third hour she'll teach you the register. She'll set you loose for the last hour and shadow you, answering any questions you might have. Let's see if there's more than just air between those ears of yours."

She smirked. "4.0 student right here." She used both her thumbs to point to herself.

"Grades mean nothing here. Only hard work means anything."

"And if I don't?" Kate put her hands on her hips.

"Then I'll hand you over to Salvatorio or even better, Marcel. Then you'll really wish you were dead." He reached around her, pulled an apron down from a hook behind her and gave it to her. Would he really do that? She wasn't sure, yet. She put the apron on. He walked away.

Lunetta smiled a bright smile and said, "Don't you pay him any mind. I'm sure you'll have no problem, and if you don't need the full hour of shadowing and you're bored out of your mind, tell me. You can start filling orders early. You're really lucky Vinny wanted you."

She didn't feel lucky. "Thanks, I'm kind of a fast learner." She'd have to bide her time until she could escape. She could do anything for a short amount of time.

"Good. Then we'll get along just fine. We only have a few rushes in the afternoon. Be glad you weren't here in the morning. We're slammed in the mornings."

Abrie would freak out if she knew the daughter she'd raised to become a huge success in life would be working as a servant in a bagel shop. A manic chuckle bubbled up inside her. It didn't seem real. If this was going to be her life, she would rather die. Seriously, though, what was keeping her here? A supposed threat to her family, her dad, and Lino? Maybe nothing would happen to them. The Bellinis didn't know who she really was, after all. She'd find a way out today. At the most she'd have to stay until next week when she could make a quick get away with the Lamberts. Marconis and Bellinis didn't exist in Texas. She'd be safe there.

She thought of Ellie and her family. Were they worried out of their minds or did they chalk up her absence as another night needing some space? She'd left a note about her plans. She couldn't keep her eyes off the street and sidewalks outside. She thought for sure the Lamberts would show up sooner or later. In a short half an hour Kate was filling orders and in another fifteen, she was taking orders, working the register like she'd worked there several weeks. It was mindless work. When a rush came, she stepped back and let Lunetta take over.

"You sure you have no food service experience?" Lunetta asked.

Kate scowled. "Yep."

Despite the fact that Lunetta seemed incredibly nice, she had to remind herself that Lunetta was a part of a crime family and most likely was not what she seemed. She couldn't be trusted.

Kate consolidated the remaining rows of bagels as a large group of teenagers came for a cheap before-dinner snack. The bagels were discounted fifty percent the last half-hour of the night. Kate acted as backup for this wave of customers, letting Lunetta take the lead.

When Kate got the opportunity, she scanned the area outside for ideas on escaping. Lunetta showed Kate the checklist for closing the bagel shop and walked her through each chore, never leaving her alone. This would be the obstacle she'd have to overcome. She'd have to either create a diversion so Lunetta had to leave her, or she'd have to take advantage when by chance Lunetta put her guard down.

Vinny showed up as they finished, and he escorted Kate back to her room. Lunetta left out the back door. One set of bunks had been removed and a table and a chair replaced it. He set a bag with take out on the table and turned to leave. "Why don't you stick around and eat with me? You could explain how everything works," Kate asked, taking a seat on the bed. Maybe if she understood that, she'd have a better chance of escape.

He stopped, turned his head around to her and said, "I can't. I hope you like lasagna." He pointed to a yellow button near the light switch. "If there's an emergency or you need help, push that button. Someone will come."

"I don't want to be here alone."

"You're going to have to learn to thrive when you're alone. Most of what you do as an earner will be solo." He had been looking past her and not at her. "I'm sorry this happened to you, but you should have listened to me and stayed away. See you in the morning." He left.

She bit back tears and screamed, "But you're my father." She would not let them take over her life. She would escape. In her mind she mapped out possible escape routes, but she knew if she couldn't get out of this room or distract her co-worker sufficiently, she would not get the chance to escape. She stewed about a way to contact her friends the rest of the night until she fell asleep.

The best idea she could dredge up involved "borrowing" someone's cell phone or finding a way to use the shop's phone to get a message out. Both seemed like long shots, but she had to try.

Someone opened her cell door and artificial light flooded in. Lunetta. She didn't look like her chipper self. Kate still felt tired and a bit weak and asked. "What time is it?"

"Two thirty."

"I slept that long? Unbelievable. I need windows to wake me earlier I guess."

"Two thirty in the morning."

"Oh." No wonder Lunetta didn't look happy.

"Time to teach you how to make the bagels."

To her surprise, Lino passed by the preparation room while she and Lunetta were cleaning it, to the front of the store. He was still working here. A piece of her soul soared in that moment. He hadn't even looked her way, but she'd seen the bright blue, purple, and black all over his face. That was her fault. She would have to beg for forgiveness and explain that she never meant to hurt him. He'd have to believe her.

***

Vinny put her in her cage as soon as the bagels were cooked and ready for sale. With hope of escape burning in her heart, she fell asleep without any trouble. She woke when Vinny brought her lunch. She was ready for a fight.

"My friends are going to come looking for me." She put her hands on her hips as she stood.

"They already have." His voice was even, dark.

Her eyes rounded, and she couldn't speak.

"Why do you think you worked in the back today?" One eyebrow rose.

"What? When? I never saw them."

"Well, they didn't come here exactly. They went to the police."

"No!" She grimaced. The Bellinis and Marconis owned the cops. Nothing would be done.

"Yes." He shook his head. "They will be given the run around and then the bad news that you simply can't be found. And even if the cops show up here, no one will have heard of you."

He squeezed his hands together. He'd brought hoagies and chips.

Heaviness crept over her body. "Are you going to keep me here forever?" she whispered.

"This is your home for at least six months."

"No. It can't be true." The distant hope that the Lamberts would somehow find a way to save her had been crushed. She had to find a way out on her own. In order to do that, she needed to get stuff from the outside world. She needed to know what was going on in the outside world.

"It is."

"Could I at least get a TV? A radio? Books? An Ipod?" She asked without any hope of getting anything.

"You've been very cooperative and hard working so far. I'll consider it."

So her comfort in this place was tied to her compliance. She could fake that, for now. She would pretend to give up on getting saved and then take the first opportunity given her.

Her life got into a rhythm for the next two nights. Around ten she heard people enter through the back of the store. She assumed they went into the gambling room. Lunetta woke her at two thirty every morning. She made bagels until six thirty. At that point she was hustled back into her room. Vincenzo brought her meals, dropping them off and heading out as quickly as he could. Each meal, Kate would ask him to stay. Each meal he'd refuse. Finally, on the fourth day, he walked all the way into her room and set two bags on the table. "I got you a few books and a simple iPod that has a couple hundred dollars loaded on it so you can order the music and videos you want."

He glanced at her and turned to go. Sensing he wanted something more, she blurted, "I understand."

He turned around again, and Kate could see the longing in his eyes, even behind his stony expression. She let out all the thoughts that had been rolling around in her brain ever since her capture. "Listen. I totally get that for some reason, you can't claim me. I guess I was on some hit list or something. At least it looks that way from the notes in that file. That my birth mom did something to put us all in danger. All I really want is for you to acknowledge me."

He didn't respond, but he didn't argue, so Kate took that as encouragement and continued, "At least when we're alone. When we're around other people, I get it. You know, to say I'm not your daughter, but to pretend when it's you and me, that's ridiculous. I saw the picture in that file of you helping me walk. Treat me however. Be as surly and mean as you have to be, but not when we're alone together, where no one can see. I lost you and now I found you." Her heart raged against its cage.

"Why. Why did you do that?" His posture slumped and his hands carved through his hair, holding it back and then releasing it. "This is not what I wanted for you. I tried to save you from this." His expression blanched as he shook his head.

"Please... Dad, sit." Kate motioned to the chair. "There was nothing you could have done that would have kept me from seeking you out."

He sat and waited for her to explain. She felt a flash of happiness. Her birth father was willing to talk. "I wasn't just curious about finding you. I thought that by finding you, I'd know better who I was."

"But why? Did he not find you a good family?"

"I have a great family. They did everything a parent should—but I need to know who I really am. Where I came from."

He didn't seem to register the longing in her voice. He focused on what she'd said about her adoptive family. "That's good. I wanted you to have a good family. I wish I could take you back to them, but it's impossible now."

She shook her head. "We can leave together."

"No!" He spat and slammed his hand on the table. "No. There is no way out for you, and there is no way out for me. Too many people will get hurt."

"Lino? We can take him—"

"You don't know what you're saying. They own me as much as they own you."

"Who? Marconi?"

He shook his head. "No. The Bellini family."

"But *you* are the Bellini family." She knew what she was saying was ridiculous. She'd seen the videos. She knew once you were in the mafia, you were in for life.

"I'm not the boss. They would find us and kill us and kill everyone who is important to us. Your adoptive family included. No. We have to find a way to keep you here and keep you safe. They can never know who you really are. Never."

"Because they believe me dead?" She didn't want to believe that the family, her family, truly wanted her dead.

"Yes."

"But why?"

"I'm not going to go into that with you now. What skills do you have?"

"Skills?"

"What are you good at? We've got to find something for you to do to become an earner as quickly as possible."

"I get great grades. I'm the president of the honor society. I—"

He cut her off. "This isn't a scholarship application. What skills do you have?"

She thought of the miniseries on the mafia and knew he was looking for skills like stealing cars, tricking people, and picking locks. She had nothing. "I'm not a mafia girl, I'm a regular girl. I play the piano."

His head shot up. "Still?"

"You knew I could play?"

"You started mimicking your mother when you weren't even two yet. Every time we had company over, you would climb up on that bench and play. Your mom was teaching you, and it was incredible to see your little hands move so deftly across the keys."

Something flashed in her mind. Her birth mom smiled down at her as she played. "That's right, Zie, you've got it." The memory faded.

"She called me Zie?"

His mouth slackened. "We all did. It seemed to fit better than your full name. You were so full of life. . . But you were so small. How can you remember?"

"How old was I when you sent me away?"

"Almost three. . . We loved you so much." His voice caught, and he stared at Kate like it was the first time he'd seen her. "How are we going to keep you safe and get you earning as soon as possible? As long as you're a gopher, you're totally vulnerable. We need to get you to associate as fast as we can."

"What do I need to do?" Kate felt a strange sense of belonging and a great desire to please this man all of a sudden. "Are you saying I can become a legitimate family member? I thought I was a slave?"

"We are all slaves except for the boss, but there are varying degrees of freedom within the ranks. You have zero when a gopher, a little when you're an earner, and a whole heck of a lot when you're an associate like I am."

"Aren't you a Bellini?" She ran a finger along her bottom lip.

"Of course I am, but even Bellinis have to rise in the ranks. And you're very lucky that Salvatorio didn't claim you. If so, you'd be at his beck and call twenty-four hours a day, doing whatever he asked."

"I didn't realize that." Now she felt a shot of fear. She wasn't sure she wanted to be an associate. They had to do terrible things. "So, I'm lucky to be with you, I guess."

He frowned. "I have to go. Think about what talents you have. I'll start looking into opportunities you could tap into to earn."

"Don't go."

He looked as if he might give in, but then he shook his head, his face going hard. "It can't be helped. See you at dinner. And if you see Lino, don't tell him about our relationship." He left, and it felt strange that he left without hugging her.

Did her dad think she couldn't trust Lino? After what she'd witnessed when she stole his keycard, she certainly did. He hadn't ratted her out before she'd shown up and he'd been beaten. He was most likely going to be disposed of and he still hadn't said anything. Or was it more than that? The knowledge that she was Vinny's daughter, who should have been dead, would definitely put Lino in danger. Knowledge was everything in the mafia. The wrong knowledge got you killed.

She tried to stop thinking of Lino, but couldn't. The one thing that kept coming back to her about Lino was his path into the family. Was he still a gopher or was he an earner? She couldn't work it out. He called them his family. Perhaps gophers were a part of the family.

Her mind wandered to escaping, and several ideas flowed into her mind. It surprised her when a heavy dose of guilt filled her for thinking of escaping. Vinny was her father. She'd found him. Perhaps she should stay with him. She shook her head. She couldn't think that way. She had to get out of there. She needed to leave with the Lamberts on Monday. The thought of them having to explain her disappearance to her parents made her cringe. She was their first child. They would be heartbroken. And her brothers and sisters wouldn't understand. Dread at never being able to see them again coursed through her. She would do almost anything to get back to them. She had four days to figure it all out. Four short days to escape.

25

It seemed like a long time had passed before Vinny returned. When the door opened, she stood up fast as if Vinny could somehow see that she'd been vainly thinking about escaping.

"Sorry," he said, hauling some bags into the room. "I didn't mean to scare you."

"It's okay, I didn't know when to expect you. What time is it anyway?"

He looked at his watch. "Nine. I was at a meeting with the other associates. They are all curious about you." He set the bags next to the table and then started emptying one with food in it. He set the boxes of Chinese food on the table.

"That doesn't sound good."

"It isn't. It got Salvatorio even more curious. He's coming tonight some time to check on you. We need a plan. Now." He sat in the only chair and started dishing food onto it while he talked. "What did you come up with?" He paused then, with chopsticks in hand, he looked at her. She stared back. She had nothing. "Aren't you hungry?" Kate nodded. "Dig in then."

"Most of the girls in the family work as receptionists, servers, do hair and nails, or work as informers. You don't want to be an informer."

None of those ideas sounded good; then she remembered Lino. "Lino told me you were helping him get to college. He said he enjoyed being a gopher, but didn't like being an earner, so you were sending him to college to work in the markets."

"He told you that?"

"Well, not in those words, but I know enough now to read between the lines."

Vinny nodded while eating a bite of lo mein. Kate had yet to serve herself any food. "Yeah. He's a smart kid, and I think he'll be good at the stock market."

"What about me. I'm smart. Why not send me to college, too? I could get my GED, go to college, and start earning money really fast."

He chuckled. "Earners have to make a ton of money, not like what you'd make at a regular job. Lino won't be getting clients like a regular broker. He'll find ways to scam people."

Kate grimaced.

"I told you it wasn't going to be easy. Well, it's not going to be pretty, either. You have all As?" He pointed the chopsticks at me.

"Yes. In hard classes, college and AP."

"I can't have both of you doing the same thing. I need to find you some business opportunity."

"You mean something like that gas tax scam?"

"You have done your homework."

"Well, I had an idea that my birth dad and birth mom were part of the mafia."

He nodded. "You are smart. What do smart people do?"

"I wanted to be an architect."

"That's not something that would help us. No. Hmm. Let me think. . . Ah. Smart people are lawyers, judges." He peered at her. "Eat. You're making me nervous."

She obeyed, putting small amounts of the boxed food on her plate.

"Ever thought of being a lawyer? Now, that would be useful to the family. You good at debating?" He didn't take another bite, but waited for Kate to respond first.

"I guess. Maybe."

"Yes. I like this. Will Salvatorio?"

Kate shrugged.

"We could groom you exactly how we want you. You're so young. Dad'll think you can be molded."

"Salvatorio is your dad?"

"Of course. Who did you think he was?"

"I didn't know. So you guys aren't under Marconi?"

Vinny laughed out loud. "No. It's not like that. They're separate from us, but we also work in tandem. We have an agreement on conduct, and they enforce our conduct and we enforce theirs."

"But from what I've seen, they're terrible people." She wanted to tell him about Cremashci and see if he knew about him.

"It's not like that. They can be as bad as they want to anyone outside the two families, but inside the families, there are rules."

His phone buzzed and he picked it up. "We'll be right there."

"He's here." Vinny's face contorted. He must've been trying to hide his discomfort.

"Already?" Kate stood up, her nerves firing. This Salvatorio—her grandfather—would determine her fate, and she didn't want just any fate. She said, "God, please help me."

"It's okay. We've got a great plan. And I hope God is on our side."

They crossed the hall and met Salvatorio in the gaming room. They sat across from each other at a poker table.

"What shall we do with this one?" He tilted his head to the side like he was analyzing her. She didn't like it one bit, but held her cool.

"We have ourselves a real smart one," Vinny said. "She takes college classes while in high school."

"But does she have any real world skills?" He pushed out his lips and put his thumbs over his mouth.

"She's not going to need those skills. She's going to be a lawyer." Vinny set his hands out on the table, a move that showed openness.

Salvatorio's eyes narrowed as he peered at her. "A lawyer?"

"Just think about it. We'll be grooming her, starting now. What could be better than that?" He shrugged.

"That's a long road. But that's thinking about the future, son. Good job."

"Yeah, and in the end, we'd have a judge in our pocket without having to bribe one." Vinny nodded as he said it.

"A judge." It wasn't a question. He tilted his head slowly from one side to the other as he openly stared at Kate. "If she's going to be ours, we need her to know how everything operates so that right from the start she can be looking for laws and such that will help us, and connections she can milk to get what we need. What do you think about becoming a judge?" He was asking Kate.

"I'd like it, I think." She pressed her hands into her legs to release some tension.

"You need to be a good lawyer first."

She nodded, hoping she looked humble.

"Show her how the bagel shop works. Then move her through all the businesses."

In her eagerness to show she was on top of things, she said, "I've already been working here for three days. I know how it all works." The disapproval in Vinny's face was apparent. Kate ducked her head, abashed.

"You know the business we want you to see. We'll show you what we're keeping from everybody," Vinny said.

"I thought you said she was smart."

She didn't feel smart at that moment, not at all, but then again, she could have revealed something even worse. She decided to count her blessings.

"Hey, we're good at keeping stuff secret. That's all."

"We'll see. We have an event on Sunday that will tell us all we need to know, I think. I want her at the club, working the room. Someone is moving in on our betting crowd. I hate poachers. I want her to uncover who they are. We want to bring down the poachers and get possible recruits checked out. I'd like to get any good ones into the back room as soon as possible. We never got Lino into the club, did we?"

"No. It's a good thing. He wouldn't have survived." Vinny grimaced.

Salvatorio chuckled. "If you hadn't saved that boy from the streets, he'd have been eaten alive."

They started speaking as if she wasn't even there.

"After Sunday, we'll know better, and we'll get her set up with one of the families. She's going to need a watch dog for a while."

"How about Lino?"

"Ah, yes. I like how you think. This way we can prove the both of them in one shot. On Monday, if I like what I see, we'll put her with Marcel."

"Hold on, there was a romantic interest there. It might not be smart to have them live together, too."

"I guess you're going to have to take her, then. Mario and Galtem have their hands and houses full at the moment."

"All right. I'll take responsibility."

"But she has to pass on Sunday. If not, she comes to me."

Kate clasped her hands to prevent them from trembling. She was going to be amazing on Sunday. She had to be.

"I'd like to get her arrested as soon as possible so that she knows how that feels."

"We can't, or she'll never be able to pass the vetting section of being nominated as judge."

"True. But she needs to be toughened up. That's your job, Vinny. Get one of the girls to teach her. She should have natural talent in persuasion and debate, or she'll never survive, either. Sunday we'll see if she's got that talent or not. Grooming up a lawyer is going to take a lot of time and money, and I want to make sure she's the one we should be grooming. Yes. She has the looks of a good persuader, but does she have the mouth?" With that, Salvatorio stood and walked to the door of the gambling room. "Part of me doesn't want her to succeed. I think it'd be nice to have her by my side all day and night." He left, his entourage leaving with him.

Dread snaked up Kate's spine.

Vinny put his index finger to his lips and gave her a look that she shouldn't say anything. "Let's get you back to your room. Two thirty will come early, and be prepared to get trained for the club later in the day."

"I'll be ready."

They left and once in her room, she said, "What was that about? Are there cameras in there?"

"Yes. But I should have told you to never be familiar with me outside of this room. Having Salvatorio show up so early threw me off, and I forgot to tell you that. Always assume someone is listening. Most of the time, someone is."

"Okay."

"I didn't want you to be a club girl, ever." He sighed and rubbed the scruff on his cheeks. "Nothing to be done, though. Now, I've got to get you trained so that you're safe. I've got to pick a few things up and see which of my cousins can come and work with you. I'll be back early. Get some sleep."

"Wait. I have a question about Cremashci."

"The old priest?"

She nodded.

"What about him?"

"He's the one that saved me, right?"

"What do you mean?" He took a step toward her. He looked completely clueless.

"He was the one you gave me to, to save me. Isn't he?"

"I have no idea what you're talking about."

Then she remembered the signature at the bottom of the green paper. Her dad hadn't signed it, someone else had. A Marconi. "Wait. You didn't send me away. Someone took me, didn't they?"

He looked at his feet. "They were going to kill you to make a point to me. A trusted friend saved you. I don't know any of the details and don't want to either."

"But didn't you want to know what happened to me?"

"Of course I did. But if I knew anything, I'd be putting you in danger, and it would be too big of a temptation to go see you."

She was starting to understand. "Tell me everything, Dad. Please."

He shook his head. "No. The past is gone. We only have the future to think about."

"I have to know!"

"No."

She could see he wouldn't budge, yet. She'd soften him up, and one day he'd tell her. "I have one more question and that's all."

"I may not answer."

"I hope you do. The priest over at St. Catharine's. Is he a Marconi?"

"No."

"But Ellie thought he wasn't a good guy, and he called McArthur's Care Center when we went there and had someone follow us."

"She was right. He isn't good. He does a lot of the dirty work for the mob. He's also an informer for both sides. If a Bellini gets in trouble, he tells the Marconis, and if a Marconi gets in trouble, he tells the Bellinis." He ran his hands through his hair, a grimace on his face. "Why did you go to the church?"

"I was following a lead."

"Great. We'll have to alter your appearance somewhat before you attend church. I don't want anyone recognizing you from before."

Fire raged in her gut. She'd exposed herself to two other Marconis. She looked at her feet.

"Oh, I don't like that look, Zie. Who else saw you?"

Her father knew her too well already. "Lenora Marconi and Andre Marconi."

He raked his hands through his hair. "How much contact?"

"Enough that they'd remember me."

"We'll find a way to keep you from them, but we will have to change your appearance." He raised an eyebrow. "Andre?"

"I thought he was my dad. Dead wife and child. . ."

He nodded, a grim look on his face. "We can't worry about that now. We need to get you ready for the club. See you in the morning." And he was gone.

In the mafia videos, the one girl she'd seen had been working in a club. They hadn't talked much about what she was doing. The sexy girl had flirted with the guys and, Kate assumed, had collected information from the men she approached. It didn't seem too difficult. What she needed was Ellie to give her points on flirting. An ache settled in her chest. She might never see Ellie again.

***

The door opened and a thrill of excitement shot through Kate. Her dad was here again. She had really found her dad. But it wasn't Vinny at the door. It was Lino. She took a sharp breath in, and her mouth remained ajar. It felt like her heart had turned to the bell from St. Catharine's and it was slamming into her ribs. Lino's bruises were a deep brown, but they seemed to be shrinking like hers were. He shut the door behind him. He gave her a pressed smile and walked to the table, setting the two bags there.

Kate gulped. "Lino. I'm so sorry. I didn't mean it—" She wanted to tell him everything, but knew she couldn't. She couldn't put him in danger again.

He held up one hand and shook his head. "Don't apologize to me. This is my fault. I should never have met with you on the boardwalk and showed you around. It was—"

Kate held up her hand this time. "What are you talking about? This was my fault. I sought you out. I thought I was a Marconi or that the Marconis were after me or—"

Then they talked over each other, each trying to prove they were at fault until they both took a breath at the same time.

"I'm as much to blame for this happening as you. I shouldn't have sought you out, knowing who I am," Lino said.

"That's not true." Kate folded her arms over her chest.

He moved to her and put a finger on her lips. "Let's agree right now that we're both at fault and it's a draw."

215

Kate shook her head.

"It's a draw." He said it with insistence this time.

Kate nodded.

"Good. The past is in the past. We move forward." She nodded again.

"But wait. You thought you were a Marconi?"

Heat started in Kate's belly and ran up her neck to her face. "Well, I, I mean." She had to come up with an explanation and quick. She could not tell him the truth, as much as she wanted to. She wanted him to understand why she took the keycard in the first place. She wanted him to know she had a good reason. "It was stupid. I'm totally not a Marconi. Looking back it was a stupid idea."

"What was it that led you to them?"

"I have this cross from my parents from St. Catharine's, and then there was the baptism and. . . Oh, I feel so dumb for even jumping to that conclusion."

"I'm sorry they weren't your family, but I'm also glad. They are pretty cutthroat."

"I thought you loved them, and they were good people. Isn't that what you told Ellie and me?"

"I did say that, but I meant it as a family member. I have to say that. Believe me, as terrible as the Bellinis can be, you're much better off becoming a part of their family than the Marconis'. And I'm sure Vinny will become something special in your life how he has in mine. He saved me, and it looks like he's decided to save you. You're finally going to have a family you can count on."

Kate nodded. She thought of her adoptive parents and siblings. They would never see her again, and she'd been so awful to them. When they found out she disappeared in New Jersey they would be swallowed up in guilt. Her mom had known there was danger surrounding her birth parents, and Kate hadn't listened and look where it got her.

"I'm supposed to keep an eye on you. It's going to be the worst job ever." He tried, but failed at not smiling.

"Who's to say I'm easy to watch?" She grinned wickedly.

He shook his head and grunted. "I want this to be fun and to enjoy our new adventure together, but I have to warn you. Now that you know what the family is capable of, you need to respect that."

"I will. I do."

"That means no running away. When you're in the family, nothing only affects you. Our fates are tied together, as is Vinny's and everyone that works here. Got it?"

"Yes. I understand." She wanted nothing more than to run away, but she knew it wasn't possible. Not yet, anyway.

"Now that we have that straight. I have to know something—was it all a game to you?" His head tilted to the side.

"No." She looked up at him through her eyelashes. "I really like you. A lot." She hoped he wouldn't ask her directly why she stole his keycard. She hadn't come up with a good lie, yet.

He grinned. "I like you a lot. And as much as I wish I could take you away from all of this, I'm glad you're here with me."

"Ditto."

He kissed her forehead. "I got these books from Maya. She's a great club girl. You need to read the passages and practice acting like these girls. You won't be working in the shop today. You need to practice, practice, practice."

"Why didn't Vinny come? I mean, I'm glad you're here and all, but—"

"Because he wanted us to meet and straighten things out before Salvatorio puts us together on Monday."

"Do I get to see you again before Monday?"

"I'm not sure. We'll see. Now, eat your breakfast, read, and practice." He turned his head to the side and looked at her with one eye.

"Wait. Are you filling in for me?"

"Me? No way. I hate early shift." He smiled and left.

All this persuasion stuff was scary. She read and re-read the passages in ten different books. She practiced, pretending her pillow in the chair was her target. She could persuade the pillow each try. Lino showed up after his shift.

"Now, practice on me. I'm someone the barkeep told you is checking things out." He tossed the pillow onto the bed and sat in the chair.

"Wait. I thought the mafia was careful with their girls. Why would they send them in as club girls?"

"Those rules are for real children or ones that have been with them forever. And they have cousins watching their back. You won't."

Kate brought him a fake glass of beer. "Here ya go. I don't think I've seen you around here before."

"Naw, this is my first time."

"And how do you like our little club?"

"Nice place, and having girls like you serve me, makes me want to spend a lot more time here." He reached around and patted her butt.

She jumped back. "That was gross."

"That was nothing. You've got to be tough on the inside. Club girls are always pretty and always get hit on. Position yourself a little differently to avoid certain types of groping."

He worked with her for the next half hour and was critical about everything she did.

"I don't know if I can do this. I guess I'm not persuasive." She slumped onto the bed

"Oh, you're persuasive, I'm just being difficult. And you persuaded me."

Kate knew he wasn't talking about their most recent conversation, but what she'd done at the carnival.

"Be that girl. You're being too timid. Too scared. You have to feel the stakes. It was easy for you to persuade me to give you my wallet because you wanted more than anything to find your birth parents. What you need to want so desperately now is to remain with Vinny, because more than anything, you don't want to end up with Salvatorio."

"I can't believe you're helping me after what I did." She stroked his cheek.

"I can't help it. You hypnotized me." He rolled his eyes around and around. He put his hand on hers and squeezed with a gentle pressure.

"Very funny. Seriously. Thank you."

"You're welcome. And thanks for forgiving me." He brought her hand to his lips and kissed it. His face moved closer to hers until their breaths mingled. She tilted her head to the side, and his lips pressed on hers. She pressed back. Fireworks exploded in her gut. For the next however long, they kissed and kissed until his phone alarm sounded.

"Shoot. I so didn't want this to end. I've got to go. Vinny will be here with someone you can practice with. Work hard. I need you to conquer this."

26

Vinny came and got Kate and took her to an abandoned warehouse for the lessons. "You ready to have some fun?" a girl said, holding her hand out for Kate to take. She was definitely not a Bellini or a Marconi. She had stick-straight blond hair with hot pink tips. "I'm Candy." Her lipstick was hot pink and so were her three-inch heels. Her skirt and top had large gold zippers going down the back, and her eyelashes were about an inch long.

Kate took her hand. "If a man holds his hand out for you to take, you take it with a gentle squeeze. Keep your eyes on his and don't let go of his hand for a few seconds longer than is natural. Smile like this." She smiled, lips together until the last second when she showed a narrow bit of white teeth. "Let your shoulders come up a bit as if you're a bit shy." From there, Candy taught her three moves to help her be more sexy and alluring to men. Then she gave her four openers that were sure to spark up a good conversation. She showed her how to walk and hold herself so that men would be willing to hit on her and believe she was looking, too.

Candy didn't leave until Kate had mastered all the moves.

"I didn't see the whole thing, but I did see the last few minutes," Vinny said. "You looked natural. Convincing. It's scary, actually. I don't want to send you into that club. I don't want men groping or hitting on you."

"It's only one night. A few hours. I can do this. I can."

"After what I saw today, I believe you. Don't be so good he wants to keep you in there, though." He grimaced. "Keep practicing tonight. I'll send Lino over. Tomorrow I'll have you work with a Bellini club girl to learn the specifics."

***

Vinny picked her up at nine. They ate breakfast sandwiches on the way. It turned out to be a very hard morning. "This girl is our best club girl. If you do what she says, you'll blow them away tonight. Her name is Veronica, and while she may seem like the girl next door, she can be very wicked. Watch it, okay?"

"Are you saying she's going to try to make me fail?"

"She might. Use your persuasive skills on her to make sure she does what you need her to. Don't take anything she does at face value. Look for the why. We're practicing in the very club you're going to be in tomorrow night."

His words had been anything but comforting or encouraging, and she was wound up when she entered the bar. He sat at a table in the back to watch.

Veronica sat at the bar. When she turned to greet Kate, Kate couldn't help but be shocked at her appearance. She was your classic preppy, cute girl. She looked seventeen or maybe eighteen. While she wore makeup, it was spare. Her clothes gave a nod to private school with a short, plaid skirt and a crisp, white button-up shirt that was open to show cleavage. She smiled, and Kate fell under her cute girl spell. "Hey," she said in a silky, fun voice. "I'm Veronica." If Kate hadn't known better, she would have thought she had fallen into a 1980's teen movie and had just met the high school's most popular girl.

She took Kate's hand and squeezed it much like Candy had taught her to yesterday. She didn't let go after the three seconds Kate thought was a bit too long. She looked hard at Kate until Kate wanted nothing more than to look away. After ten seconds she let go and said, "Did that feel natural to you?"

221

"No." Kate wanted to laugh at how absurd it had been.

"Tell me what about it wasn't natural."

"You held on too long and kept eye contact too long." Kate hadn't needed the lesson yesterday to teach her that.

"I thought the same thing." Somehow she smirked with her eyes, her mouth still in a beautiful smile.

"What?" She had thrown her off. This girl freaked her out.

"You held on too long and kept eye contact too long. It was like meeting a curious monkey or something." There was a slight twitch in her left eye. Her lessons would not be fun like with Candy.

Lesson learned. Know your prey.

"Let's try it again." This time she did smirk.

By two o'clock when workers started showing up, Kate felt like she'd been run over by a steamroller. This girl was unapologetic about what she did and downright nasty, but not overtly. Kate could see why she was so good at what she did. But Kate didn't believe she had to be so awful in order to be effective. She did have to admit that she learned a ton. What to look for, where to stand, how to find the right guy, tricks about getting them to talk. Veronica had been effective in her teaching, but she'd made an enemy in the process.

"That was great, Veronica," Vinny said. "I appreciate that. I think Kate has learned a ton." He looked at Kate and she said, "Yes. I did. Thank you."

She raised her eyebrows and smirked. "I don't know, Vinny. I think she needs a couple more weeks. When does she hit the floor?"

Kate wanted to smack her for that comment.

"Tonight, actually."

"Seriously? The boss said tonight was super important, and that he needed me to be in top form. I can't be looking after a newbie tonight."

"No need. She'll be fine," Vinny said. Kate wanted to give him the biggest hug ever. "She'll stay out of your way, and you stay out of hers. The boss is coming tonight." The threat was explicit. "Between the two of you, he expects all the poachers and newbies to be brought in."

"Well, I'm not going to let him down." Veronica eyed me.

Vinny nodded. "You never do. Like I said, you were great today. Thank you." He turned to Kate. "Let's go." He started out.

Veronica hissed at Kate, "Stay out of my way tonight. I get first pick."

"Whatever," Kate said in her normal voice.

Vinny turned again. "You coming?"

Kate wasted no time in following him this time.

Once in the car, she told Vinny about it.

"Did you convince her you needed first pick since you're new at this?"

She stammered. "I-I-I-"

Then Vinny started laughing. "She's scary, right?"

"You got that right." But he'd been correct with his comment. She should have tried to persuade Veronica. A terrible cold shifted through her. What if Salvatorio was setting her up to fail tonight? If she was in competition with Veronica, Veronica would be named the winner, hands-down. For the first time since hearing about this challenge, Kate felt completely unprepared and unable to accomplish it.

***

She hardly slept, tossing and turning all afternoon. She thought about the escape ideas that she'd come up with the first few days she'd been there. She now knew how futile they all had been. Her chances of escape were even smaller now that she wasn't working day shift. Veronica taunted her in her dreams, and she woke more than once thick with sweat. She'd thought about pushing the yellow button, but she had no idea who would show up and even if Vinny showed up, she wouldn't be able to tell him her fears or get his opinion about any of the escape ideas she'd come up with.

Monday was her last day to escape, at least with the Lamberts. Their flight left early in the morning. Was it six or seven? She couldn't remember. She thought about the club and the chances of escape from there. She thought it might be possible depending on where the boss and his cronies were sitting. She'd have to be quick and exit with a patron somehow. The circumstances would have to be perfect. She thought of all the coincidences that had occurred since her arrival in Jersey and decided she wouldn't give up on them. If she had been able to find Lino, she would also be able to find a way out of that club.

When she woke, she noticed a book on her table that hadn't been there earlier. She snatched it up. It was some romance novel and she was about to flick it back to the table, disgusted, when she noticed a yellow piece of paper sticking out of it.

Her hands trembled as she read the note.

Roses are red. Violets are blue. They come in the night. Only for you.

She dropped the note. It fluttered to the cement ground. The threat was clear. Someone was coming for her tonight. She read the note again and again. She lay back, her head hitting her soft pillow. Her mind filled with fearful thoughts. Who was coming for her? It couldn't be the Bellinis. Veronica? Had the Marconis discovered who she was? Had Andre and Lenora talked and made the connection? It was a possibility. If any Marconi had laid eyes on her and described her to Lenora Marconi, the priest at the church, or even Andre, they could have made the connection somehow.

She bolted up and picked up the note, scrutinizing it. Who had written it? No clues presented themselves. Her birth mom popped into her head unbidden. If her birth mom was alive and if she worked for the FBI, it could have come from her. She imagined they had to be cryptic in case someone found the note before Kate did. If that was the truth about the note. She couldn't be sure. Everyone seemed to think her mother was dead. The idea faded the more she considered it.

She hoped she would see Lino again before the club. She wanted to trust him and have him help her escape. He could come with her.

Lino brought dinner. Kate fell immediately into his arms.

"Oh, Lino. I'm so scared. I can't do this. You have to help me escape or something."

He stroked her hair and chuckled a little. He obviously didn't understand how extremely upset she was. "I'm serious."

"You're nervous. Don't think about your fears, okay? Think about the possibilities. It will be over before you know it. You can do this. I believe in you." He was annoyingly calm. Irritation flooded her. Even Lino was no help.

Kate sniffed, fighting tears.

"I wish I could stay, especially when you feel scared, but I can't. I have to work in five minutes, which means I have to leave now, and I won't see you again before you leave."

Kate grabbed him into a tight hug. "Don't go."

He pulled back and kissed her hard on the lips. "I have to. You'll see, tonight will open all kinds of doors for you. I'll miss you. I can't tell you how much I adore you."

He stood, kissed her again and left. She could have sworn he had tears in his eyes.

He was as worried as she was. This was not good.

Not long after that, Vinny took her to shower and get ready. The water was warm, hot even, as she showered, but she had to work to control her trembling. Using positive self-talk, she was able to shower and do her hair and makeup. She worked hard to continue to hide the small traces of bruises on her face. She reached for the clothes she'd brought in, but couldn't find them. On a hook on the door leading to the hall hung a black clothes bag and some two-inch heels on the floor.

She put the clothes on and they weren't half bad. The mini skirt was long enough that she could still get something from the floor if she bent her knees and that she could sit crossing her legs without it shimmying up to her waist. The blousy, navy blue shirt looked a lot like a peasant shirt. She kept her hair down and straight. She slipped into the comfortable heels and felt a surge of relief that they fit. If she had to wear them all night or even run in them, she'd be able.

"Dad," Kate whispered in the car as they drove.

"Why are you whispering?"

"I guess since we're out of my room. I have a question. A quick one, and I want you to answer it."

He nodded once.

"My mom was a nark, I get that. But she wasn't a prostitute or anything, right?" His hands gripped the steering wheel hard. He didn't glance at Kate at all.

"She wasn't what I told you she was that night in the car. I wanted to scare you away. I didn't want you to be a part of this madness. I loved your mother, and I loved you. I didn't want to lose you, and I really don't want to lose you again." He didn't say any more and Kate didn't feel like she could push. Little by little she'd find out about her birth mom.

27

Kate had to let her eyes and ears adjust to the club. Loud music pounded on her eardrums, and the dim lighting had her squinting. Smoke swirled about and liquor flowed freely. Raucous laughter could be heard over some sections of the music. A few girls danced around large men, who simply smiled, enjoying the attention. The men didn't even bother to move with the music. Vinny took her to the back of the establishment, motioning to the barkeep to join them as they passed.

"This is my niece, Kate. She's going to be working with Veronica tonight."

The barkeep looked her up and down and then said, "Serious?"

Vinny gave him look that could kill. "Watch out for her. She's new at this stuff."

"The boss doesn't want me to interfere tonight."

Vinny flared his nose and huffed. "I said watch out for her, not interfere with her."

"Look, Vinny, I gotta follow orders just like you do." The big man put his hands in the air and shook them. Vinny had clout, and this man would usually listen to him, but not tonight. That was for sure. Vinny excused the barkeep, who gladly went out to the front.

"Look," he rubbed his hand over his chin. "I'm not allowed to be here tonight. I told you you'd be alone, but I thought I'd at least have Carlo to back you up if needed. Looks like that's not going to happen. Keep that little purse on you at all times. There's some pepper spray in there if you find you need it, but don't use it unless you really have to. I'm pretty sure using it will prove you don't have the skill of persuasion. And put this on." It was a star brooch. "Lino sent it. Hopefully it will give you luck." The diamonds glittered and sparkled in the light. She pinned it on her blouse, a warm feeling filling her chest. "That looks great. Why do I feel like I'm sending my baby off to college?"

"I don't know, seriously, this is nothing like school." She wanted to tell him about the note, but his earlier words about not wanting to lose her stopped her. She didn't want him to worry more than he had to. Instead, she patted the cute little brooch. He was worried about her, but he believed in her.

"You got this." His tone was serious. "Good luck. I love you." He disappeared before she had a chance to say anything back. Could she have returned the same words? The words felt so final, so odd for tonight. She guessed it was nerves making everyone crazy. Lino had been the same way.

She took in a deep breath. One step at a time. She could do this. She'd get to the far end of the bar and order ginger ale or sparkling water. Both could be confused for alcoholic beverages at first glance. She'd get control of her nerves and get to work.

Not long after Carlo filled her glass, Veronica walked in. All eyes fell on her, including Kate's. She was disgusted, but at the same time impressed. Veronica walked the walk for sure.

There was a steady stream of large guards taking various women and men to a back room. The guards knocked each time, and someone inside opened the door. The guard then returned to the front of the club, but the escorted person disappeared behind the door. Is that were Salvatorio and the other Bellinis were?

Kate took a drink of her ginger ale and looked around for her first target when she noticed something unusual. A guy with short cropped blond hair tapped the right corner of the back of the chair next to him four times. She looked around, but couldn't find a bookie of any kind, but she did notice Veronica giving Carlo a longing look. The man's movements were so practiced, and yet so insistent, she knew it wasn't incidental contact. He had bet four hundred big ones on whatever the bookie was offering. Now all she had to do was find the bookie. She thought he had to have paper and pen. But then again, he could use a cell or something similar to record the bets.

Veronica was up working the room, and Carlo's eyes rarely left her. After two more ginger ales, Kate realized she needed to pretend to drink instead of actually drink. Her bladder was painfully full. She got up and went to the bathroom. Before she was done, she heard a voice coming from the stall next to hear. The voice was a whisper, and Kate almost stopped listening to flush, thinking something she didn't want to hear was about to happen in that stall, but then she thought she heard numbers. "And 400 from AXL." The toilet flushed and Kate peeked out one of the cracks in the stall door to see who it was.

The woman was tall and wore a bright yellow dress. Kate wouldn't be able to miss that. She flushed the toilet and came out. The lady was gone. Kate had found her first poacher. She went to the counter and ordered a sparkling water. She reached in her little purse and pulled out a small pen and wrote: *Lady in yellow is poacher. At least two gamblers. Have one.* Kate tapped the counter five times in a row, alerting Carlo that she had information. Before he could get the napkin, the lady in yellow was being led by a bulky man into a back room. Kate narrowed her eyes. Carlo touched her hand as he took the napkin. He said, "Veronica already took care of it." Kate scanned the crowds. The guy who'd been gambling was also gone.

A new spirit of competition grew in her. She would not let Veronica get the next one. That's when she realized what she was being tested on, her persuasion skills. Finding the gamblers and poachers had nothing to do with that. How hard would it be to convince a gambler to gamble in a better place? Not so hard. But this barkeep, he'd been told not to interfere with her tonight. What better way to showcase her persuasion skills than by convincing the barkeep to help her?

She ordered another drink and wrote a note on it. *Meet me in back. Something interesting.* When he took it, she winked at him and strutted to the back. To her surprise, he came. That hadn't been hard. The hard part was yet to come.

The din of the music lessened when the door closed behind her. When Carlo got there, she said, "Look. I'm behind in every way possible. This competition isn't fair, and I know everything is stacked against me, but if you helped me a little, I could do something for you."

He smirked at her. "There's nothing you have I want." He started to walk away from her.

"I could get you a date with Veronica."

Carlo stopped in his tracks. "Impossible." But he turned toward her. Dishes in the kitchen clanked in the background.

"I'll even get her to ask you out."

He narrowed his eyes, obviously thinking. "Sure. I got nothing to lose. But no one can know."

"Are you kidding? If anyone found out I'd cheated, you think they'd let me win?"

"You're on. Get her to ask me out, and I'll guarantee a win for you tonight." A server passed them with some food on a tray.

She held out her hand, and he shook it. "Deal."

She went straight out to the table Veronica was perched on. "You like it here, don't you?"

"Piss off. I told you not to get in my way tonight." She didn't even look at Kate.

"I just wanted some advice, and then I'll move on." Every table in the place was occupied and the dance floor rocked with dancers.

"Forget it. I gave you all the help I was going to yesterday." She sneered at Kate, but only for a quick second. Her charming smile quickly replaced it.

"No, it has nothing to do with our little competition. It has to do with Carlo."

"Carlo?" Her head whipped to him. He was wiping up the bar in the far corner. "He asked me out, but I wasn't sure what to say."

A little twitch formed in Veronica's right eyebrow.

"I mean, he seems nice and all, but I wasn't sure about dating a bartender, ya know? I mean you've been out with him, right?"

"Uh, yeah. Right. When did he want to go out with you?"

"Next Tuesday. He wants to go to the Amity concert." Kate grinned. Veronica's face went a light shade of red.

"He's hot, there's no doubt, but should I?"

"You should do what you want." Veronica scowled. "Who cares?"

"Okay, I will. Hey, is there somewhere to go for some fresh air around here that isn't out front?"

Veronica's eyes flicked to Carlo. She indicated a door past the bathrooms. Kate walked that way, hoping her words had had the desired effect. When she peered around the corner, Veronica was flirting with Carlo. Kate forced herself not to laugh.

It felt good to be outside in the cool air. Unfortunately, tall, ornate wrought iron fencing surrounded the patio. There'd be no escape this way. If she were able to escape, she now had information she could give the FBI that could make them help her save Vinny and Lino.

As soon as she could see that the date was set, she walked toward the bar. Veronica was already leaving it. "Sorry, honey, you're too late— he's taken Tuesday." She bit her lip and moved past her, triumph in her eyes, but it was Kate who was truly triumphant.

An hour later, Kate had bagged five prospective clients, who were happily gambling away in the back room already and one poacher. Because Carlo was the bartender, he overheard a lot of stuff that she couldn't. Not only was she neck and neck with Veronica, she had the bartender in her pocket, too. That made her ahead in her book. As she ate, her mind wandered to Lino, and she touched the brooch. She couldn't wait to see him in the morning. Unbidden, the note sprang to mind. Suddenly alert, she looked all around. Carlo got close and took her glass with the pretense to fill it. "Purple tie. Easy recruit."

Kate focused on the guy. He hadn't been there long and was sipping on a beer, looking all around, his eyes stopping on each person in the room. Yeah. He was looking for action other than drinking.

She walked up behind him and put her hand on the table to the side of him. "Hi." She bit her bottom lip. "Want to dance?" She rotated slightly side to side, a flirty gesture. His eyes fell on her cleavage and she knew she had him, but it wasn't her cleavage he was looking at, it was the brooch. Great, she thought, a thief. He wouldn't be getting this piece of jewelry. No way, no how.

"Sure, but I need to check this text first." He leaned in close and whispered. "I'm supposed to be working. Don't tell."

She pretended to have a key and lock her lips shut. She felt like a total idiot. She sat next to him while he typed on his phone. Once done, he took her hand and led her to the dance floor. He turned out to be a great dancer, but the dance was short. He led her off the dance floor. She pulled on him, wishing she were someone else and not having to seduce this guy. "Aw, come on. That was too short. One more."

"I'll tell you what," he said, after pulling out his phone again and looking at the display. "How about I buy you a drink over at the bar, and you wait for me while I hit the little boys' room."

She felt a blow off. This was not good. What was she doing, anyway? Getting Carlo to help her had been smart, but how was she going to pull out ahead of Veronica? She was tanking again. But she couldn't tank. She couldn't live with Salvatorio. She'd never have a decent future. It was going to be bad enough, even being with Lino and Vinny, being told what she could and couldn't do. The future had been so promising for her back home, and now she had nothing. Sure, she would become an awesome attorney, but being an attorney chained to the mafia? That wasn't the life she wanted. And yet, she didn't have a choice. She was stuck in a life she would hate.

She'd confront this guy directly. She didn't have time to mess around. "No, come on. Let's dance. I want to dance." He pulled on her.

"I promise, I'm not giving you the slip. I really need to use the head. Come on." He was stronger than she was, and she finally gave up on resisting. She'd watch him to make sure he kept his promise. He deposited Kate at the end of the bar closest the entrance and gave her ten bucks to order what she wanted. She saw him head for the bathroom, but then look her way. She held up her new glass of ginger ale. He smiled and stepped inside.

There were only two people who knew she existed. Only one who knew who she really was, and if she didn't get this guy in the backroom, she'd lose both of them. What more could she do to show them she could be persuasive? She knew she could be a great judge, but she didn't want to be the mafia's puppet. Kate glanced at the exit door. It was only about six steps from her. It would be easy to walk out, but once she was out, she'd run into the bouncer, who would bounce her right back inside and then she and everyone she knew would be punished.

As Kate watched the door, a couple guys were trying to get out of the club, but the door seemed to be locked. They stumbled over to the bar and said something to Carlo. Carlo went to the big metal door and spoke with the guy standing next to it. She couldn't hear what was being said, but they shook hands and laughed before Carlo pushed on the door. The door didn't budge and he pushed harder, using his shoulder. Still, it didn't budge.

The guy at the door laughed and took a shot at the door. He got the same result. His voice raised in frustration. "What the..." He tried again and then pulled out his phone. He yelled into it and then said to Carlo, "Marcel isn't answering. Something's up." The two of them walked about five feet from the door. Kate slid around the bar, sensing trouble. The men then ran at the door, shoulders low, preparing to ram the door open. Kate covered her eyes with her hands. She heard no thud, but screams instead. She turned to see the door wide open and the men on the ground with someone holding them down, knees in their backs.

As that scene registered, men and women with FBI jackets and shirts, guns drawn, rushed into the establishment. Out of the corner of her eye, she saw the man with the purple tie exit the bathroom, but instead of a purple tie and jacket, he now wore a shirt with the letters FBI on it. As they came inside, the first agents in stopped, pointing their guns at people. Another couple of special agents stopped every ten feet, securing the area. They kept pouring in and securing until a horde of agents pushed that back door where the thieves and gamblers had been taken, and rushed inside. Gun shots fired in the backroom and the people in the front flinched, many crouching to the ground in fear. Two large men and one scrawny one came barreling out of the room, guns firing, not caring who they hit.

Everyone crouched now, even the special agents, dodging bullets as they went down. In mere moments, the men were already to the middle of the room. Cries of pain echoed through the room as several people were shot. The determined, frantic looks on the faces of the three men told Kate that this would not end well. She balled up on the floor behind a chair, hoping to avoid the chaos as much as possible. As the men passed the special agents, the agents regrouped and shot at the men while at the same time a few agents entered the front door, aimed at their three targets and sent bullets into them. The three men fell. An eerie silence fell over the room, but only for a few seconds at the most as voices of fear, pain, and relief began to rise.

The FBI had come. Had the Lamberts gotten through to them or was her mother alive and had found out about her and was helping her? But how did they know she was there, at the club? For a moment, hope surged within her. Then she realized—if they'd been coming for her, they would have gotten her out, protected her. This raid had nothing to do with her, at all. She was going to be arrested along with everyone here. They'd never believe her that she was there against her will. That was probably everyone's story.

A wave of hopelessness crashed over her. When all this was over, she'd just be sent back to the Bellinis, and now even her chance to become a lawyer and judge was dashed. She was going to be at the whim of Salvatorio. She hid behind the bar. Maybe she could escape out the back. She headed for the backroom, but someone grabbed her. She turned to find the special agent she'd danced with holding her. "Not that way, darling." He cuffed her and held her elbow. Kate's whole body shook.

Starting at the back of the room, each person was cuffed and led out. Kate's mind filled with terror at what was about to happen. She thought of the note she'd found about someone coming for her tonight. Whoever it was would have to wait their turn.

Once outside, she was led into a big van with others from the club. Chaos was widespread, but there were enough agents to control it. The yelling and complaining from the captives in the van gave Kate a headache. She wanted to scream out to the agents who she was—anything to convince them she was a victim, she didn't belong in jail. But she knew it was too risky—if they didn't believe her, the Bellinis and Marconis would punish her for trying to escape. Her only hope was to talk to one of the agents alone.

Kate went along numbly as the agents unloaded the van and herded her along with all the others into the FBI field office. They took her picture and fingerprints, but she was always surrounded by other people from the club. She shifted in her seat, worry making her hot and uncomfortable. She sat in a long line of chairs, waiting for a detective to question her, when a man walked in wearing an expensive suit and perfectly shined shoes. He held out a paper to the receptionist.

"You mean you'd like us to round all of these suspects up and put them in one room with you during questioning?" She put one fist on her hip. "You're representing all of them?"

"Yes. And it better be done now." Kate realized he must be the lawyer for the mafia families.

"I'm sorry, sir, it will take some time. Some of these names are already with detectives, while others are waiting their turn. We'll move as quickly as we can."

"I want the questioning of anyone on this list stopped immediately." Kate looked at the man and considered him. That could be her in ten years. Or would they keep her away from the family affairs until she became a judge? That seemed the smarter path. No one would vote for a judge who regularly worked with the mafia. The man had a scar going down his left cheek, and he scowled at the receptionist. She had no doubt her name was on the list. If she couldn't talk to an agent alone, there was no hope for her. Her chance to escape was dwindling.

The receptionist huffed, but said nothing more as she took the list he'd supplied to the head agent. The agent swore when the paper landed on his desk. A huge shuffle ensued. In a flurry of activity, people in interrogation rooms were brought out while others, including Kate, were moved in. Mass confusion took over, with some suspects yelling, some trying to escape, while still others tussled with the agents detaining them.

Kate was brought to a small room with a narrow table and three chairs. As soon as the special agent took her hand off Kate's arm, Kate sat in the chair nearest her wishing someone would take the cuffs off. She opened her mouth to speak, to explain who she was, but fear paralyzed her. If she managed to convince them—what would happen to Vinny? What would happen to Lino?

The agent walked past the table and to a door on the other side of the room. She knocked twice, waited a few seconds and knocked once more. She then came to Kate. "Don't sit now. We've got to move. That bull attorney will be breaking down the door to find you any minute."

Kate stood and the special agent grabbed her arm, leading her around the table and out the now open door. She was met by two other FBI agents, one of them the man from the bar with the purple tie. "Kate Hamilton?"

Relief made her knees weak, and she nearly fell. They knew who she was. "Yes. Yes! I'm Kate." Tears started to drip down her face, though she barely noticed them.

"I'm Special Agent Tyler, and this is Special Agent Long. We are here to remove you from the care of the Bellini family."

She didn't know whether to sob or to laugh. What came out was more like a hiccup. "The care?"

He grinned. "You do want us to rescue you, right?"

"Did my mother send you?"

Confusion played across the agent's faces. "I'm sorry, who's your mother? This tip came from inside the family. Whoever gave you that brooch. That's who you need to thank."

Her hand flew to the brooch. Lino. Her heart lurched. Would he be all right?

"Right now we need to get you back with the Lamberts who are on their way to the airport as we speak."

It was Monday morning, the day the Lamberts planned to go back home. She had been rescued. Time had seemed to speed past, but at the same time, mouse along.

"We'll need to escort you to the car in disguise—or rather, covered. We're going to bulk you up, shackle you, and put a shirt over your head so no one knows it's you."

"Okay." Kate took a deep breath, and nodded, trying to gain control of her emotions.

With her help, they got her ready in a matter of minutes for transport. They'd done well disguising her. She didn't look anything like herself. She shuffled down a hall and out a door. The only indication she had that she was outside was the hard cement under her feet. They shoved her into the waiting car, careful not to let the shirt over her head fall from its place.

The door clicked shut behind her, and relief filled her. She was free.

28

Kate broke away from the special agents when she spotted the Lamberts inside the airport. She ran with all she had to Ellie, who only had a few seconds warning that Kate was about to smash into her. After the initial collision, the rest of the family joined in a group hug, squealing and rejoicing in Kate's return. It felt beyond wonderful to be back with them. The agents came shortly after and encouraged them to celebrate once they landed in Texas. While the teens calmed down, the special agents spoke with the parents.

"It's time you go and get on the plane. We'll watch from here, and as soon as you get on that escalator, we'll go deal with the chaos at the office." Kate and Ellie hugged the men and then rushed to the escalator to go upstairs to get in the security line. The Lamberts had checked everyone in online the previous night. Streams of people rode the escalators down and up, either returning from vacation or just starting it. Kate was the last one on the escalator, each separated from the person in front of them by a step or two. As each person reached the top, they turned down the long hallway leading to the security check in.

A young man who'd run up the escalators bumped Kate as she stepped off the escalators, making her fall. The teen yelled his apology as he sped up and cruised to the security checkpoint. Kate could see Ellie's feet disappear into the security line, a bunch of other passengers getting in line behind her.

"So sorry. I'm going to miss my flight. So sorry!" He didn't look back as he yelled the words, and Kate couldn't help but chuckle. Nothing was going to make her sad now. In a few minutes she'd be through security and in less than an hour she'd be on her way back home.

A hand reached out to her, and she took it gladly. The hand pulled her up so hard that she sprang through the air.

"What are you doing here, Kate?" The gruff voice asked, his hand not letting go of hers. Galtem was here.

Dizziness swept over her and an ache in the back of her throat came alive. He'd been the one who had beaten her that first night when she turned herself in to the Bellinis. She whimpered as he grabbed her by the back of the neck. Her arms flailed, and her whimpering became uncontrolled. All she could think about was escaping, but her body wouldn't respond to the commands her mind was sending. She scanned the hallway for the Lamberts, but she couldn't see them.

Once she was standing, Galtem put his arm around her shoulders and pulled her in close, like they were good friends. He whispered, his hot breath sliding over her cheek, "What. Are. You. Doing. Here?" He grabbed her ticket from her hand and led her to a far corner, away from the crowds and lines of people coming and going from the airport.

Salvatorio was not here. She would not give him power over her again. "What are *you* doing here?" she spat. She had to figure this out.

"Benito," Galtem said to the other big guy across the hall, "Call Vinny. We have a runaway here. Kate thinks she's heading for—" he consulted the top of her ticket. "Dallas, Texas. I think we have other plans for her." She snatched the ticket from him before he could see her last name. "You won't be needing that, honey." While keeping hold of her, he pushed her toward the other guy. "Just don't take your eyes off the people arriving. If we miss Ricco, the boss will kill us."

For some reason, knowing they hadn't come to specifically find her gave her hope. They were here to pick someone up. They obviously didn't even know what had happened at the club. She shoved her ticket into her pocket.

She thought of a way out. "Let go of me! I wasn't escaping. I can't believe you don't know. There was a raid on the club last night and everyone was arrested. Me included. They quickly discovered I didn't belong and were sending me home."

The men looked at each other and Benito said, "How did they know who you are? Did you snitch?" Benito grabbed Kate's jaw and squeezed.

She had to work the angle hard. She would not give up yet. As soon as a fresh batch of people arriving started shuffling through the hall, she said, "I'm serious! It wasn't my choice to go home. The FBI is sending me. If I don't show up, they'll come after you guys again."

Galtem reacted by squeezing her neck tighter. She stomped on the arch of his foot, he bent a bit forward and she bit his forearm, which now pressed against her face. Instead of jerking his arm out of her reach, he pushed hard into her mouth, gagging her. She tried to pull back, but he didn't allow it. He pushed still harder and she screamed, but the scream was lost in his arm. He must have been in enough situations like this one that it didn't even faze him. He was used to such assaults.

She drew hard for breath. She couldn't believe everyone was so focused on whatever they were doing that they didn't see her distress, but then again, they were back a good thirty feet from the masses moving in snakelike lines here and there.

"I see him," Benito said. "I'll retrieve Ricco. You think you can manage her? She's a wild one."

"Of course," he said, with a determination and enthusiasm that soured her stomach. "The wilder, the better." And with that, he squeezed a bit harder, taking what little breath she had out of her. If he hadn't relaxed only a moment later, she would have died of asphyxiation. Perhaps death was preferable to what was to come. No. She couldn't give in. She'd been fighting to find her parents for all this time and now it was her time to rise up and be her best self despite her discovery. She needed to deal with it.

It had only been maybe two minutes since she'd been separated from the Lamberts. She searched for them and liked what she found. They were pushing through the lines of people around them and coming in her direction. They must've discovered her absence was not temporary. They would get to her and save her.

Galtem's phone rang. He loosened his grip on Kate and answered it, keeping one arm around her neck.

"What?"

She couldn't hear the other end of the conversation. "Yes. I have Kate. At the airport. Says the FBI raided the club." He pushed her toward the snaking lines of people leaving the airport. Pause. "I knew there was something going on when I saw her." They entered the queue. She could barely breathe, his arm crushing her neck. "They arrested him? Seriously?" He grimaced at Kate. They were only feet from the escalator, their path made easy as people moved out of the way to accommodate the huge man. She had no choice but to go with. She glanced at the Lamberts, who had only now burst through the masses of people and were running toward her and calling to the guards, yelling for assistance. The guards joined the race, talking on their radios as they advanced, calling for support. She could only hope that they had seen her and knew where she was. She was determined to escape, but had no clue how. She only had TV shows and movies to draw on. Where she lived was totally safe. Nothing bad ever happened. The need for self-defense was nonexistent. She waited for the right moment.

One more step and they'd be on the escalator and most likely lost to everyone. Galtem pocketed the phone, but then she felt a jab in her side. He glanced back. He must have noticed the disturbance coming their way. "Keep moving. Be a good girl and pretend that we're together. No problems. The club was raided, but you should have stuck up for us. I bet you told them everything you knew. You sang like a bird." He jabbed the barrel of the gun into her side and stepped on the escalator.

"No. No. I didn't. They fingerprinted me and found out who I was." If she stepped on that escalator, she could see her chances of rescue disappearing. In less than a minute he'd have her out the door and into a car, never to be seen again.

"We'll see about that," he snarled.

The Lamberts and guards were too far from her to stop it from happening. Her chance arrived with his step onto the escalator.

She let herself go limp. It made him stumble. With one hand on her neck and the other on the gun, he had no way to steady himself. He released her neck and the gun almost simultaneously, his survival instincts kicking in. His hands clawed for the side rails and Kate's arms wheeled, trying to stop her fall. He tumbled into the person directly in front of him, bowling the person down with him. He put his hands out, trying to grab onto the next person, but his weight and frenzy only pushed that person and the next two down, too. Kate slammed into the bodies of the people as they fell, but Galtem didn't stop despite his best efforts, momentum dragging him down with ten others in a heap at the bottom. The bite of the teeth of the escalator dug into her as she tried to get up. She was moving ever so slowly toward him. Crawling over the people underneath her, she finally found a clear stair. She jumped up and ran up the steps, glad that the traffic had stopped once Galtem fell. The way was clear. She pushed hard until she reached the top. Pained, bruised, and broken. She'd taken her only chance, and it'd paid off.

She bent over, heaving, trying to catch her breath. The police had arrived at the bottom of the steps and were cuffing Galtem, his gun confiscated. She pushed through the crowds to the Lamberts, eyes gawking all around them.

The airport security detained them in a room off to the side of the security scanners. Once their story was corroborated by the special agents who had brought her there, they were released, barely making it on the plane as they were rushed in a small electric cart to their gate.

29

The five of them were rushed onto the plane, Colby handed Kate her carry-on as she took her seat. She was curious what they had packed in it. The flight attendant brought around orange juice and bottled water, a great perk of being in first class. She happily accepted both while buckling in. The three kids all had single window seats on the same side of the plane without anyone next to them. Mr. and Mrs. Lambert sat in the middle two seats on the same row with Ellie.

After the requisite safety announcements, the plane backed out and headed for the runway. Kate opened the bag Ellie had most likely packed for her. Right on top was a new pack of gum. She stuck one piece in her mouth, happy to be back with friends who would know she needed that.

Just under the gum was her journal. She pulled it out and looked over each page. Ellie had taped in the pictures of her and her mother as well as the notes she'd found in the folder and all other pictures she'd taken on the trip. Kate's fingers caressed the picture of her mom and the one of her dad helping her walk.

Then she wrote down everything that had happened since finding the folder. As she wrote about getting caught and being forced into the mafia, a feeling of worry settled over her. She fingered the diamond star. She hoped Salvatorio would never find out that Lino had tipped off the FBI. She hoped her dad wouldn't be held responsible either. The FBI was smart, right? They would cover their tracks nicely. Surely they knew that any information they recorded about her and anyone else could be accessed by someone who really wanted the information. If not, she'd be right back with the Bellinis before she could settle in at home.

She dedicated a few pages to her father. She wrote, FOUND, at the top of the page. Underneath the heading, she wrote Vincenzo (Vinny) Bellini. Father. She wrote what some might call a eulogy for him, full of all the things she'd learned about him. She felt a sense of peace come over her. She knew who her birth father was. He wasn't perfect, but he had tried to help her. And he loved her in his own, imperfect way.

She wrote a page about Lino and what he'd done for her, risking everything, but being smart enough not to leave a trail. She even dedicated a page to each of the other people she met and dealt with, including all the Marconis and every Bellini she knew. And she didn't forget to write about the new priest or Savino Cremashci, the savior of children, the savior of Kate.

Then she wrote, NOT FOUND and underneath the heading, she wrote, Carmela Bellini. Mother. She then wrote, Dead? Alive? It's still a mystery.

Kate fell asleep with her hand still on her mother's picture. She woke to Ellie shaking her awake. "Kate. Wake up. You were screaming."

Kate's rapid breaths slowed.

"It was a dream," she said shakily. "I'm fine."

"Was it the piano dream?" Ellie asked.

Kate nodded, what she didn't tell Ellie was that she knew why the people were in a panic at the performance. The room had been full of applause and the audience had been thrilled with Kate's performance. Many stood and called encore. Encore. And that's when it happened. Blood splattered on Kate's face. The woman next to her slumped down. Was it her birth mother?

The captain spoke over the intercom that they had begun their descent into Dallas. Kate pulled out a fresh stick of gum and thought about her adoptive parents. They would be so upset. They might not even let her come back home. She'd broken so many rules. She tapped Ellie, who looked back at her. "Do you think I can stay with you guys for a little while at least? I mean, I don't know how my parents are going to react to all of this."

"Of course. You know my parents will be happy to have you."

Kate glanced at them, both watching movies on their screens. She knew they wouldn't mind. She'd used almost every cent of her savings while in New Jersey. She had no way to live on her own, nor did she want to.

After deplaning, Kate and the Lamberts headed for baggage pickup. Kate's head whirred with what could only be called dread at going home. Her parents were going to hate her. She didn't know if she could handle that. She loved the Lamberts and living with them would be a continual party, but was that what she really wanted? What she'd wanted was to find her birth parents, but she didn't really bargain for losing her adoptive parents in the process. Shame and regret washed over her when she thought of how she'd lied to them. She knew now, they'd only been trying to keep her safe. She felt sick and looked for a bathroom, but found none. Maybe in the baggage area she'd find one.

As they rounded the corner into the large area, she stopped in her tracks, tears springing to her eyes. Her entire family stood only ten yards away with signs and balloons welcoming her and the Lamberts home.

Ellie leaned into her and said, "I hope you don't mind. I called them."

Kate hugged Ellie, "No. Not at all. Not at all." Then she ran to her family.

"Mom! Dad!" Her mom grabbed Kate first and then her dad, then all the kids piled around her, hugging her and laughing and talking.

"My dear, sweet, Kate. Kate. Kate. Kate." While affection wasn't sparse in their house it wasn't something that was enormous and overwhelming like this. "Kate!" "Kate's home!"

"We thought we'd lost you forever," her mom said, placing her hands on the sides of Kate's face and sighing. She stepped back and took

Kate Unmasked

Kate's hands in hers, looking her over from head to toe. Then her questions and commands came out like a machine gun firing. "Are you hungry? You must be starving. We brought some water and grapes, but we can stop on the way home."

Kate squeezed her mom's hands. "No, Mom. I don't need any of that. Let's get my bag."

"We'll get it," the twins called out before running to the carousel.

"No! We'll get it," the girls yelled, chasing after the boys, leaving Kate alone with her parents. The smile in her heart grew, and warmth radiated throughout her whole body. This was family, no fear. Only peace. Only love.

"I don't know what Ellie told you, but I found my birth dad and it didn't turn out so well."

"We know."

"Everything?"

"We think so. Ellie thought you were dead, and she told us everything she knew."

"I'm so sorry." Kate hung her head. "I understand now why you kept everything from me, and I'm okay with that. You only wanted to protect me. I don't care what you knew or what you didn't, just know I forgive you and I love you."

"We love you, too, Kate," her dad said. "We want you to know that we didn't know about your birth parents. Your mom just had a strange feeling about the whole adoption. We disregarded our fears that maybe someday someone would come for you because you had been kidnapped or something because we so desperately wanted a baby. And when we got you, we decided to create a safe, normal world for you here, a place that no one would ever find you. We hid those things from you, because we didn't want you to go looking for anything that would hurt you."

"Ironic, I guess," her mom said. She was smiling, but her eyes were filled with regret.

Kate hugged her. Even if they hadn't done it the way she might have wanted, they had tried to keep her safe. "Can we make a promise to each other right now, that we will be honest with each other, no matter what?"

They both nodded, and Kate smiled.

The twins came running with one bag and the girls came with the other. Kate was going home, and she could hardly wait.

30

"I can't believe how well it went either," Kate said into her cell. "Of course, I didn't tell them everything, like my mom being an agent."

"But you don't know that for sure."

"No. But I'm expecting a call from the FBI any minute to confirm my suspicions."

Kate's phone buzzed. It was Special Agent Johansen—Mr. Purple Tie. "It's them. I'll call you back."

"Kate, listen. I know I promised you answers today, but I don't have them. I've asked all around, and no one knows about your mom. It's possible she was an agent, but it seems that if she were, I'd be able to find some indication of it. There is no record of her."

"But—her name. Could she have worked under a different name? I'm sure Carmela couldn't have been her real name if she was undercover."

"That's just it. We have no record of a Carmela as a snitch, as an alias, or as an employee. We sent out a company-wide email asking every agent still working with us about your mom. There's been no response."

Kate's world spun. A mystery she thought she'd solved hadn't been solved at all. "Oh. I thought..."

"I know this is hard, and I'm not saying she wasn't an agent. Her file could be sealed, but as far as we can tell, she is no longer an agent if she ever was one."

"Oh. Thanks. I'm sure you put a lot of work into looking for her. Thank you."

"If I hear anything, I'll let you know, but don't get your hopes up."

"Okay. Thanks.

"Bye."

"Bye." Her mom could've gone into hiding. Her records could have been sealed. She would not submit to the idea that her mom was dead. She couldn't. Curiosity burned inside her. She called Ellie.

"There's no record of her."

"I'm sorry. Sometimes there really are no answers."

Kate pulled out a fresh journal as Ellie spouted about things they had to do that summer. She pulled out colorful paper and markers. She cut out a rectangle that fit perfectly to the outside of the journal and she wrote,

Carmela Bellini

In beautiful swirly script. Underneath she wrote,

My journey to finding my birth mom.

And the first thing she put in it was the notepaper with someone's signature on it. If she could find the person who saved her, maybe he would also help her find her mom.

Thank you for leaving a review!
It helps me more than you know. Big Hugs!

Pick up *Kate Concealed (Code of Silence: Book 2)* the next book in the trilogy.

If you loved this book, try these fun novels and series:

Jump into the exciting adventures of the *Watched Trilogy*
Up the stakes and suspense with *Adrenaline Rush*
Dive in to great mystery in *Gravediggers*
Laugh and cry with Brooklyn in *Sweet and Sour Kisses:**
*Formerly called Confessions of a 16-Year-Old Virgin Lips

Know Cindy's news before anyone else by signing up for her newsletter http://eepurl.com/GL2HL Get sneak peaks and free stuff!

Visit Cindy on her website:
cindymhogan.com
and on Google plus: Cindy M. Hogan

For series trivia, sneak peeks, events in your area, contests, fun fan interaction, like the Watched Facebook Page: Watched-the book

Follow Cindy M. Hogan on twitter: @Watched

About the Author

Cindy M Hogan is inspired by the unpredictable teenagers she teaches. More than anything she loves the time she has with her own teenage daughters and wishes she could freeze them at this fun age. If she's not reading or writing, you'll find her snuggled up with the love of her life watching a great movie or planning their next party. Most of all, she loves to laugh.

She is the bestselling and award winning author of the *Watched trilogy*, a YA suspense series with a dash of romance. She has since branched off to write a mystery, *Gravediggers*, that won Best YA novel of 2013, a contemporary romance, *Sweet and Sour Kisses*, and three in a spy series, *Adrenaline Rush Hotwire,* and *Fatal Exchange.*

To learn more about the author and the books she has written, visit her at cindymhogan.com